The

We hope you enjoy this book.
Please return or renew it by the due date.
You can renew it at **www.norfolk.gov.uk/libraries**
or by using our free library app. Otherwise you can
phone **0344 800 8020** - please have your library
card and pin ready.
You can sign up for email reminders too.

NORFOLK COUNTY COUNCIL
LIBRARY AND INFORMATION SERVICE

NORFOLK ITEM

3 0129

D1350588

The
YEAR
of The
RAT

CLARE FURNISS

SIMON AND SCHUSTER

First published in Great Britain in 2014 by Simon and Schuster UK Ltd
A CBS COMPANY
This edition published 2017

1 3 5 7 9 10 8 6 4 2

Simon & Schuster UK Ltd
1ˢᵗ Floor, 222 Gray's Inn Road
London
WC1X 8HB

Simon & Schuster Australia, Sydney
Simon & Schuster India, New Delhi

A CIP catalogue record for this book is available from the British Library.

PB ISBN: 978-1-47117-100-0
EBook ISBN: 978-1-47112-029-9

Typeset by Hewer Text UK Ltd, Edinburgh
Printed and bound by CPI Group (UK) Ltd, Croydon, CR0 4YY

www.simonandschuster.co.uk
www.simonandschuster.com.au

For Marianne, Joe and Ewan, with love

'I meant to write about death, only life came breaking in as usual.'

Virginia Woolf's diary, 17 February 1922

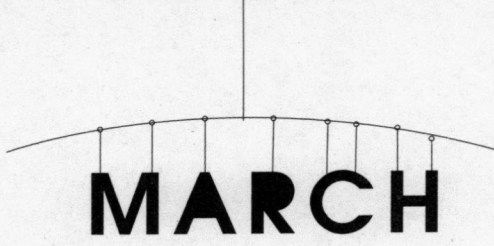

The traffic light glows red through the rainy windscreen, blurred, clear, blurred again, as the wipers swish to and fro. Below it, in front of us, is the hearse. I try not to look at it.

My hands fidget as though they don't belong to me, picking at a loose thread on my sleeve, stretching my skirt down so that it covers more of my legs. Why did I wear it? It's way too short for a funeral. The silence is making me panicky, but I can't think of anything to say.

I sneak a sideways look at Dad, his face blank and still as a mask. What's he thinking? About Mum? Maybe he's just trying to find something to say, like me.

'You should do your seat belt up,' I say at last, too loud.

He starts and looks at me in surprise, as though he'd forgotten I was there.

'What?'

I feel stupid, as though I've interrupted something important.

'Your seat belt,' I mutter, cheeks burning.

'Oh. Yes.' Then, 'Thanks.'

But I know he's not really listening. It's as though he's listening to another conversation, one that I can't hear. He doesn't do his seat belt up.

We're like two statues, side by side in the back of the car, grey and cold.

We're nearly there, just pulling up outside the church, when he puts a hand on my arm, looks me in the eye. His face is lined and pale.

'Are you OK, Pearl?'

I stare back at him. Is that really the best he can do?

'Yes,' I say eventually.

Then I get out of the car and walk into the church without him.

I always thought you'd know, somehow, if something terrible was going to happen. I thought you'd sense it, like when the air goes damp and heavy before a storm and you know you'd better hide yourself away some-where safe until it all blows over.

But it turns out it's not like that at all. There's no scary music playing in the background like in

4

films. No warning signs. Not even a lonely magpie. *One for sorrow*, Mum used to say. *Quick, look for another*.

The last time I saw her was in the kitchen, an apron tight over her enormous bump, surrounded by cake tins and mixing bowls, bags of sugar and flour. She would have looked quite the domestic goddess if it hadn't been for the obscenities she was bellowing at the ancient stove, which belched smoke back at her.

'Mum?' I said cautiously. 'What are you doing?'

She turned on me, pink-faced, her red hair wilder than ever and streaked with flour.

'The tango, Pearl,' she shouted, waving a spatula at me. 'Synchronized swimming. Bell-ringing. What does it look like I'm doing?'

'I only asked,' I said. 'Don't get your knickers in a twist.'

Which wasn't a wise move. Mum looked like she might actually explode.

'I'm baking a frigging cake.'

Except she didn't say frigging.

'But you can't cook,' I pointed out reasonably.

She gave me a glare that would have peeled the paint off the walls, if it hadn't already flaked away a hundred years ago. 'That oven is possessed by the devil.'

'Well, it's not my fault, is it? You were the one who insisted on moving into a falling-down wreck of a house where nothing works. We had a perfectly good oven in our old house. And a roof that didn't leak. And heating that actually *heated* instead of just clanking.'

'All right, all right. You've made your point.' She examined an angry red stripe down the side of her hand.

'Perhaps you should run that under the tap.'

'Yes, thank you, Pearl,' she snapped, 'for the benefit of your medical expertise.'

But she hoisted herself over to the sink anyway, still swearing under her breath.

'Aren't pregnant women supposed to be all serene?' I said. 'Glowing with inner joy and all that?'

'No.' She winced as she held her hand under the cold water. 'They're supposed to be fat and prone to unpredictable mood swings.'

'Oh.' I suppressed a smile, partly because I felt sorry for her, and partly because I wasn't quite sure where the spatula might end up if I didn't.

There was a muffled snort of laughter from the hallway.

'I don't know what you think you're laughing at,' Mum shouted at the kitchen door. Dad's head appeared from behind it.

'Laughing?' he said, eyes wide and innocent. 'No, not me. I was just coming to congratulate you on mastering the mood swings so magnificently.'

Mum glared at him.

'Although, from memory,' he said, keeping well out of reach, 'you were pretty good at them before you were pregnant.'

For a moment I thought she was going to throw a saucepan at him. But she didn't. She just stood in the middle of the dilapidated, egg-shell-strewn, cocoa-smeared kitchen and laughed and laughed until there were tears streaming down her face and none of us were really sure whether she was laughing or crying. Dad went over and held her hands.

'Sit down, will you?' he said, leading her over to a chair. 'I'll make you a cup of tea. You're supposed to be taking it easy.'

'Bloody hormones.' She wiped her eyes.

'Are you sure that's all it is?' Dad sat down next to her, looking anxious. 'Are you sure you're OK?'

'Don't fuss,' she said, smiling. 'I'm fine. Really. It's just – well, look at me. I'm already so huge I practically need my own postcode. God only knows what I'll be like in another two months. And my ankles look like they belong to an old lady. It's most disconcerting.'

'It'll all be worth it,' Dad said.

'I know,' she said, her hands on her bump. 'Little Rose. She'll be worth it.'

Then they sat smiling at each other nauseatingly.

'Oh *yes*,' I said, grinning. 'All those sleepless nights and smelly nappies. It'll be well worth it.'

I pulled my jacket from where it was hanging on the back of a chair and turned to go.

'Are you off out?' Mum said.

'Yes. I'm meeting Molly.'

'Pearl, wait,' Mum said. 'Come here.'

She held her arms out and smiled, and it was just like it always was with Mum. However unreasonable she'd been, and however much you tried not to forgive her, she'd sort of dazzle you into it.

'Sorry, love. I shouldn't have shouted at you before. I've got a splitting headache, but I shouldn't have taken it out on you. I'm a miserable old crone.'

I smiled. 'Yes you are.'

'Do you forgive me?'

I dipped my finger into the bowl of chocolate cake mix on the table and tasted it. It was surprisingly good. 'Definitely not.' I leaned over her bump and gave her a peck on the cheek. 'Put your old lady feet up. Watch some crap telly, will you? Give the poor baby a bit of peace and quiet for once.'

She laughed and took my hand. 'Stay and have a cup of tea with me before you go.'

'I really can't. We're going to the cinema. Molls has booked the tickets.' I gave her hand a squeeze. 'I'll see you later.'

But I was wrong.

It's cold in the church. I hide my hands inside my sleeves to keep warm, but as the service goes on the chill starts to feel as though it's inside me. I imagine ice crystals forming in my veins. All around me there are people crying, but I can't feel anything, except cold.

It's all wrong. Mum would have hated it: the solemn music, the droning voice of the priest. I don't listen. I'm still trying to work out how I got here: how the world tipped and I slipped out of my comfortable, predictable life and landed here, in this cold, unfamiliar place.

At last it's nearly over. Everyone's singing the final, dreary hymn, but I can't join in. I just stand, jaw clenched, wondering why I'm still not crying, panic rising inside me. Why can't I cry? Will people notice and think I don't care? I untuck my hair from behind my ears and let it fall like a long dark curtain around my face. The coffin goes past, all shiny brass and lilies, the smell of them sweet and overpowering. Why lilies? They look so stiff and formal. Mum loved flowers that grew wherever they pleased. Honeysuckle tangled pink and yellow in hedges. The neon flash of poppies on motorway verges.

And suddenly I know that she's here. I *know* that if I look round I'll see her all alone in the middle of the furthest pew, and she'll wave and give me a big grin and blow me a kiss, like I'm five and in the infant school nativity play. My heart pounds till I'm light-headed. My hands are shaking.

I turn round.

I see rows and rows of sombre, dark-clothed people. I stand on tiptoes to see beyond them. Molly's there with her mum, red-eyed. She sees me looking and gives me a sad smile. I don't smile back.

The furthest pew is empty.

Outside, the rain has stopped. I stand, breathing in the damp, fresh air, trying not to be noticed while Dad is surrounded by a gaggle of dark-clothed people. A tall woman wearing a hat like a dead crow is telling him how sorry she is. He's not listening though. I can see his hand edging to his pocket for his phone. He wants to call the hospital to find out how the baby is, I know he does. When he's not actually with her, which is hardly ever, he phones practically every hour. I can tell he's panicking about what might happen if he doesn't. Even now, when all he should be thinking about is Mum.

I hang back as the group makes its way down the hill, keeping away from all the hat ladies and their sympathy, putting off the silent journey to the cemetery. By the time I get to the shiny black funeral parlour car, Dad's already inside, waiting for me. I look in through the window, but I can't see him properly behind the darkened glass, just the shape of him framed by my own reflection. My face is distorted, long and thin. My eyes, close to the glass, are huge. They're the one bit of me that looks like Mum. I always wanted her hair. *Do you know how much stick I got at school for being a redhead?* she'd say. But I did get her eyes: green, dark-lashed. For a moment it's as if she's staring at me through the window.

'I've got to go back,' I say. 'I've left my umbrella.' Dad can't hear me, but instead of opening the window he says something to me; I can make out his lips moving silently on the other side of the glass. For a moment we stare at each other helplessly. He might as well be on the other side of the world.

We've always been so close, me and Dad. I hated it when people called him my stepdad. Right from my earliest memories he's always been my dad. I didn't think anything could change that.

I can pinpoint the moment it happened. We were standing next to the baby's incubator. It was two hours after Mum died.

11

'Just look at her,' he whispered. I didn't know if he was talking to himself or to me, but even though I didn't want to, and my hands were shaking and I felt sick, I made myself look.

In my mind I could still see the dimpled, blonde, nappy-advert baby I'd imagined when Mum first told me she was pregnant, the baby me and Molly had picked out tiny shoes, dresses and furry sleepsuits with teddy bear ears for.

Then I saw *her*. And for a split second all I could think of was how, when I was five, our cat Soot had kittens. I'd been excited for weeks. I'd told everyone at school and Mum had given me a special book explaining how to look after them. Each night before I went to sleep I'd look at the pictures of those kittens: fluffy, wide-eyed. Then one day Mum took me into the back room and pointed to an open drawer at the bottom of the dresser. And there were these pink, wrinkly little rats, squirming blindly, and I looked at Mum in horror because I thought there'd been some terrible mistake; but she just stood there smiling and not understanding, and I ran out of the room crying because I hated them.

And, as I looked down at the mass of tubes, the paper-thin, purple-veined skin, the skeletal, alien crea-ture inside the incubator, I realized it wasn't shock making me tremble. It wasn't grief. It was hate: big and dark and terrifying. And I felt like I was falling and I needed something to hold on to, and I was so scared and I turned to Dad—

And he was hunched over her, the rat baby, *the reason Mum was dead*, focused on her as though she was the only thing in the world.

And all I wanted to do was hurt him. 'You love her more than you love me, don't you?' My voice came out clear and cold. 'Because—' I made myself say it. 'Because she's yours and I'm not.'

And it worked. He flinched. It was as if I'd hit him.

'How can you think that?' His eyes were wide with the shock of it. He took hold of my arms. 'You're my *daughter*. You know I could never love anyone more than you.'

And he was right. I *had* always known it. The biology of it had never made any difference. But now . . .

I broke myself free of his hold and turned away from him. What did his tears matter now?

He loved her.

Hours later, we drove home from the hospital through familiar, unreal London streets. It was already light: a sleepy Sunday morning, curtains drawn. The sky was clear blue, frosty rooftops glinting in pale, cold sunlight.

Dad opened the front door and behind it was our life, like an exhibit in a museum: perfectly preserved, hundreds of years old.

I walked through to the kitchen, trying to ignore Mum's discarded slippers on the hall floor, the photo on the fridge of us in Wales last summer.

Sitting in the middle of the kitchen table was the chocolate cake.

We stared at it, dazed. How could it still be there? Perfect and round and delicious. The flour she sieved, the eggs she beat.

And it was like something collapsed inside Dad. I could see it: sudden, but in slow motion, unstoppable, like an avalanche. He made this weird noise – a sob or a shout, scared and angry. Then he picked up the cake and threw it at the wall. Thick dark gobbets splattered and oozed and slid slowly down the wall.

I looked at the shattered mess. And something broke inside me too.

'She made that! She made it for us!' I was screaming, but it didn't sound like me. I ran at Dad and pushed him in the chest so hard he staggered backwards, eyes wide with shock. Then I ran out of the room.

And suddenly, with a force that scared me, I wished it was him that was dead.

Back in the church, I walk up the aisle to where we were sitting. It seems huge in here now it's empty. I kneel down to pick up my umbrella and put it in my bag. For a moment I feel so heavy and tired I think I can't get up again. It feels comfortable here. The silence isn't stifling like it was in the car. Just peaceful. I close my eyes and bow my head. I don't pray or anything. I just feel the dark pressing against my eyelids. I don't want to go back outside. I don't want to sit in that car with Dad, go to the cemetery, eat dry, curly sandwiches with everyone like at Nanna Pam's funeral. I can't. I just want to kneel here with my eyes closed.

But Dad's waiting outside.

With an effort I stand up and turn to go.

And there she is. Sitting all alone in the middle of the furthest pew.

Her eyes are fixed on me and for a moment I catch a look on her face I've never seen before: a fierce look of joy and longing. But as our eyes meet it vanishes. She smiles and stands up, holds out her arms to me.

I can't move. I don't dare. Any sudden movement and she might take flight like a bird or fade into the shadows. I hardly let myself breathe.

'It's OK,' she says and despite the smile there's a catch in her voice. 'It's only me.'

At last, slowly, I walk towards her. The click of my shoes echoes quietly into the still church. I reach the back pew and I stand facing her, just staring, taking in every last detail: her red curls twisted untidily up in a clip, the tiny amber flecks in her green eyes, the frayed laces of her old baseball boots.

'What are you doing here?' It comes out as a whisper.

For a second she's silent. Then she laughs, till it rings round the church right up to the vaulted stone of the roof, happy peals of it filling the cold space around us.

'It's my *funeral*, Pearl. Of course I'm here.'

My head is spinning. I put my hand on the pew to steady myself. Mum's here. I can see her.

'But you're . . .'

I can't say it.

'Dead?' She grimaces comically. 'Well, yes. That *is* the downside of attending one's own funeral.'

I stare at her, outraged.

'Don't you joke about it,' I shout. 'Don't you *dare*.'

My anger echoes round the dark hollows above us.

She doesn't say anything, just reaches out and cups my face in her hands and watches me silently till her fingers are wet with my tears. Then she pulls me to her and hugs me tight, kisses my hair.

I can't speak. Great sobs rise from deep inside me, shaking my whole body. Even when the tears stop, I keep my face pressed into her. I know it can't be real, but I don't care. Somehow she's here. I breathe her in, the warm, familiar smell of her.

16

'How?' I try to say, but she doesn't answer. I don't ask again. Asking might break the spell. And anyway perhaps I don't want to know. I must be mad. Or perhaps I'm dreaming and if I think about it too hard I'll wake up.

I don't care. It doesn't matter. She's here.

Then I push her away.

'Why did you miss that midwife appointment? They said if you'd gone they'd have known something was wrong. They'd have done tests. Why didn't you tell someone you were feeling ill?'

She shrugs impatiently. 'It was just a headache for God's sake. I didn't know it was serious.'

I look at her and more tears slide down my cheeks. 'You didn't even say goodbye.'

'I know.'

She says it quietly and I'm suddenly scared.

'Is that why you're here? To say goodbye?'

She doesn't say anything, just smiles a little. But the smile makes her look sad. Then she sits down, deflated.

'Oh, Pearl, I'm sorry. What a fucking mess.'

'*Mum!*'

'What?'

'We're in church.'

'Yes, about that,' says Mum, 'whose idea was it to give me a full bloody requiem mass? It went on for hours. By the end of it, I bet everyone was wishing it was them in the coffin.'

'Well, Granny suggested it actually—'

Mum rolls her eyes. 'Oh,' she says. 'Oh *well*. Yes. I might have known. Interfering as usual. You know what she's like.'

I shrug. I haven't seen Granny since I was a little kid. I can't even really remember her. Mum and her didn't exactly Get Along. Dad would phone her every now and then when Mum was out. She'd pretend not to know he kept in touch. 'Dad says she's really upset—'

'Oh, she is, is she? I notice she couldn't actually be bothered to turn up. I suppose she had something more important to do. One of her Pilates classes, was it? Her weekly manicure? Or was my funeral not worth forking out the train fare down from Scotland for?'

I stare at her in wonder. She's dead. She's here. And she's still having a go at Granny.

'Mum—' I've heard the rant she's about to launch into a million times before, but there's no stopping her.

'She never liked me, Pearl. Never thought I was good enough for her precious son. Horrible single mother turning up with a mewling, snotty baby—'

'Excuse me, that's *me* you're talking about.'

'Stealing her darling boy away. She's probably breaking open the champagne as we speak.'

'Actually, Dad told her he thought it would be best if she didn't come, what with everything that's gone on. He said he wasn't sure you'd want her there. She did send some flowers.'

'Oh. Well.' Mum looks taken aback and sits down again, unsure what to say for once.

'Anyway, you can't just blame Granny. Dad agreed it was for the best. Having it in church I mean. I told him you wouldn't like it, but he said *just in case.* You know. Doesn't do any harm, does it?' I looked at her, wondering suddenly. 'Or does it?'

Mum sighs. 'It's always so bloody cold in church.' She shivers and reaches absently into a pocket, bringing out a packet of cigarettes.

'*Mum!*'

'What? Oh right. Yes. Church.' She shrugs. 'It's my funeral.'

She smirks at her joke and looks hopefully at me to see if I'm laughing too.

I'm not.

'You've given up, remember?'

She gives me a look.

'Pearl, give me a break. One of the few advantages of being dead is that you can *finally* stop giving things up.'

19

And of course she's not pregnant any more. I push the thought away. I don't want to think about The Rat. I certainly don't want to talk about her. I want Mum to myself.

She takes a long drag and blows a smoke ring. We watch it together as it floats upwards, expanding, growing fainter and fainter until it's gone.

How can she be here? The question still echoes round my head; but there's something more important that I need to know.

'How long can you stay?' I whisper it, hardly daring to say the words out loud.

She's about to speak when the church door slams, echoing loudly. The sound makes me jump and I spin round to see Dad.

'Come on, we've got to go,' he says impatiently. 'We can't keep everyone waiting.'

I whirl back to where Mum was standing, but I know already that she's gone.

'What are you doing in here anyway?' Dad asks.

'What?' I stare at him blankly, hardly hearing him. She's gone. It's all I can think of. There were so many things I needed to ask her. And now I might never see her again. 'Why did you come back?' he says, his voice gentler.

'I left something behind,' I say, fighting back tears.

'Did you find it?'

'Yes,' I say, following him out of the church. 'I found it.'

As I step through the door, I look back to the space where Mum had been.

A shaft of light streams suddenly through a stained-glass window above me, making a pool of rainbow colour on the stone floor.

The sun has come out.

APRIL

'Right. I'm off to the hospital.' Dad has a last swig of coffee and takes his toast with him in his hurry to leave. 'And I'll be going there straight after work too, so I won't be back till late. Rose had a good night last night apparently.'

He's trying to make his voice all bright and breezy, like he can fool us both that everything's OK. But his face is lined and pale. Sometimes I wake up in the night and I hear him crying quietly. I lie in the dark, feeling like I'm eavesdropping, wishing I knew what to do about it. Once I've heard it, I can't get back to sleep. Those nights stretch on and on until I'm not properly awake or properly asleep. Sometimes I think it will never get light, and I'll be stuck on my own in those in-between, shadowy hours forever.

'Are you sure you won't come with me?' He asks the same thing every day, just as he gets to the door, like he's trying not to, but at the last minute he just can't help himself. He wants it to sound like he doesn't mind one way or the other. I can't look at his face because I know it won't match his voice, and seeing how much he wants me to care about The Rat makes my insides squirm. Instead, I poke at the soggy cornflakes in my bowl with my spoon.

'Are you going to eat those?' he asks. But he already knows the answer.

'You have to eat, Pearl.' He can't keep the frustration out of his voice. 'I've got enough to worry about without you—' He stops himself, but his words hang between us in the chilly air.

'Sorry,' he says. 'I'm sorry, love. I just meant . . .'

He searches for a way to finish the sentence, but he needn't bother. I know what he meant.

'Pearl,' he pleads. 'Look at me.'

But instead I look at four small rainbow squares painted on the flaking grey kitchen wall behind him. Mum painted them months ago when we first moved in, trying out different colours from tiny sample paint pots. She'd had great plans for redecorating when we first looked round the house. She was always coming back from the shops with curtain swatches and wallpaper. But like always with her projects she lost interest after a while. The move dragged on for so long, with things going wrong down the chain and Mum shouting at solicitors and mortgage people on the phone, that by the time we moved in her energy and enthusiasm quickly vanished. As she grew more pregnant, she just got tetchy and tearful about the state of the house: the grubby old wallpaper, the draughty, rattling windows, the leaking roof.

I wrap my dressing gown a bit tighter round me.

'I thought you were going,' I say.

'OK,' Dad sighs, too tired to push it. 'Try and get some revision done then. I know it's hard, Pearl, but you'll be back at school next week. Your exams will be here before you know it.'

I don't reply. It's almost a month since I was at school. With the Easter holidays coming straight after Mum's funeral I haven't been back since she died. While I've been here, hidden away on my own, everything has stopped. I hate the thought of being out in the real world again, of life carrying on without Mum. And I know exactly how it will be at school: everyone knowing, watching but pretending not to, whispering when they think I'm out of earshot, like when Katie Hammond's dad went to prison or when we first found out Zoe Greenwood was pregnant. The thought of going back makes me feel sick.

'Don't look like that,' he says. 'Molly'll look after you, won't she?'

Molly always has. Before this.

'I'll stop at the supermarket on the way home tonight,' Dad says. 'Get us something nice for tea if you don't mind eating late. Or I could get us a takeaway?'

I get up and scrape the cornflake mush into the bin. 'Don't bother,' I say.

'I'm trying to help,' he says wearily, and for a second I'm so breathless with anger that I have to turn my back on him. I grip the side of the sink and look out of the window at the grey-green wilderness of the back garden.

'How can you possibly help? How can anyone?' The words stick painfully in my throat. Of all people he should know, he *must* know what an empty, pointless thing that is to say.

But when I turn round he's already gone.

I try to feel pleased that I'm on my own, but instead I just feel small. The silence and emptiness of the house weigh down on me, room after dingy room of it. And now I'm alone I can't ignore the tense, sick feeling in my stomach. I switch on the radio. I boil the kettle and make a cup of tea that I don't drink. I force myself to take a shower, turning my face against the hot spikes of water. I pull on yesterday's clothes. But none of it works: I try not to, but all the time I'm waiting for her.

Almost three weeks have passed since the funeral and there's no trace of her: not a glimpse or a whisper or a

28

sign that she might have been there while I wasn't looking. I leave the patio doors open sometimes, half hoping she'll close them. She always had a thing about draughts. But Dad just gets annoyed. *For heaven's sake, Pearl, what are you playing at? This house is cold enough without any help from you.*

One night, when Dad had to stay over in the hospital, I found her perfume in the cupboard under the sink and I sat on my bed and sprayed it into the air in the hope of conjuring her up. I closed my eyes. And for a moment, breathing in the scent of her, I thought she was really there. I thought that when I opened my eyes she'd be standing there watching me, saying, *Don't waste that, it was bloody expensive I'll have you know.* But she wasn't, and the smell of the perfume made me ache inside so that I could hardly breathe and I had to close my eyes again to stop the tears escaping. So I've put it away now, back in the cupboard under the sink.

I even went back to the church. I thought that if I knelt in the same place and bowed my head and closed my eyes she'd have to come back. But the church was all locked up. A woman in a headscarf turned up with the key saying she was there to do the flowers for a wedding tomorrow. Did I want to come in? I just shook my head. Why had I come here? It was stupid. Of course she wasn't here. What was I thinking of? But still, as the woman pushed the door open with a woolly-gloved hand, I peered in, half expecting to see a movement in the shadows, or a telltale trace of cigarette smoke. I can't help it. It doesn't matter how many times I tell myself she won't come back or I imagined it or I'm mad. All the time, I'm waiting for her.

As I walk down the stairs, taking care not to catch my feet on the bare carpet tacks, I hear a rustling sound from the small room next to my bedroom. I stop dead. It's the room that Mum had planned to turn into her study. For a moment I stand completely still, palms prickling, listening to the silence. There it is again! I run back up the stairs, my heart thudding.

'Mum?'

I reach out, my hand shaking. But when I push the door open the room is empty apart from Mum's desk and chair and several removal company boxes, still unopened, marked STELLA'S STUDY in Mum's brash handwriting.

Soot appears from behind one of them, purring loudly.

'You,' I say. She saunters over and winds herself round my legs and, despite my disappointment, I sit down on the chair and settle her on my lap.

We've been here more than four months now, but it still feels like someone else's house. There are packing boxes everywhere, left where the impatient removal men dumped them on the icy day we moved in, a couple of weeks before Christmas. We've taken out the essentials: pots and pans, duvets, alarm clocks. But Mum said it wasn't worth unpacking everything until we'd sorted the house out a bit, redecorated. So the rest of our old life is still in the boxes, safely packed away out of sight. The bareness of the rooms just emphasizes how shabby and depressing they are. The whole house looks like it was last redecorated when dinosaurs roamed the earth.

'You don't half exaggerate,' Mum had said when I voiced this opinion the first time we looked round the house, late last summer. 'It just needs a bit of TLC.'

'And about twenty grand thrown at it,' Dad had muttered. 'There's no way . . .'

But Mum just laughed and kissed him on the cheek and said, 'You'll see.' And as we traipsed from room to gloomy room she transformed them, imagining jewel-coloured walls and velvet cushions, polished floorboards and oriental rugs and roaring log fires with Soot stretched warm in front of them, dreaming of mice.

'Dreaming of them?' Dad said. 'I bet this place is infested with them.'

But the estate agent stared at Mum, impressed. 'Blimey,' he said. 'You should do my job. Don't fancy coming to my next viewing with me, do you?'

In the end the only room she got round to redecorating was the baby's. She was determined it would be perfect. She sanded and varnished the floorboards. She cleaned the dusty paintwork and painted it glossy white. She stripped the mildewed wallpaper, Dad lurking anxiously by the door as she teetered on top of the step-ladder. 'Let me do that,' he pleaded, but she wouldn't. There was a lot of crashing about and swearing, but she got it all done. Then she pasted up smooth, pale lining paper and painted it the colour of bluebells. She hung mobiles and fairy lights and even made curtains on Nanna Pam's old sewing machine.

'I didn't know you could sew!' I said.

'Course I can sew,' she replied. 'I used to make all my own clothes when I was at art school.' I stared at her, as amazed as if it had suddenly turned out she could levitate. She just smiled and said, 'There's more to me than meets the eye, Pearl.'

It's like it belongs in a different house, that room, or perhaps this house in a parallel universe where everything turned out different. Going in there feels like that bit in *The Wizard of Oz* when everything changes from black and white to colour.

Not that we ever do go in now. The door – painted shiny white – stays shut.

My phone buzzes. I know before I look at it that it's Molly. She phones and texts every day to see how I am, desperate to meet up. But every time she phones I just let it ring. I don't know why. I thought I'd want to see her. She's always been there for me, ever since we were little kids first starting school together.

I look at her text: *Can u meet tomorrow? Hope u r OK xxx*

She'll want to talk, about Mum and the baby. I can't tell her about Mum. She'll think I'm mad. And I know she won't understand about The Rat. Molly loves babies. All that time we spent looking at baby clothes and thinking up names . . .

I don't want to talk. Not to Molly. Not to anyone. Except Mum. But I know she'll be hurt if I don't get back to her, and school starts next week. I can't hide away in here forever. *OK*, I type, but then my thumb hovers over the send key. Perhaps later. I put the phone back in my pocket.

Soot jumps off my lap, giving me a reproachful look, then leaps up on to a box marked STELLA'S STUDY (PERSONAL) and settles down into a cat-shaped hollow she's made there. PERSONAL. What's in there? I wonder. But I think of the perfume and how it made me feel and I know I can't open it.

I walk over to the window. The greyish net curtains left by the old couple who used to live here are still hanging there. Mum hated them, but I like the way everything looks soft and blurred through them, no sharp edges. I pull them back for a moment and everything comes glaringly into focus: the pale pink blossom unfurling on the cherry trees that line our road, the buses thundering past, graffiti etched on their windows. The old dear next door is out in her front garden, tending to the flower beds. As I watch, she stands up, grimacing with pain as she straightens her back, and catches sight of me at the window. She smiles and cheerfully waves a pair of secateurs at me. I let the net curtain drop down again.

Dad will be at the hospital by now. I imagine him, rushing through those awful green corridors that I remember so well, eager to get to *her*. What does he do there, all day every day? Just sit staring at The Rat? Does he talk to her, tell her things?

'Mum?' I say one last time. 'Are you there?' But all I hear is the cat purring and a car alarm going off down the road.

It's raining so hard I get the bus to meet Molly. As I stand at the bus stop, I wish I hadn't agreed to meet her after all. Maybe I should text her and say I can't make it. But then the bus pulls up and the old man in front of me says, 'After you, dear,' and ushers me on so there's no getting out of it.

The bus is pretty empty when I get on, but after a couple of stops it's crowded and the air is thick and damp. A very wide woman laden with shopping sits down next to me so that I'm all squashed up against the window. Her wet carrier bags rest against my leg, making my jeans clammy and cold.

I think about the last time I met up with Molly; remember the two of us stumbling out of the dark cinema that day, into the dazzling afternoon. It was only a few weeks ago. *That's weird*, I'd said, switching my phone back on. *Dad's phoned fifteen times. What's he playing at? He knew we were going to see a film . . .*

The bus windows are so steamed up it's like being in a cave and I start to feel claustrophobic. I make a small clear square on the steamed-up window with my finger so I can see out to the rainy streets. The doctor's surgery, the chippy, the petrol station. Everything, inexplicably, just the same as it's always been my whole life.

This bus route goes past the end of the street where we used to live. There's a little boy in yellow wellies at the corner, holding his mum's hand and jumping in puddles. I peer at them through the gap on the window which is starting to cloud up again. As I do, I see the back of someone, a dark figure with an umbrella, turn into our old road. Was it Mum? Yes! Wasn't that a glimpse of red hair I saw before she disappeared from view? Suddenly I'm certain of it. It must be her. I know it was.

'I've got to get off!' I blurt at the wide lady. I jump up, pressing the bell and clambering over her shopping as she tuts at me.

'Watch it,' she says as I dash for the doors. 'There's eggs in there.'

Outside, the rain's still bucketing down. I don't have an umbrella and before I've even sprinted across the road, a car blaring its horn at me, I'm soaked. I don't care. I run round the corner and down the street and, spotting the dark figure ahead of me through the rain, I speed up.

'Mum,' I call out, but she's too far ahead to hear. I'm out of breath, but getting closer. 'Mum, it's me,' I call again as the figure turns to cross the road—

—and I realize it's a man. Way taller than Mum. No red hair. How could I have thought it was her?

My whole body burns with humiliation as I slow my pace to a walk and try to catch my breath. How could I have been so stupid? What if someone had seen me? They'd think I was mad. And worse than that – my stomach lurches – they might be right. What am I doing? Am I really losing my mind? People were always going mad from grief in history and Shakespeare. Maybe that's what's happening to me.

I look around me and realize I'm standing right outside number 16, a house just the same as all the others, in the middle of the terrace. It doesn't look like our home any more. In the few months since we moved out they've painted the door white and paved over the small square front garden. All trace of us is gone.

The rain plasters my hair to my head and drips from my eyelashes, my nose. My reflection looks back at me from the bay window: a ghost girl. Sometimes, when I can't get to sleep and it gets to that shadowy, unreal time of the night, I think that somehow I split off from the real me in that moment in the wintery sunshine outside the cinema when I listened to Dad's message on my phone and everything changed. The other me is living my real life with Mum and the perfect, pretty baby sister that should have been mine. And I'm trapped here with The Rat, unable to escape.

The ghost girl in the window watches me, water trickling down her face. I turn away from her and walk slowly back up the road.

When I get to Angelo's Cafe, Molly is already inside, sitting at a table in the window. She looks almost luminous through the rain, tucking her long blonde hair absently behind her ear as she watches anxiously for me. She waves frantically as she sees me and my stomach flips and my nails dig into my palms. I want to be pleased to see her, but I just want to turn round and go home.

As soon as I walk inside, she jumps up, sending a tomato-shaped ketchup holder rolling across the floor, tears running down her cheeks.

'Oh, Pearl.' She hugs me and even though I'm soaking wet she won't let go. 'I can't believe it,' she sobs. I stand there stiffly, staring over her shoulder at the endless traffic on the main road. I don't want Molly to cry over Mum. She's got no right.

Eventually, she lets go and looks at me.

'I'm so sorry, Pearl.'

'I know.' I sit down, dripping on to the wood-effect plastic table. Molly sits too and takes hold of my hand.

'Look at you. You're soaked to the skin. I'll go and see if they can bring you a towel or something.'

Before she can move, a waiter dashes over, all smiles. Waiters always want to impress Molly. In fact, the whole male population wants to impress Molly. Not that she notices. She thinks they're just being nice, that they're like that to everyone, regardless of whether they happen to be tall and blonde and extremely attractive. Mum always used to worry that it would bother me. *You're beautiful too*, she'd say. *Just in a . . . different sort of way*. But it doesn't bother me. People assume there's nothing more to Molly than being pretty. That's why we've always been best friends: I've always known different.

'I can help you?' the waiter says hopefully in an eastern European accent, even though everyone else has to order at the counter.

'Don't fuss, Molls, I'm fine,' I say, clenching my teeth to stop them chattering.

'You're not,' she says, full of concern. 'You're wringing wet. Look at you. You're shivering.'

'You want me to bring a towel? It's no problem,' he says.

'No.'

But he's not even listening to me, he's transfixed by Molly.

'Could you?' she says. 'Thanks so much.'

'I said I'm fine,' I say too loudly. A man on the other side of the cafe looks up from his plate of egg, bacon and beans and I huddle down into my wet clothes, trying to look inconspicuous. 'Just a cappuccino thanks,' I mutter and the waiter drags himself away, still grinning stupidly at Molly, though she's far too busy fussing over me to pay any attention.

'I've been so worried about you,' she says. I can't think of anything to say. I'm still half thinking about the house, the girl in the window, the figure I thought was Mum. I was so sure it was her.

'I wanted to wait and speak to you after the funeral, but Mum said we should just go,' Molly carries on. 'I've been thinking about you all the time. What you must have been going through.' She shakes her head. 'It must have been so awful, Pearl. I've been so desperate to speak to you.'

'Well, sorry,' I say harshly, thinking of all the times she's phoned and I haven't answered, all the texts I've ignored, sitting on my own in the house waiting for Mum. 'I've been kind of busy.'

She stares at me and goes red.

'I know ... I didn't mean ...' she stumbles, confused. 'I just wanted to see if there was anything I could do ...'

Water is still trickling from my hair, cold down the back of my neck.

'You can't do anything,' I say.

She watches me, her eyes big and puzzled.

'I thought you might want to talk. I know I can't change anything, but it might make you feel better to talk about how you're feeling.'

We've always talked about everything. Right from when we were little kids. But how can I now? What would she say if she knew what I was really feeling? *I hate the baby. It should be her that's dead.* Even lovely, kind, understanding Molly might find that a bit hard to take. *I saw my mum at her funeral and now I'm waiting for her to come back again?* I don't think so.

'I was going to come round, but I didn't know ...' She trails off and her eyes fill with tears again. I look away. I know I'm being cruel, but I don't seem to be able to stop.

'I just can't believe it,' she says again.

The smiling waiter brings our coffees. I make patterns in the top of my cappuccino with my spoon.

'How's the baby?' Molly says at last. My heart thuds. I knew she'd ask eventually.

I shrug. 'Dad thinks she'll die.' I hold a sugar cube in the coffee and watch the brown stain climb till it almost touches my fingers. 'She won't though.'

'No.' Molly pounces on something she can be positive about. 'Course she won't. She must be a fighter, to have survived till now. Every day she'll be getting stronger.'

The sugar cube disintegrates and falls into the coffee. 'How long will she be in hospital?'

'Dunno. Weeks. Months probably. That's what they told Dad.'

'It's like a kind of miracle, isn't it? That she's alive.'

I knew I shouldn't have come. I want to just get up and run out, away from Molly and the lurking waiter and the smell of frying bacon, into the rain. But I've embarrassed myself enough for one day. I look out of the window and watch the cars go by.

'Mum used to bring me here when I was a little kid,' I say, more to myself than to Molly. 'This really old Italian guy used to run it then. Angelo, I suppose. He was funny.'

Mum used to practise her Italian on him. She used to tell him he was mad for moving to London. She said one day we were going to run away to Italy, me and her and Dad, and we'd live in a crumbling villa and she'd have an artist's studio surrounded by lemon trees and live on olives and red wine. I remember how worried I

41

was. I was too young then to know that most of Mum's grand schemes were just talk. I didn't want to move and I didn't like olives or lemons or red wine. Angelo would wink at me and say, 'You like the *gelato* though, no?'

I can feel Molly watching me, wondering what I'm thinking. 'You OK?' she says tentatively.

'She'd always sit at one of the window tables and tell me to see how many red cars I could count. She told me if I counted thirty she'd buy me an ice cream.' I almost smile. 'Took me ages to realize it was just so she could read a book in peace.'

There's a pause.

'Pearl. That day—' Molly stops and I know from her face which day she means. 'After we'd been to the cinema . . .'

'What about it?'

'After you got the phone call from your dad . . .'

I remember again how I listened to my voicemail outside the cinema in the bright sunshine, and how something in Dad's voice made me stop so sharply in the middle of the pavement that a woman ran into my ankles with her buggy. The bruise lasted for days after, but at the time I hardly noticed; all I could think of was Dad's voice. It sounded so – wrong. *Pearl, you need to get to the hospital. It's Mum. Get a taxi. Just be as quick as you can.* He didn't sound like him. Time slowed down. I just stood there in the busy street full of Saturday afternoon

42

shoppers with their kids and dogs and cans of Coke, and it was like I was on my own.

'Did you get there in time to see her?' Molly asks.

I close my eyes and I'm back, running down those green hospital corridors, lungs bursting . . . I open them again. I watch the cars, but they're all black and silver and white. No red ones.

'Yes,' I say to Molly eventually. 'I did.'

'Did you speak to her?'

'Yes. She gave me a hug and told me she loved me.' I feel like I'm listening to someone else saying it. 'And then it was like she just fell asleep. Peaceful. She was even smiling.'

'Oh, Pearl.' Her tears flow again.

The besotted waiter looks over, maybe hoping to offer his shoulder to cry on.

'Can we pay?' I say. I feel faint suddenly. My stomach is empty and the coffee is making my brain buzz. 'I need to go.'

The rain has stopped at last. We stand awkwardly outside the cafe, neither of us knowing what to say.

'I'm going to meet Ravi,' Molly says. 'But I can walk back with you first if you like?'

'Ravi?' I say, surprised. 'You're not still seeing him, are you?' Molly had met him at a party we'd been to just before Mum died. I'd assumed she wouldn't see him again. Molly could have her pick of anyone. Ravi looks like his ambition is to be the youngest ever Chancellor of the Exchequer.

'I am actually,' Molly says shyly. 'It's been more than a month now. It's going really well.'

'Oh.' Strange to think of life going on without me.

'You don't like him, do you?' Molly says.

'It's not that,' I say. 'I don't know him. I only met him that one time at Chloe's party. He seemed a bit . . .' I try to think of a polite way of saying 'dull', '. . . serious.'

'You'll like him when you get to know him,' Molly says. 'I know you will.'

We walk along in silence, the noise of the traffic loud around us.

'School was weird without you,' Molly says, filling the gap. 'And the holidays have been a nightmare. My family's driving me mad. Liam plays his music really loud all day. Jake wants a pet snake, keeps on about it the whole time. Callum keeps wetting the bed. Mum and Dad aren't talking to each other. *Again.* I'll be glad to get back to school. And it'll be great to have you back.' She takes my arm.

I've never really heard Molly's mum and dad say much to each other, except for stuff like *Where are the car keys?* or *I told you I'd be late tonight, it's not my fault if you don't listen.* But Molly looks really down.

44

'I've really missed you,' she says, linking arms with me. I wonder if she expects me to say I've missed her too. A massive lorry thunders past, spraying the puddles at the side of the road up towards us so we have to dodge out of the way. Molly lets go of my arm and we walk side by side.

'Do you go and see her every day?' Molly asks. 'The baby?'

'Dad does. He practically lives there when he's not at work. I never see him.'

'Don't you go too?'

I shrug. 'I've been revising.'

'Me too,' she says. 'But it's so noisy at my house. Everyone's rowing all the time. Once we're on study leave, we should go to the library together.'

We walk in silence for a while.

'Maybe I could come with you to visit the baby some time,' Molly says. 'I can't wait to see her.'

I imagine Molly seeing The Rat for the first time. I imagine her face lighting up, softening into a smile as she whispers to her—

'No,' I say. 'You can't.'

Molly looks confused. 'When she's well enough I mean.'

'You might as well leave me here,' I say. 'I'll get the bus.'

'You sure?' She's disappointed. 'I really don't mind walking with you.'

'There's one coming now,' I say, spying a bus in the distance, and before she can say anything more I dash out across the road. Molly waves as I stand in the queue, and then turns and walks off in the opposite direction. She's out of sight when the bus eventually pulls up.

I decide to walk after all.

By the time I get back to the house, the sun is shining. I go inside to peel off my damp clothes and get dry ones on, still thinking about Mum, how sure I'd been that it was her. I feel panicky suddenly. She's slipping away from me, every second taking me further away from her. What if I wake up one day and I can't remember what she looked like? Already, sometimes, I have to concentrate to think of what she sounded like when she spoke, to try and hear it in my head. I have to keep her with me.

I remember the box in her study. PERSONAL it had said. I hurry through and stare at it. What's in there? I shoo a deeply unimpressed Soot off the lid of the box. Then I take a deep breath and carefully peel back the brown tape that seals it.

Inside, there are letters and cards, photos and postcards, bunches of them tied up with string or ribbon or held with elastic bands, some in old shoeboxes, others loose. There must be hundreds of them. I stare at them, overwhelmed, hardly able to breathe. It's like the story of Mum's life all here in this box. I pick out one of the envelopes of photos and look through them. They're all muddled up, some of Mum when she was a little girl and then a teenager, one of her with Nanna Pam before she got ill. Looking at them makes me cry, but I keep on looking.

The last picture is of Mum lying in a hospital bed, looking young and exhausted, holding me, all new and crumpled. Not like The Rat though. I look like a real baby. I think of The Rat in her funny plastic box with the tubes going in and out of her. Is she still in it? Does she still look the same? I examine the photo carefully. Dad wasn't there; he and Mum had been friends since before I was born, but they didn't get together until a few months later. My real father hadn't been there either. He and Mum had split up before I was even born. I think of how Dad looked at The Rat when we first saw her and I wish suddenly that someone had been there to look at me like that.

I put the envelope back in the box and press down the tape. There's plenty more to see, but I can't look any more. Perhaps another day.

The sun's shining now and I go outside into the garden. It was a mess when we moved in and now spring is here it's grown completely wild. I pick my way across the overgrown meadow of the lawn, yellow with dandelions, to the little bench under the trees at the end, surrounded by a mass of lily of the valley in among knee-high weeds. I close my eyes, just like I did in the church when Mum appeared, and I try to reach her with my mind.

This was where it all started: where she told me about The Rat, that day we first looked round the house last summer. I picture it in my head, trying to remember every tiny detail. The estate agent had taken Dad up to look at the loft space.

'Plenty of room for a master bedroom and en suite up there if you ever wanted to convert it, Alex,' he said as they started up the stairs. 'You don't mind me calling you Alex, do you?'

Mum had done a disappearing act. I thought maybe she'd gone outside for a cigarette so I went out to explore the overgrown tangle of back garden and found her, sitting where I am now, almost hidden from the house. But she wasn't smoking.

'What are you doing out here?' I'd asked. 'It looks like it's going to chuck it down again any minute.'

'I just needed some air,' she said. 'I felt a bit—' She stopped and put her hand over her mouth suddenly, as though she was going to be sick.

I looked at her. 'Are you OK? You look terrible.'

'Of course,' she said, attempting a bright smile. 'Just . . .' Her skin was pale and waxy, smudged dark under the eyes. She tried to smile. 'I'm absolutely fine, really.'

I looked at her, surprised. I knew from years of watching Mum lie that she could fib without a flicker. Never about anything serious. Just about parking tickets or library fines, or imaginary disasters that meant she was going to be late for work. When I was a kid, she'd have me believing her, even though I knew what she was saying bore absolutely no resemblance to the facts. Afterwards, she'd give me a big wink and say, *Just a little white lie, Pearl.* But this wasn't a little white lie. This was something big; so big she couldn't hide it.

'You're not fine. Why are you lying to me?'

Now I thought about it she hadn't seemed right for a while. Tired all the time. Not eating much.

'Oh my God. You're ill, aren't you?'

'Honestly, Pearl, you're such a drama queen.'

But she looked nervous, not meeting my eye.

I started to panic. 'It's something serious. That's why you're lying.'

It seemed obvious now. The tiredness and the sickness. Three mornings that week I'd been hopping around outside our toilet while Mum vomited. She'd said it was food poisoning, but, oh Christ, it all made sense now. Dad fussing round her all the time. She'd even given up smoking. It had to be something serious. What else could explain it? The tiredness. Giving up smoking. Sickness . . . every morning . . .

49

Oh.

I looked at her, disbelieving. 'You're *pregnant*,' I breathed.

'No,' she said. 'Well . . . Yes. Dad'll kill me for telling you. He wanted us to do it together. You'll have to pretend it's all a big surprise when we do.'

I stared at her. 'You're going to have a baby,' I said, still not really believing it.

'That's the general idea.'

'And you're always telling *me* to Be Careful.'

She looked embarrassed. 'Actually, it wasn't an accident.'

I tried to take all it in. 'But you're too old.'

'No I'm not,' she said, frowning. 'I'm thirty-seven. Which is very young *actually*, Pearl.'

I tried to get it all straight in my head.

'When is it due?'

'Not for ages. I'm only a few weeks gone.'

'Is it a boy or a girl?'

She shrugs. 'I don't know. Dad's convinced it's a boy.'

We sat in awkward silence for a moment. I didn't know what to say.

'Are you pleased?' she asked. 'About the baby?'

'I don't know.' The whole thing was freaking me out a bit. She looked disappointed.

'I don't mind,' I said. 'It's just a surprise.' I thought about it a bit more. 'Are *you* pleased?'

'I would be if I didn't feel so sick,' she said. 'Dad's over the bloody moon.'

We sat there a while longer, the scent of rain on dry earth hanging in the air around us.

Funny how things get linked in your head. When I smell it now, that smell of rain and mud and things growing silently, it feels like a warning that you don't know what's coming; that the world can tip. At the time it just smelt fresh and clean and new.

'Wow,' I said at last, smiling. 'A *baby*.'

'I know,' she said. 'Amazing, isn't it?'

'Yeah,' I said. 'It is pretty amazing.'

She reached out and squeezed my hand. 'I'm so glad you're pleased,' she said. 'You'll make a fantastic big sister.'

'Can I have your leather jacket?' I said. 'You'll be too fat for it soon.'

It seems like another life, thinking back on it now. I open my eyes. Has it worked? Surely she'll be here. But the garden is still.

'Mum?' I say at last. '*Mum*. Are you there?'

I wait.

'*Please*.'

There's the lazy buzz of an aeroplane overhead. A tear slides down my nose. Why should she be any more reliable now she's dead than she was when she was alive? The thought flashes, unwelcome, into my head and suddenly my patience has gone.

'Why did you let him persuade you to have a stupid baby in the first place?' I shout at the empty garden. 'Why aren't you here when I need you?'

Shouting feels good.

'You're a selfish bitch!'

I'm so angry my hands are shaking. But rage feels good. It feels hot and powerful and fierce and I feel alive. I shut my eyes again and breathe deeply and slowly. As the anger drains away, I feel limp and exhausted and a bit ridiculous. The garden sounds very quiet now I've stopped ranting. And yet – I open my eyes – not as quiet as it should. There's a shuffling sound in the leaves on the other side of the wall. I sit up, tensed.

'Who's there?' For a second I think maybe it's Mum. But no, if she'd heard me shouting at her, she wouldn't be hiding behind a wall, she'd be yelling right back at me. But if it's not her . . .

It's probably just Soot, I tell myself, trying not to panic. Then the shuffling stops and someone clears their throat in a slightly embarrassed way.

I'm guessing it's not the cat.

Christ. Whoever it is must have heard everything. It must be Dulcie, the old lady next door. But no, it didn't sound like an old lady kind of cough at all—

'Are you all right?' says a male voice abruptly.

I freeze. I think about scuttling back into the house and hiding there forever. I think about lying down on the ground and pretending to have had some kind of fit, or a bang to the head or attack, that would explain everything or at least provide a distraction and mean I didn't have to speak. I think about invisibility cloaks and stories in the news about sinkholes opening up and swallowing people whole. But disaster never strikes when you want it to.

'Hello?' says the voice uncertainly.

In the end I decide the only option is to pretend it never happened.

'Yes, I'm fine,' I say, trying to sound surprised that he's asking such a stupid question, whoever he is.

There's a pause.

'Are you sure?' It's a gruff voice, with a northern sort of accent.

'Yes. Of course I'm sure.'

'You sounded a bit . . .' He's obviously trying to think of a diplomatic way of saying 'insane'. 'Upset.'

'I said I'm fine.'

Another pause.

'Right.' Is he being sarcastic? I stand up and stare at the wall, trying to get a sense of the person on the other side. Is he laughing at me? My fists clench. I'm not having him laughing at me, and attack, as Mum was fond of saying, is often the best form of defence.

'What the hell are you doing there anyway? Hiding behind walls, listening in on people's private—' I stop. Private what? You could hardly call it a conversation. '. . . Stuff,' I finish lamely.

A head appears over the wall and it doesn't look impressed. Also, it's the head of someone younger than I expected, with rather wild dark hair. He can't be that much older than me, two or three years at the most, which just makes it all worse, if it could possibly get any worse than being caught shouting abuse at shrubbery.

'I'm *gardening*. You know, like people do in gardens? Well,' his eyes scan the jungle of weeds behind me, 'some people do anyway. That all right with you?'

It really couldn't be any more excruciating.

'S'pose,' I say. I sound like a five-year-old. He pushes back the dark hair hanging over his eyes and it stands up in mad corkscrews on top of his head. We stand there awkwardly for a moment.

'Right,' he says uncertainly. 'Fine.'

'You just carry right on with your *pruning* or whatever,' I say, unable to let him have the last word. I try to make it sound like a faintly perverted activity. 'Don't let me stop you.'

He stares at me and opens his mouth as if he's going to say something. Then he shakes his head and disappears behind the wall again. I sit down on the bench, but before I can feel relieved up he pops again like an angry jack-in-the-box.

'What's your problem? I was only trying to help.'

'I thought you'd gone.' I try to sound bored, inspecting my nails.

Out of the corner of my eye I see him shake his head again.

'Suit yourself.'

He disappears behind the wall once more.

I sit for a minute or two, trying to pretend I'm just having a nice relaxing time in the privacy of my own garden and not at all concerned about the fact that he's on the other side of the wall, a few metres away from me, thinking I'm deranged. But in the end I have to admit defeat. I get up and trample my way through the undergrowth back towards the empty house. As I do, my phone buzzes with a text message. It's from Dad.

Hope you're OK. Rose is doing so well the doctors think she should be home in the next few weeks! See you later x

I stare at the message and suddenly all the anger and frustration and humiliation is just too much. Without thinking about what I'm doing I throw the phone into the fishpond. I don't need it. I'm on my own now. It makes a satisfying *plop*, then its light disappears under the thick layer of green algae, sinking into the dark without leaving a trace.

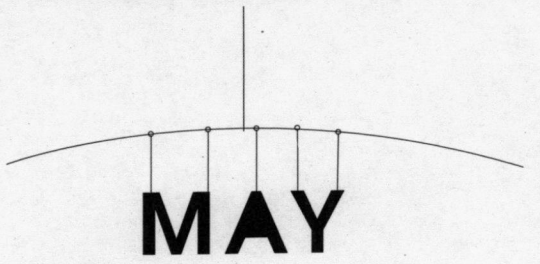

'Bollocks!' says Mum.

There's a cracking, scraping noise over by my bedroom window as I sit up in bed, suddenly wide awake.

'Jesus Christ,' I gasp.

'No,' she grins, holding a cigarette between her lips and rummaging about in her pockets for a lighter. The sun streams in through the window, making her hair glint amber. 'Just little old me. See. No beard.'

I stare at her. I'm so relieved to see her I feel faint, so angry it's taken her this long I could scream.

'*Mum!*'

But she's not even looking at me; she's too busy leaning against the window of my bedroom, pushing all her weight against it.

'I can't get this damn thing to open. Some idiot's painted it shut. Give us a hand, will you?' She's talking as though we saw each other yesterday, not weeks ago, and definitely not as if she's, well . . . dead. Typical. I bet it hasn't even occurred to her how upset I've been.

'*MUM.*'

'What?' She turns to look at me, noticing at last that I'm furious. Her eyes do the wide, innocent *Oh, I think there must be some mistake* thing that she used to use on traffic wardens. 'I thought you'd be pleased to see me.'

'I AM!' I shout as loudly as I dare; I can hear Dad clattering about downstairs in the kitchen. 'Of course I bloody am.'

'Well, you could've fooled me. Come on. Spit it out. What have I done now?'

I take a deep breath. 'Well, apart from scaring the life out of me *and* waking me up—'

'Well, exactly. That's precisely why I'm here actually.' She smiles indulgently. 'But then you looked so sweet and peaceful lying there asleep that I thought I'd give you five minutes while I had a cigarette. Except then the window . . .' She gestures at it as if it explains everything.

'No.' I shake my head. 'Stop. Go back. What's precisely why you're here?'

She looks at me as if I'm stupid. 'I'm your wake-up call. Come on. Rise and shine, sleepyhead. Spit spot.'

I blink at her.

'First day of your exams and all that?' she says slowly, as if to a small child. 'Shouldn't you be up and about by now?'

In fact, I'd been lying in bed, pretending to myself that I was still asleep, trying not to think about this very thing, when she appeared. Not that I care about the exams. How could I now? But the thought of the lines of desks in the hall, *You may turn your papers over now*, everyone scribbling away like mad and then gabbling on about it afterwards . . . I could do without it. But I'm not going to let her distract me from my anger.

'Never mind that,' I say, trying to keep my voice down. '*Where the hell have you been?*'

'Oh,' she says vaguely. 'Well. The thing is I can't really talk about that.'

'I thought you weren't coming back.' As I say it, I feel my eyes fill with unexpected tears and I get up and turn away from her. I take my dressing gown from the hook on the door and wrap it round me.

'Did you?'

'*Yes.* I've been waiting for you. Ever since the funeral.'

'Don't remind me about that funeral, Pearl,' she groans. 'Wasn't it dreadful? I wanted one of those funerals in a field where everyone has fun. You know. People wear yellow—'

'Yellow?'

'And everyone would have to tell stories about how marvellous I was. Beautiful and hilarious, that kind of thing. Kind to animals and a friend to the downtrodden and—'

'OK, I get the idea.'

'—and then dance and get drunk. *That's* the kind of funeral I wanted.'

'Well then, you should have made a will,' I snap. 'Apparently, it's very inconvenient that you didn't. There's all sorts of forms and stuff you didn't fill in. Dad's been doing his nut. Anyway, I hate yellow.'

'That was just an example obviously. Not black was what I meant.' She frowns. 'I don't think you're really entering into the spirit of this, Pearl.'

'I like black. Anyway, you've changed the subject.'

There's a pause.

'Well, I'm sorry if I upset you. I didn't realize you'd be worried.'

'Are you? You don't seem very sorry.'

'Yes, of course I am, darling. I don't want you to be upset. But I'm here now, aren't I?'

'I suppose.'

She's finally got the window open and is sitting on the sill, blowing a plume of smoke into the clear morning. I watch her, wondering.

'So go on then,' I say at last. 'What's it like?'

'What?' she asks.

'You *know* what.'

She gives me a caustic little smile. 'You'll have to wait and find out for yourself.'

'Oh great. That's really cheered me up.'

She laughs. 'You asked.'

'Where then? Just tell me where you've been since I saw you in church.'

She sighs impatiently. 'I told you, Pearl. I'm not going to talk about any of that.'

'Why not?'

'Because.'

'Because what?'

'Because it's not for you to know. It's not for anyone to know.' She says it with an air of finality. I think about it for a while.

'Would it rip a hole in the space-time continuum?'

'No.'

'Would my head explode?'

She raises an eyebrow. 'Do you really want to find out?'

'Oh, come on. Can't you just give me a clue?'

'A clue?'

'Without actually saying anything.'

'You want me to do a *mime* of the afterlife?'

'Maybe.' I suppose it does sound a bit feeble.

'Oh, OK,' she says. 'Sure. And then maybe you could try to express infinity through the medium of – oh, I don't know – tap dance?'

'No need to be sarcastic.' I lie down on my bed and put my hands behind my head. 'I just want to know what happens.'

'And you will, my love, you can be sure of that. But for the moment *life* is complicated enough. Just concentrate on that for now.'

She turns, blowing smoke out of the window. 'How's it been anyway, at school?'

I think back over it. I've been back for three weeks now. The first few days were excruciating, everyone either talking loudly about nothing in particular in case they upset me or squeezing my arm in a heartfelt way. Then they all forgot. Miss Lomax, the new Head, had called me to her office for a 'chat'. *It must be hard coming back to school, especially with the exams coming up, but a bit of normality will probably help.* Normality! I almost laughed out loud when she said that. But I didn't. She gave me a big spiel about the school counsellor and how important it was not to bottle things up. *And of course I'm always here if you need to talk*, she said, looking at her watch as she ushered me out.

I'd rather chop my own leg off, I said, but only to Molly afterwards.

'It's been fine,' I say to Mum.

'I'm so glad you've got Molly to look after you,' she says. 'She's such a good friend. I always said she was like a second mum, didn't I? Reminding you about your homework. Making sure you had everything you needed for school. She's a treasure that girl.'

'We're on study leave now anyway,' I say quickly, trying to steer the conversation away from Molly. Not that I've been doing much studying. Molly keeps trying to get me to go to the library to revise with her, but I can't face it. Anyway, Ravi's always there too, studying for his A levels, and I don't want to play gooseberry, thanks very much.

'And how's . . . everything else?'

'Like what?'

'Well, you know. Rose? Is she OK?' She says it lightly, as if she's just making conversation. But I know she's not.

What if that's the only reason she's here? To make sure The Rat's OK? Maybe she hasn't really come to see me at all. I start to panic. What if she realizes how much I hate The Rat? She'd disappear then for sure, and I'd never see her again. I can't let her know.

I don't look at her. 'Oh,' I say. 'Yes, she's fine.'

'But she's not home yet,' Mum says. It's a statement, not a question.

'How do you know?'

'Too quiet,' she says. 'Houses with babies in are much noisier than this.'

'She's still in hospital,' I say. 'Dad too, most of the time. But she's fine.'

Mum watches me, waiting for me to say something more. 'Anyway,' I say quickly, trying to move on from the subject of The Rat, 'you're right. I'd better get going or I'll be late.'

She pauses, as though she's going to say something, but then seems to change her mind. 'Yes of course. What is it today?'

'English,' I say, but I just lie there looking up at the patch of brown on the ceiling where rainwater must have seeped through, years ago by the look of it. I don't want to leave her.

'Well, go on then,' she says. I sit up and look at her.

'I thought you'd come when I needed you,' I say at last. 'But you didn't.'

She watches me, perched on the window sill. 'When have you needed me?'

I think about it. 'All the time.'

She laughs. 'I can't be with you all the time.'

'Why not?'

'Well, apart from anything else, it would drive us both completely stark staring mad. You'd kill me if I wasn't already dead. Or vice versa. You know how we argue, sweetheart, if we have to spend more than two hours together in a confined space.'

'No we don't.' I think about it. 'Not really.'

She raises an eyebrow. 'Remember that week in Barmouth when it rained non-stop and we couldn't leave the caravan? You said you needed counselling after that holiday. You said you were suffering from post-traumatic stress disorder.'

It's funny, I'd forgotten about that bit. I'd remembered the one sunny day when we all had ice cream on the beach and Mum and me buried Dad in the sand. But I can't deny she's right.

'And what about when you had your appendix out and I took a week off work to look after you?' she continues. 'You said you'd pay me to go back to work. You got on your knees and begged me.'

I groan, remembering. 'You kept trying to cook me things.'

'Yes.'

'And then expecting me to eat them.'

'Yes.'

'And you kept making me watch *The Sound of Music* and then you'd sing along.'

'Of course.'

'Really loudly.'

'Exactly.'

'And out of tune.'

She stops and stares at me. '*Out of tune?* I don't think so, Pearl. I have an excellent singing voice. Loud perhaps. Out of tune, no.'

'Flat as a pancake,' I laugh. 'And that's being kind.'

She's about to retaliate when she stops herself and smiles. 'You see? You're just proving my point. We're arguing already.'

'You're arguing.'

'Look. No one wants to spend twenty-four hours a day with their mother, dead or alive. Now come on. Shift. You need a good breakfast before exams.'

'I'm not hungry.' I haven't really been able to face food since Mum died, but today it's even more true than usual. 'Anyway, I don't care about the exams. What's the point?'

She stares at me.

'The point is you're brilliant, my love, and I don't want you messing everything up because of me and my bad timing. I'm not having everyone blame me. "Poor Pearl, she'd have gone to Oxford AND Cambridge and won the Nobel Prize and written a string of international bestsellers—" she breaks off to take a breath, "if it hadn't been for that no-good mother of hers kicking the bucket at the wrong moment." I won't have it. Now come on. No more self-pity. Go and have a shower.'

I haul myself off the bed.

'But come and give me a kiss first,' she says. I walk over to her and let her kiss me on the cheek. Then I lean on the window sill with her. It's been raining during the night, but the sky is a perfect pale blue now, and the air so clear and fresh that everything looks new and bright.

'Are you nervous?' she asks.

'Not really. I just want it to be over.'

She puts an arm round me and I rest my cheek against hers for a moment. She smells of smoke and perfume.

'How?' I say. 'How can you be here?'

She shrugs. 'You wanted to see me, didn't you?'

I know she's avoiding the question.

'You will come back, won't you?'

'Course.' She flicks her cigarette stub out of the open window. It soars in a perfect arc and lands in the fish-pond, disappearing under the algae to join my mobile phone. 'Now go on. You'll be brilliant, my love.'

When I come back from my shower, the bedroom is empty.

I knew it would be, but I cry anyway.

As soon as I hear the sound of Dad's key in the front-door lock, I switch off my bedside light and my iPod and pretend to be asleep. He's late back from the hospital tonight; it's almost ten thirty. I always make sure I'm in bed by the time he gets back otherwise he just goes on and on about The Rat: what amazing progress she's making and how he can pick her up and give her cuddles now, and how the nurses are dying to see me and maybe I can go in soon. It doesn't matter how bored I look, he just keeps on and on.

69

The front door slams and I hear his footsteps on the stairs. Every night my bedroom door opens. A rectangle of light from the landing falls across the dark of my room, but it doesn't quite reach me. He never says anything, just watches me for a few seconds. I'm rubbish at pretending to be asleep; I always was, even as a kid. I always forget to breathe. I don't know whether he knows I'm pretending. In the end the door always closes.

But tonight something's different. The door doesn't close.

'Pearl?' Dad whispers. My heart thuds. Something's happened. I open an eye a tiny bit to try to see his face, but I can only make out his silhouette against the landing light.

'Pearl?' He says it louder this time. Panic rises inside me. What if something's wrong with The Rat? What if I'm pleased?

He walks over to the bed and sits down. 'Are you awake?'

I don't speak.

'They've said she can come home soon, Pearl.' I can hear the excitement in his voice. 'Rose. They've said she's nearly strong enough to leave the hospital. If she keeps improving it could just be weeks till she's here at home with us.'

He couldn't wait to tell me. I lie there, not breathing.

'Pearl?'

He wants me to sit up and smile and hug him. He wants me to be happy. I want it too. But I don't know how.

'Mmmm,' I say, trying to sound as though I'm still asleep. I roll over, away from him, to face the wall.

He doesn't move for a moment. I can feel his eyes on my back. I can feel his disappointment. A hot tear trickles sideways down my nose. I want him to say something. I want him to stroke my hair like he used to when I was a kid and I'd had a nightmare. He'd always be the one who came when I woke up, and then he'd stay with me till I went back to sleep. I didn't have to tell him that I needed him; he just knew. He understood then how scared I was, how alone and lost I felt, lying in the dark.

But now he just gets up and walks away. Through my closed lids I see the room go dark as he shuts the door behind him.

'Do you need any help at all?'

The shop assistant gives Dad a bright smile. She can obviously see we haven't got a clue. We're standing in front of the fleet of buggies on the shop floor, lined up against us like an army.

Yes. We need help.

'What is it you're looking for today? Do you have any particular requirements or was there a specific model you were interested in?'

71

Dad looks at her, bewildered, and a hot wave of embarrassment washes over me. All the other customers in the Baby Department seem to know what they're doing: women resting their hands on their big smug baby bumps, men holding wriggly toddlers. Dad and I are all wrong: too sad and thin and quiet. I worry that they'll notice, the happy, noisy people. They'll sense we're bad luck. Or are they too busy holding hands and laughing and wiping their children's noses? I shrink down into my clothes.

'We need a pram,' Dad says. He goes red as he says it and he can't look the smiley assistant – Julianne, her badge says – in the eye.

'Certainly, sir,' she says. 'Was it an actual pram you wanted or a travel system?'

'Oh,' says Dad. 'I, um . . .'

Julianne waits, smile fixed.

'I don't know.'

'Oh. Well, it depends what you're going to be using it for really,' says Julianne helpfully.

'For putting a baby in,' snaps Dad. I stare at my feet. I should never have let him talk me into coming. But he'd looked so desperate. *Please, Pearl. I don't think I can face it on my own.*

Pathetic. And I was all ready to tell him so. *You're the one who wanted a baby.* If it wasn't for him, we wouldn't have to go shopping for a buggy. If he could just have been happy with how things were . . . But then I'd had a sudden feeling that Mum might be watching from behind the curtains, or through the window, and that she'd give me an earful about it later. So, sulkily, I'd let him persuade me.

'Is it . . .' Julianne pauses, her eyes flicking from Dad's face to mine, down to my distinctly not-pregnant middle and back again. 'Is it for yourselves?'

Dad doesn't say anything. Along the aisle a couple and another shop assistant are applauding as a toddler pushes his chewed-looking rabbit toy along in a lurid green pushchair.

'Oh, well done, Harry,' the heavily pregnant woman gushes. 'I think you and Bunny have chosen for us, haven't you, darling?'

I hate them. All of them. Even Bunny.

'Yes,' I mutter to Julianne. 'It's for us.'

'OK,' she says brightly. 'Well, let's start with something simple. Did you want baby to be forward facing or facing towards you?'

Dad still doesn't say anything.

'Of course if it's for a newborn . . .' She looks at us questioningly and Dad nods. 'Well then, you'll be wanting something that can go completely flat, either with a carrycot that fits into the frame like this one or . . .'

Julianne carries on talking. I watch her mouth move and I hear the words, but they mean nothing at all.

73

Dad's face is as blank as mine. And suddenly I remember the two of us in the relatives' room at the hospital the day Mum died. The doctor had talked and talked at us. *Pre-eclampsia. Cerebral oedema. Caesarean section.* Words and more words that meant nothing to me.

'Facing you is great when they're little,' Julianne says. 'Helps with bonding . . .'

I can remember the doctor's face so clearly: smooth dark skin, short greying goatee. It was a kind face. At the end he'd asked us if we had any questions.

'. . . pneumatic wheels are great for bumpy terrain,' Julianne's saying. 'But of course they do add weight . . .'

Is she definitely dead? I'd asked.

The doctor had looked at me, surprised. *Yes,* he said at last, his eyes sad behind his glasses. *I'm sorry.*

'And of course this one,' Julianne rests her manicured hand on the handle of yet another buggy, 'has the option of an additional seat which can be added for a little brother or sister if you should need it in the future.'

She beams at Dad. He stares at her, but I'm pretty sure he's not really seeing her. He just stares and stares till it's awkward and I have to pretend to look for something in my bag.

'I didn't realize it would be so difficult,' he says at last. His voice sounds strange. I look up and my stomach clenches. There are tears running down his face.

'Dad!' Christ. Please don't let anyone see.

74

Julianne's not smiling any more. 'Are you OK, sir?' she says.

The stupid kaftan-wearing Bunny woman looks over then quickly looks away again. I've got to get him out of here before anyone else notices.

'Would you like to sit down?' Julianne says. 'Can I get you some water?'

'No,' Dad says, trying to get it together. 'I just—'

And he walks off, leaving me and Julianne staring at each other.

'Is he OK?' she says.

'What do you think?' I mutter and then go after him. I follow him down the escalator; he's going fast and I have to run to keep up. I finally catch up with him in the kitchen section. I grab his arm and turn him round to face me.

'How could you do that? How could you humiliate me like that?'

For an instant he looks so angry that I think he's going to shout at me right there in the middle of the shop, surrounded by kettles and sandwich toasters. Then it's like he just hasn't got the energy.

'I need a coffee,' he says wearily. 'Come on.'

I hesitate.

'Don't argue with me, Pearl. Just this once.'

So I trail after him, back through the store, till we get to the huge airy coffee shop. I sit at a table next to a wall

75

of windows, looking out over the car park while Dad gets the coffees.

He brings the tray over and we sit in silence for a while. Dad sips his coffee. I stare out over the rows and rows of cars, stretching almost as far as I can see, sparkling in the sunlight.

'I'd pictured it all, you know,' he says at last.

'What?'

'All this. Coming here and buying all the kit. Moses baskets and little Babygros. Before. When Mum was pregnant. I imagined how it would be. Mum pretending not to be excited, moaning about her sore feet, getting all the shop assistants to run around after her. And you acting like you didn't want to be there, texting Molly half the time, and then picking out all the most expensive stuff. And me just . . . happy.'

He looks through the window into the distance, seeing things that I can't, memories that never happened. It's hot outside. Summer has arrived suddenly and everyone's in T-shirts and shorts or summer dresses. But in here the air conditioning is fierce and I shiver.

'Every day is a collection of tiny little things that don't happen,' Dad says.

'What are you talking about?'

He's silent for a minute, thinking. 'I thought I'd tidy up the CDs yesterday,' he says at last. 'You know how

76

Mum would always put them in the wrong box or just leave them lying around. And I'd have to go through them and put them all back where they should be. Used to drive me mad.'

It was true. I'd go into the kitchen and he'd be there, all red and annoyed, waving CD boxes around, saying, *She's put her bloody Abba in with my Wagner! Again!* as if anyone cared or even knew what he was talking about. And Mum would snort and roll her eyes and say, *Of course Hitler was a big fan of Wagner you know.*

Dad looks at me. 'But yesterday they were all there. On their shelves in the right boxes in the right order. Just like they should be. Just how I'd left them.'

I don't say anything.

'You can go along day to day. You can get through it, convince yourself you're doing OK. But it's the unexpected things . . .' he says, faltering.

Please don't let him cry again.

He gives me a tentative look. 'Do you find that?'

I look back at him. 'I don't know why you don't just get an iPod.'

He blinks. 'I'm not your enemy, Pearl,' he says. 'Why do I feel as though you think I am?'

'I don't know what you mean,' I say, but I can't meet his eyes.

We finish our coffees in silence.

We don't go back to the Baby Department.

'I'll order a pram on the website,' Dad says as we drive home.

But I can't help feeling it's a victory, as though fate has stepped in. As though no pram equals no baby.

Dad drops me off at home and goes on to the hospital. He doesn't bother to ask me if I want to go with him. I get out of the car in silence and he doesn't say goodbye. I go up to my room and get out my revision notes to read through, but I can't concentrate on them. All I can think about is The Rat. While she's been in hospital, I've almost been able to pretend she doesn't exist. But soon she'll be here, in the house, all the time.

I walk out on to the landing and stand in front of the glossy white door of her room. Slowly, I push it open and go in. I haven't been in here since Mum died. Next to the cot there's an old rocking chair. Mum had painted it and stacked it with cushions that she'd covered with scraps of the old curtains from my room when I was a baby. I'd forgotten all about them till I saw them: elephants carrying balloons with their trunks. I'd felt pleased that she would have something of mine, the plump, smiling baby with the blonde curls. I picture her sleeping peacefully in her cot under the little embroidered quilt Molly and I had picked out, her thumb in her mouth and her cheeks flushed pink. I sit down in the chair and rock myself gently to and fro. I close my eyes and imagine I'm holding the baby that should have been. She smiles, gurgling, reaching out her tiny perfect fingers towards me—

I stop the chair abruptly with my foot. Then I get up and leave the room, closing the door behind me.

This is her room, not The Rat's.

The Rat is an imposter.

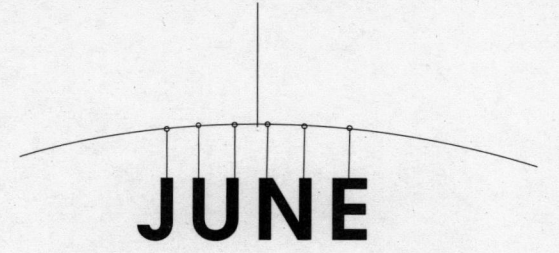

JUNE

JUNE

'I can't believe it!' Molly squeals, hugging me as soon as we're out of the exam hall. 'We never, ever have to sit another exam again in the whole of our lives if we don't want to.'

The noise around us is deafening, everyone chatting excitedly, hugging each other or comparing notes.

'Are you going to come and celebrate?' Molly says, taking my arm as we all file out into the afternoon sunshine. 'A load of us are going over to the park later.'

But all I want to do is be somewhere quiet on my own.

'Sorry,' I say. 'I've got to get back.' I know she'll assume it's something to do with the baby, and I don't put her right.

'Oh.' Molly's face falls. 'That's a shame. Haven't you even got time to come and have a quick coffee with me and Ravi? He's got his last A level tomorrow so he can't stay long.'

'I can't.'

We walk down to the school gates together.

'How is everything?' Molly asks. 'How's little Rose?'

'Fine,' I say. 'She's coming home next week.'

'That's fantastic,' she says.

'Yeah,' I say. 'Fantastic.'

She looks at me curiously. 'You don't sound very pleased.'

I shrug.

'I wish you'd talk to me, Pearl,' she says. She's quiet for a moment, a little frown creasing her forehead. 'Does it feel strange, the thought of having Rose with you at home?' she says at last, tentatively. 'Does it make you think about your mum?'

I don't say anything.

'I mean, I know you must think about her all the time, but do you think it will make it worse? Having Rose with you, but not your mum?' I stop dead still and stare at her. How does she know that's what I'm feeling? Could she understand about The Rat? Could I tell her?

'You can talk to me you know,' she says.

'Oh look,' I say, grateful for an escape route. 'That's Ravi, isn't it?'

84

He's easy to recognize even though I've only met him once, mainly because he's just so tall, about a head taller than everyone around him, gangly and slightly awkward. He's standing by the school gates. I'd forgotten about his stupid, lopsided quiff. His face lights up when he sees Molly and she runs over and kisses him. He has to stoop down to reach her.

'You two haven't really met properly, have you?' she says, smiling as I reach them. 'Ravi, this is Pearl, my best friend in the whole world, Pearl, this is Ravi.'

'Hi,' he says nervously, looking even more awkward. 'Pleased to meet you.' He holds out his hand. I look at it and laugh.

'Bit formal, isn't it?'

'Oh yes, of course,' he says, looking embarrassed. 'Sorry.' Molly puts her arm round him.

'Ravi's really been looking forward to meeting you, Pearl.'

I doubt it somehow.

'Yes,' Ravi says, smiling. 'I've heard so much about you from Molly.'

'Oh dear,' I say. 'Well, don't believe a word of it.'

He laughs loudly as if I've said something side-splittingly hilarious.

'Don't worry,' he says earnestly. 'It's all good.'

'I should hope so too,' I say, trying to sound like I'm

joking. But suddenly I can't help wondering what she *has* said to Ravi about me. She'd have told him about Mum obviously. Maybe that's why he's trying a bit too hard to be nice. But what else? *We used to be really good friends, but . . .* But what?

. . . but we've grown apart?

. . . but Pearl's been behaving like a psycho bitch from hell since her mum died?

. . . but I don't need her now I've got you?

Maybe she doesn't even talk about me. I guess they have other things on their minds when they're together. A disturbing image pops into my head of Ravi with very few clothes on, all skinny legs and knobbly knees, glasses steamed up and slightly askew.

'Anyway,' I say firmly, trying to banish Naked Ravi from my mind, 'I've got to go.'

'Oh,' the real, fully clothed Ravi says. 'Aren't you coming with us? Molly thought you'd want to celebrate. I've been looking forward to meeting you properly.' He actually looks like he means it.

'Can't, I'm afraid,' I say.

'Not even for a short while?' Molly says. She takes hold of my hand. 'Please?'

I look at Molly, her kind, pleading face, and I realize how much I miss her.

'Well . . .' I say. Maybe I could. Maybe I should give Ravi a chance. He might not be so bad.

'Oh, go on,' Ravi says. 'Otherwise we won't be able to get together till Molly and I get back from Spain.'

I stare at him. 'What?'

'Oh yes. I was going to tell you,' Molly says awkwardly. 'But I haven't had a chance.'

I know she's right; she hasn't had a chance to tell me. We've only seen each other in the exam hall. I still haven't got a mobile and I never pick up the phone at home. I haven't looked at my laptop in weeks. But it doesn't stop me feeling that she's kept it a secret from me.

'You're going to Spain? Together?'

'Ravi's parents have an apartment there. They go for a month every summer and they asked if me and Ravi wanted to go too.' She looks at me, anxious.

I remember suddenly all the things we'd planned to do the summer after our GCSEs. We'd been thinking about it since last summer. Festivals. Maybe a bit of travelling. InterRailing round Europe if Molly could earn enough money and could get out of looking after her brothers. Dad had been worried. *Lighten up*, Mum had told him. *She's a big girl now. Let her have a few adventures.*

'But you always have to look after the boys over the summer holidays.' My voice comes out a bit choked.

'Mum's doing a lot of late shifts at the moment so she'll be around during the day. The little ones are going to the childminder the rest of the time. Dad says I'm being selfish and we can't afford to pay someone when I could be doing it for free.' She looks upset. 'Mum says it's OK. Yet another thing for them to argue about.'

'Don't feel guilty,' Ravi says, putting his arm round her. 'You look after your brothers all the time. You can't let your parents take you for granted.' I used to tell Molly this all the time. Now it's Ravi telling her. I stare at his stupid gelled quiff and his stupid designer glasses and I hate him.

We stand there awkwardly for a moment, people filing past us, some shouting and slapping each other on the back, others still comparing notes about the exam. Then I realize Ravi's probably waiting for me to back him up, to reassure Molly.

'I really can't stay,' I say instead. 'I've got to go.'

I turn and walk off towards the Heath before Molly can even give me a hug.

'Pearl!' she calls after me. 'Will you phone me later? I don't like calling you at home in case I'm interrupting . . . or something. I wish you'd get a new mobile.'

But I won't.

When I look back, she and Ravi are walking off down the hill, hand in hand, laughing together.

When I get home, the front door won't open properly. It crashes into something big standing behind it in the hallway. I push it as far as it will go and squeeze in through the gap. Standing in the hall is a massive pram, so big you could fit triplets into it. It's one of those posh, old-fashioned ones, but it's brand-new, all navy blue and shiny silver with bright white wheels. Julianne had shown us one like it in the shop. '*If money is no object, you could think about something like this* . . .' It looks totally out of place in our dilapidated hallway. I stare at it, hating it. Why couldn't Dad just have bought a normal buggy like everyone else? Nothing but the best for his little girl obviously.

I walk through to the kitchen, closing the door behind me so I can't see the pram. Even though it's bright daylight outside, the kitchen is gloomy, full of shadows. On the table there's a note.

Will be late at the hospital again tonight. Didn't get to supermarket. Sorry, love. Here's some money for a takeaway. Dad x

Scrawled at the bottom as an afterthought is:

Hope your exam went well.

Underneath I write:

No it didn't, thanks very much for asking

I sit and look at it for a while, then scrunch it up and throw it in the bin. I put the takeaway menus back in the drawer and slip the money into my pocket. Then I pour myself a glass of water and sit at the kitchen table, ignoring my growling stomach, watching the dappled shadows of the trees dance on the kitchen floor.

'Well,' Mum's voice comes from the shadows behind me. 'You certainly know how to celebrate.'

'Bloody hell,' I say, trying to disguise how relieved I am to see her. 'Don't sneak up on me like that.'

'Well, it's lovely to see you too, my darling daughter.' She gives me a dazzling smile. 'But tell me, why are you sitting alone in the gloom? Wasn't it your last exam today? Shouldn't you be out celebrating in some debauched way I don't want to know about?'

'I'm tired,' I say.

'But I thought you'd be out somewhere with Molly.'

'No. She's off with her new boyfriend. *Ravi.*' I say it with as much contempt as I can manage.

'Call me Sherlock Holmes,' Mum says, 'but do I detect a certain lack of enthusiasm for the love of Molly's life?'

'You know what she's like,' I say. 'Her boyfriends are always a total disaster.'

'Oh dear, poor Molls,' Mum sighs. 'She's a smart girl. Why does she always go out with boys who treat her badly?'

'Oh no,' I say quickly, thinking of Molly's last boyfriend, Jay, who turned out to have several other girlfriends and a pregnant fiancée, and the one before that, Ozzy, who worked on the market and stored pirate DVDs at her flat. She'd had no idea till the police turned up. 'He's not like that at all.'

'What's wrong with this one then?'

I think for a minute and don't really come up with an answer. 'It's hard to explain,' I say finally.

She pulls up a chair and sits down next to me. 'Is he arrogant?'

I think about it. 'No.'

'Creepy?'

'No.'

'What then? Grotesque? Shifty? Domineering? Unhygienic?'

'No. No. Nothing like that. It's just . . .'

'What?'

I get up and pour myself some more water, trying to pinpoint what it is I don't like about him. 'You know what Molly's like. She sees the best in everyone. She could go on a date with a mass-murdering bigamist and she'd find something good to say about him. He had a nice smile or something. He had an unhappy childhood.'

'But you still haven't explained what the problem with this particular one is. I assume he's not actually a mass-murdering bigamist?'

'No.'

'So what's wrong with him?'

The annoying thing is that I can't really think of anything. 'He goes to that posh school up the hill.'

'So?'

'He shook my hand when I met him,' I add lamely. 'And . . . he's too tall.'

Mum laughs. 'Well, if that's the worst you can say about him, Molly should count herself very lucky. And you should be pleased for her, given her track record of attracting losers and reprobates.'

'He laughed at all my jokes even though they weren't very funny,' I say, still trying to put my finger on what's so annoying about him.

'Oh well. *Now* I understand. He's clearly mad.'

'Ha ha.'

'Do you not think he might just have been a bit nervous? Boys are terrified of their girlfriends' best friends. And rightly so. They know if they do anything they shouldn't, it's the Best Friend who'll turn up on the doorstep ready to relieve them of a testicle or two.' She laughs. 'Do you remember when you and Molly bumped into her horrible ex at the market and you told him exactly what you thought of him in front of everybody?' That was Ozzy. I smile. Yes I do remember. 'Got a round of applause, didn't you?'

'Yeah.' It had been a good moment. Molly had been so embarrassed and upset when we saw him, and he'd been so obnoxious, smiling and winking at me, doing the whole cheeky chappie bit and completely blanking Molly. I'd just lost it: told him exactly what I thought of him.

Afterwards, Molly had been so grateful. *I'm so lucky to have a friend like you.* It brings me up sharp to remember it. I'd almost forgotten what it felt like, that bond.

'But this Ravi,' Mum muses, 'he sounds rather sweet. To be honest I really don't see what the problem is.'

I sigh. 'I just think she could do better.'

Mum smiles. 'Do you remember when you were going out with that awful what's-his-name . . . Baz?'

'Taz. And I wasn't really going out with him.'

'And I could see he was a complete – well, I won't say what.' She smiles a saintly smile. 'But I didn't say anything – I *wouldn't* say anything – because I didn't want to interfere.'

I choke on the water I'm drinking. Mum comes over and thumps me on the back. 'I'm afraid, Pearl, that when we love people we have to be supportive of their choices even when we don't agree with them. I knew I had to let you make your own mistakes so I kept my opinions to myself.'

'No you didn't! When have you ever kept your opinions to yourself?'

Mum looks surprised. 'Well, I certainly meant to.'

'You called him a – let me get it right – a "self-obsessed pillock".'

'Did I?' Mum says vaguely.

'Yes. While he was *still in the room.*'

'Oh. Well.' She walks over to the fridge and opens it so that I can't see her. 'That was different. I'm your mother. And anyway—' She sticks her head round the door. 'I was right, wasn't I?'

She disappears from view again and there's some clattering from the fridge, followed by tutting and muffled swearing.

'You're still interfering even now,' I mutter.

She sticks her head round the fridge door again. 'What?'

'What are you *doing*?'

'Why is there no food in the fridge except this . . .' she holds up a rather flaccid-looking cucumber in one hand, 'and this?' With the other hand she bashes a lump of ancient cheese against the wall and it makes the sound of stone hitting stone. A bit of it splinters off and clatters on to the tiled floor.

I shrug. 'Dad hasn't been able to get to the supermarket. He's at the hospital pretty much every night.'

Mum is still suddenly.

'At the hospital.' She says it quietly, to herself. 'With Rose.' For a moment it's as if she's forgotten I'm there. Then she looks up at me. 'Is that where he is now?'

'Yes.'

She's watching me closely. 'And you're not?'

'No.'

Mum's eyes search my face. 'Do you ever go and see her?'

I feel myself tense. I can't let her know the truth. She'd never forgive me, I know she wouldn't. She always was infamous for her ability to bear a grudge.

'I've been really busy,' I say, not meeting her gaze. 'Revision and everything.'

'But she's OK?'

'Yes.' I pause. 'She'll be out of hospital soon.'

She puts her hand to her mouth and turns away from me. It's a while before she can speak. When she turns round to me, her eyes are wet.

'Oh, Pearl,' she says. 'That's wonderful. That's just wonderful, isn't it?'

I hesitate. 'Yes.'

'You don't sound very pleased.'

'I'm just tired.'

'And Dad? He's OK?'

'Yes.'

'You never talk about them.' There's an edge to her voice. 'Why is that, I wonder?'

95

She takes out her silver lighter from her pocket and sparks a flame into life. It glows in the gloom and she holds it out towards me so it lights up my face.

'You know I'm actually really tired,' I say turning away. 'I might just go and have a bath.'

I think she's going to try and stop me, that she's guessed I'm just avoiding talking about Dad and The Rat. But instead she snaps the lighter shut and leans over to give me a kiss.

'You've earned a rest. Goodnight, love.'

I look back at her as I leave the room. 'Night, Mum.'

She smiles at me through the shadows.

But as I squeeze past the stupid pram and make my way up the stairs I can feel the panic rising. I can't just walk off and leave her. I hurry back to the kitchen. 'You will come back soon, won't you?'

But I'm talking to the shadows. Mum's gone.

As I make my way downstairs after my bath, just to check Mum hasn't come back while I was away, Dad arrives home, crashing the front door into the pram again.

'You got a pram then,' I say to him. 'You sure it's big enough?'

'Ah,' he says uncomfortably. 'Yes, it arrived this morning. It is quite big, isn't it? We might need to rearrange the hall a bit.'

'Quite big? We could practically move into it. Why didn't you just get a normal buggy like everyone else has?'

'Actually, I didn't buy it.'

'What do you mean?'

'It was . . . a gift.'

'A gift? From who?'

He hesitates. 'From Granny.'

'Granny?'

'Yes.'

I stare at him, imagining Mum's reaction. 'Well, you'll have to send it back.'

'Of course I'm not going to send it back. We need a pram.'

'But Mum wouldn't want *her* to buy us a pram.'

'Rose is her granddaughter, Pearl. I know Mum and Granny had their differences, but Granny cares about us. She knows things are hard for us and she wants to help, that's all. Mum would appreciate that, I'm sure.'

'No she wouldn't. She'd think it was a betrayal. She wouldn't want you to have anything to do with her.'

He shakes his head. 'She's my mother, Pearl.'

'Yes. And she hated mine.'

'That's not true. I know they didn't see eye to eye, but Granny didn't hate Mum at all.'

'Yes she did,' I shout. 'You needn't bother trying to cover it up. Mum told me all about it. Granny thought Mum wasn't good enough for you and she was always putting Mum down. She hoped that you'd split up. That's why they fell out all those years ago.'

'That's not quite how it was.'

'Oh really? Are you saying Mum was a liar now?'

'No,' he says. 'Of course not.'

'Well, that's what it sounds like to me.'

'Look, you're upset. Can we talk about this later?'

'Why?' I turn away from him and stamp up the stairs. 'There's nothing more to say.'

'This is it,' Dad says as we walk through the hospital car park. He's carrying the empty baby seat as proudly and carefully as if it already had a baby in it. 'Can you believe it's finally happening?'

'No.' I'm trailing behind, and he looks round at me to try and read my expression, but the sun is shining directly in his eyes. He waits for me to catch up.

'I know this is strange for you,' he says as we draw close to the huge revolving doors of the foyer. 'I know you must be feeling anxious. I'm a bit apprehensive myself to tell the truth. But honestly, love, once she's home and you get to know her, you'll feel differently.'

I have no intention of getting to know The Rat, but I can't be bothered to have another argument and the sharpness of Mum's voice when we talked about The Rat is still fresh in my mind. So I just let Dad talk. He's so nervous and excited the words just keep tumbling out of his mouth. He looks different. Or maybe it's that he's stopped looking different. He looks like Dad again; older, with silver hairs around his temples, lines around his eyes, but it's like inside he's remembered who he was before all this. I feel a pang of envy. I want to know how he did it.

'It's going to be fine,' he says as we go through the door and he puts his hand on my shoulder and for a tiny fleeting moment I almost want him to be right.

It's the smell that does it; as soon as we're inside the hospital, I think I'm going to be sick. My clothes stank of it, that hospital smell, for days after Mum died. I washed them and washed them, but I couldn't get rid of it. In the end I put them in a black bin bag and chucked them out with the rest of the rubbish. But the weird thing was the smell didn't go; for weeks it was like it was on my skin, or in my hair.

I follow Dad, but all I can think about is the last time I was here, running along these same corridors, and the nausea rises in my throat and I start to feel faint.

'I can't go up with you,' I call to Dad.

He turns round. 'What?'

'I can't. I'll wait outside.'

His face changes from surprise to disappointment.

'Why are you doing this, Pearl?' he says, and I can see how hard he's trying not to raise his voice. 'Why do you have to make everything so difficult?'

I stare at him. He doesn't understand. He's not thinking about Mum. Just about The Rat. I turn and run. I run back along the corridors, past nurses and shuffly old people and anxious relatives and trolleys with people on and trolleys with medicine on, through the foyer with its coffee shop and horrid plastic plants, and out into the car park.

Outside, I lean against the wall, trying to catch my breath, surrounded by all the people who have come outside for a cigarette: doctors, visitors, patients in wheelchairs, all congregated on the little paved area outside the entrance.

I close my eyes for a moment, trying to clear my head.

'Hello,' says a voice. 'It's Pearl, isn't it?'

When I open my eyes, there's a very old, frail-looking lady standing in front of me. It takes me a moment to recognize her: the old dear from next door.

'Dulcie,' she says, holding out a tiny fragile hand. Her eyes are unexpectedly blue and alert in her lined face. 'Your next-door neighbour. We haven't met properly, have we? Though I've spoken to your

100

father a few times. I hope everything's OK? You're not ill?'

'No,' I say. 'Dad's just here to—' I break off. I can't even bring myself to talk about The Rat. 'To pick someone up.'

She looks at me with a curious expression, then covers it with a smile.

'The baby?' she says. I feel my face flush, aware that she knows I was trying to avoid mentioning The Rat. 'He said last time I saw him that the doctors were hoping she'd be well enough to come home soon.'

I try to smile. 'Yes. That's right.'

'Well, you must bring her round to see me soon. You'll do that, won't you?'

'OK,' I say, not meaning it.

'And perhaps you can meet Finn again,' she says. 'My grandson. He's coming to stay with me over the summer after he's finished his exams, before he goes off to music college in September. He'll be helping me out with the house and garden now I can't cope with it all. Such a good boy. You met him once before, I think, when he was down for a few days?'

I'm about to say no, thinking perhaps she's a bit senile, when I realize who she means: the horrible, wild-haired gardener, who overheard me shouting at trees. He's her grandson.

101

'Oh,' I say, going red. 'Yes. I did meet him once.' The memory of it makes me cringe.

'Well, you must pop round when he's here. I'm sure he'd be delighted to see you.'

I doubt it somehow.

'Anyway,' she says, 'I'd better go. I'm keeping the consultant waiting again.'

She grimaces slightly as she says it, as though she's in pain, but she covers it well.

'Are you all right?' I say. 'Do you want me to walk with you?'

'No, dear,' she says. 'You wait here for your sister. I'll be fine. This place is my second home; I'd know my way blindfold.' She smiles. 'See you soon I hope.'

I watch her make her way inside, so slight, her back bent, her movement slow and pained. Once she's gone, I go and sit on one of the benches over by the bus stops to wait for Dad. I don't have to wait long before he appears through the automatic doors, clutching the car seat, this time with The Rat in it. It's a shock seeing her. She's changed so much. She doesn't look like an alien any more. She's still tiny and scrawny, but she looks like a baby now, with dark hair and big eyes as she looks at the outside world for the first time. There's nothing cute about her though; no rosy cheeks or dimples. We walk to the car in silence.

As soon as we're in the car, she starts to yell. It's a weird noise, a kind of hoarse scream, over and over again. In the small space of the car it's incredibly loud.

'I expect she'll stop once we get moving,' Dad says. 'She'll probably go to sleep.'

But she doesn't. She doesn't stop screaming for a single second of the journey home.

'Perhaps you should take her back to the hospital,' I say. 'There might be something wrong.'

'Babies cry, Pearl,' Dad snaps. 'She's fine. It's just new for her, that's all. She's probably scared.'

It's new for me too, I want to say. I'm scared too.

Once we get home, Dad takes The Rat out of her seat and at last she stops crying. But every time he tries to put her down again the yelling starts up just as loud. In the end she falls asleep in Dad's arms. I leave them sitting together in the sitting room, both exhausted on the sofa.

But I can still hear the sound of her crying in my ears.

I'm running. I'm running down corridors, identical green corridors, but the further I run the longer they get and I'm trying to run faster, but I can't move my legs and I'm not going to get there I'm not going to get there . . .

I sit up in bed, heart pounding, head still half in the dream. I try to breathe slowly. The corridors fade, leaving blank darkness. For a second relief floods through me; but that second disappears into the dark too and now I feel that there are tears on my cheeks and I remember why. I scrub them away with my sleeve and I hate myself for forgetting, even for that tiny moment, just like I do every morning. Except – I stare into the darkness, slow to catch up . . . Except this isn't morning. The clock says 3:17.

Something is strange. It takes me another moment to work out what it is.

It's the silence. Every single one of the ten nights since she came home the noise of The Rat has filled the house. But tonight there is nothing except the pipes clanking and a dog barking in the distance. My brain is still half in the panicky dream. Perhaps something has happened while I've been asleep. I get up and pad across the cold floorboards along the landing to Dad's bedroom. I push the door open a crack. His bedside lamp is on and he's in bed, propped up on some pillows, fast asleep, with The Rat also asleep on his chest. His hand rests protectively on her tiny back. They seem to glow in the circle of lamplight.

I stare at them for a moment longer; somehow I feel like I'm intruding on something private. I force myself to look away and head back to my room, but I can't stop thinking of them, together on the other side of the wall, their gentle breathing.

Eventually, I give up on trying to sleep and go downstairs to make a cup of tea. I bring it back up with me and go to sit in Mum's study. I don't expect her to be there this time. I just want to feel less alone.

I put my tea down on the desk and carefully open up the STELLA'S STUDY (PERSONAL) box again.

There are old letters from Nanna Pam, Mum's mum, and more recent cards from Mum's best friend Aimee in Australia and other people I don't know. There's a photo of Mum and Dad looking young and happy, one with me on Dad's shoulders at London Zoo. There's an old biscuit tin with things from when I was a baby: the hospital wristband, some little soft shoes, a tiny knitted hat. I hold the hat to my face. It's soft and smells very faintly of washing powder.

I place everything carefully back in the tin and go to put it in the box. As I do, I notice a strip of passport pictures, slightly creased, lying at the bottom of the box. I pull them out. They're of two teenagers, a girl and a boy, not much older than me I'd guess. The girl is Mum, but I don't recognize the boy. On the back it says: *With James*. I look at them in wonder. *James*. I say the name out loud.

It's my father's name. My real dad. These pictures are of him.

I've never seen any photos of him. He's always just been a name: James Sullivan. Mum told me his name when I was a little kid. She told me he knew about me, but that they'd agreed from the start that he wouldn't be involved. She'd said if I ever wanted to know anything more I could ask, or if I wanted to contact him we could talk about it. But even then I sensed that really she hoped I wouldn't. And, anyway, I was never interested. Molly asked me about it once. 'Aren't you curious?' she'd said. 'He might be a billionaire or something.' But I had a dad, one who took care of me and comforted me when I was upset and was always there when I needed him. Why would I care about some stranger who had never met me?

But now I'm intrigued. I study the pictures closely, trying to work out what kind of person he is. He looks fun, I decide. Kind of mischievous. Interesting too, with his punky goth haircut. In two of the photos he's smiling and it's a real smile, you can tell: it goes right up to his eyes. In the next one he and Mum are doing serious faces, gazing off at different angles, as if they're looking into the distance and thinking very deep thoughts. In the last one you can't really see their faces because they're laughing so much. James is bent forward, his hair flopping forward over his face, and Mum's thrown her head back.

Does he look like me at all? I squint a bit, focus on his eyes then his nose and his mouth, but he just looks like some guy I don't know.

I'm starting to feel cold and sleepy, so I put every-thing back in the box. Everything except the passport pictures. I take them with me back to my bedroom and I put them in the drawer of my bedside table. And when I switch the light out and close my eyes I don't see Dad and The Rat curled up together in the room next door.

I see James.

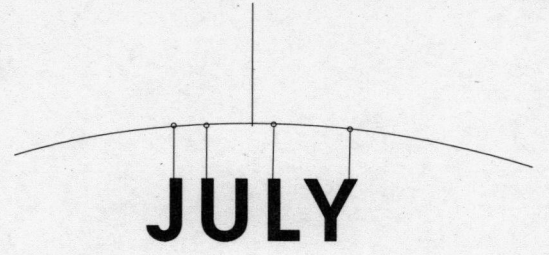

'Are you listening to me?'

'What?' I hadn't even realized Dad was there; I'm watching a story on the news about a man who was struck by lightning walking his dog in the park. I never really paid much attention to this stuff before. But now . . . I imagine the man in the blurry photo on the TV putting on his raincoat, getting the dog's lead off the hook in the hall, grumbling about how, when they got the dog, the kids had promised they'd walk it and now here he is, every night, whatever the weather. He never even wanted a bloody dog. '*Paying tribute to Mr Davies today, his wife said, "He was a loving husband and a wonderful dad."*'

The world can tip at any moment—

'Pearl! Switch that off, will you? This is important.'

I do as he says and turn round to look at him. The Rat is in his arms, her dark eyes fixed on him as he speaks.

111

'Look, Pearl,' he says, coming to sit down on the sofa. 'The thing is – well, the thing is money.'

'What about it?' My mind is still on the lightning man.

'Well, basically, we haven't got any. I don't know when we're going to see any of Mum's insurance money. That's if we ever get it at all.' He rubs his head as if it's aching. I've heard him on the phone going on about forms and liability and cover. It made me angry to think of a bored call-centre person talking about Mum.

'What does it matter?' I say. 'No amount of money is going to bring Mum back.'

'I know that, Pearl,' Dad says, trying to keep his voice calm. 'But we need money to live, if you hadn't noticed. Anyway. Work have been brilliant letting me take unpaid leave since we brought Rose home. They didn't have to. But I've got to start earning again. I need to go back to work. Now. Or we're in danger of losing the house.'

'Right.'

'And we can't afford any childcare.'

'So who's going to look after her?' I nod to The Rat.

'Well, that's the thing.' He pauses and shifts uncomfortably and suddenly I realize what he's going to say. But no, surely he wouldn't? He takes a deep breath. 'Until I can sort out something more permanent, I'm

112

going to need your help, Pearl. I'm going to need you to keep an eye on your sister.'

'*Me?*'

'I wouldn't ask if I wasn't desperate, Pearl.'

'But I can't.'

'I know it seems daunting. But you'll be fine. You've done babysitting before, haven't you? And this will be easier really because you know Rose and she knows you and you'll be in your own home.' He doesn't even sound totally convinced himself.

It's true, I have done babysitting a few times, but only ever as a favour to Molly when she was supposed to be looking after her brothers and only if she promised me the kids would be in bed before I got there. Then I just sat there with the TV on really quiet, hoping they wouldn't wake up. I didn't have a clue what I'd do if they did.

'You'll be able to phone me any time. I've talked to work about it and they're very understanding.'

God, he's got it all worked out. How long has he been planning this?

'And that's supposed to make it all OK? What if I've got other plans?'

'Like what?'

He's got a point. I've hardly got a packed social diary.

'It won't be for long,' he says. 'You could see if Molly could come round and help. She'd be company for you and she's good with children, isn't she?'

113

'Meaning I'm not?'

'No, of course not,' he says uncertainly. 'I just meant – well, she's got younger brothers, hasn't she? She's used to looking after them.'

'Well, she's in Spain with her posh boyfriend and his family,' I snap. *Getting an amazing tan and eating way too much tapas!!!* according to the postcard which arrived yesterday. *Really missing u though!* 'So she can't.'

'Oh,' he says. 'Well, never mind. Dulcie next door has said she'll keep an ear open and you can go round to her if there's any problem.'

I actually laugh out loud. 'Dulcie from next door? Are you kidding me? She's ancient. She must be a hundred at least. I expect she's deaf as a post. Probably senile too.'

'That's uncalled for, Pearl. Really. You're being very unreasonable.'

'*I'm* being unreasonable?'

'Yes!' He yells it. The Rat's face crumples and she starts to cry. 'Yes you are. You're being unreasonable and selfish and I just don't understand why. I'm going out of my mind with worry, just trying to keep everything together, and I thought I could rely on you to help.' He's so angry he's shaking. 'I feel like I don't know you any more, Pearl. I feel let down. And so would Mum.'

I'm so shocked I can't speak. Dad never shouts at me. I honestly can't remember a single time, except

114

for once when I was about five and I ran out into the road after a football and a car almost hit me. I can still hear the screech of the brakes. He'd yelled then all right.

He stands up abruptly and turns away from me so he's face to face with the hideous 1970s orange and brown zigzag wallpaper that adorns the sitting-room walls, which I can't help thinking isn't going to cheer him up much. He rocks The Rat to try and calm her down, but it's like she knows he's upset and her roars just get louder.

I stare at his back, trying to work out what to do.

'All right,' I manage to say eventually. 'Keep your hair on.'

When he turns round, there are tear tracks on his cheeks. My insides squirm.

'I'm sorry,' he says at last over The Rat's cries. 'I shouldn't have said that. I shouldn't have shouted at you.'

But the truth is I know he's right. Mum would never forgive me if she could hear this conversation. And suddenly the nagging doubt is in my head again: what if she can? What if she's listening in without me knowing? I've been getting it a lot, the sense that she could be sneaking around after me; that she might know more than she was letting on. I haven't seen her since The Rat came home. What if it's because she knows how I feel? What if she's angry with me and never comes back?

'Look,' Dad says, struggling to make his voice calm, cradling The Rat and swaying to and fro till at last she stops crying and sucks her tiny thumb instead. 'I know it's a lot to ask. But now your exams have finished it would make things so much easier if you could keep an eye on her during the day. Just for a week or two until—' He stops himself.

'Until what?' I'm convinced suddenly that there's something he doesn't want to tell me.

'Well.' He looks uncomfortable. 'Until I can sort something else out.'

'Like what?'

'Let's not worry about that now,' he says. 'What I need to know is, are you prepared to do it?'

I imagine Mum out in the hall with a glass to the wall. I wouldn't put it past her.

'Doesn't look like I've got much choice, does it?' I say ungraciously.

His face is so full of relief that I think he's going to cry again.

'Thanks, love,' he says as The Rat's eyelids droop and then close.

'I'm not changing any nappies though,' I say quickly. 'No way.'

*   *   *

116

'So,' Dad says for the billionth time, 'these are all the phone numbers here. If you have to call me at work and they say I'm in a meeting, just tell them it's you and that it's urgent.'

He's pacing up and down the kitchen, waving lists and schedules at me in a slightly unhinged way, while I sit at the table, pretending to read a magazine.

'That's the number for the GP's surgery. Call them if you think she's got a temperature or if anything doesn't seem quite right. And obviously if it's an emergency—'

'Call 999,' I say, not looking up from my magazine. 'Yes, I know, Dad. I'm not a total idiot.'

'And Dulcie says you can go round any time.'

'Great.' Dad's too busy imagining scenes of doom and disaster to notice my sarcasm.

'So, like I said, Rose's routine is on this piece of paper here,' he picks one out of the sheaf and puts it next to me on the table, 'so you know roughly when she might want a feed or a nap. But we've been through all of that already anyway, haven't we?'

'Yes, two minutes ago. And two minutes before that.'

'And each of the bottles is on the side labelled with the time to give it to her with the powder already measured out. And—'

Christ. 'Dad, just go, will you?'

'OK, OK.' He pulls on his jacket. 'But remember about checking the milk's not too hot before you give it

117

to her in case she scalds her mouth. And don't let her get hold of anything small in case she puts it in her mouth and chokes. I've put all these things on another piece of paper here, just in case.'

The piece of paper is headed *Miscellaneous Dangers*.

I roll my eyes. 'Dad. You're doing my head in.' All his fussing is just making me more jittery; not that I'm going to let him see I'm nervous.

'Right. Sorry.' But he hovers, not wanting to leave. 'You remember what I said about making sure Rose is on her back when she has a nap. And making sure she's not too hot. That's really important.'

'*Dad.* Honestly. Loads of sixteen-year-olds have babies of their own to look after.' I'm telling myself as well as him. 'Why are you so convinced I won't be able to manage? I mean, how hard can it be?'

I look down to where The Rat is sitting in her bouncy chair, dribbling. Dad looks at her too and I can tell he's still imagining every possible disaster and probably some impossible ones too.

'She doesn't even *do* anything yet,' I add.

Everything I say just seems to make him more worried.

'Perhaps this is a bad idea,' he says to himself, absently twisting his wedding ring round and round.

'It's a very bad idea,' I say, flicking through the pages of the magazine without really seeing them. 'I could still

118

be in bed instead of listening to you blithering on about nap times and feeds. But it's better than being homeless.'

He sighs. 'You know I wouldn't ask unless I had to.'

'So you keep saying.'

'And you might even find you enjoy it. Might be a chance to – well, you know. Bond.'

And, you never know, hell might freeze over. It could happen.

'Anyway, it won't be for long. Just this week and maybe next. I might even be able to swing working from home for a couple of days.'

'And you've definitely sorted out something else after that? A nursery place or something?'

'I'll talk to you about it later,' he says. 'Got to dash now or I'll miss my train.' He kisses the top of my head and I pretend not to notice. 'Are you sure you'll be OK?'

'I'll have to be, won't I?' I say.

He crouches down to say goodbye to The Rat. I can see how much he doesn't want to leave her.

'Your train,' I say.

He dashes out, still calling back over his shoulder. 'Any problem, just call me straight away. And remember what I said about not putting her chair near anything she can pull down on top of her—'

And then the door slams.

119

I stare at The Rat and The Rat stares back at me and a cold, heavy feeling settles in my stomach. The room seems to shrink around her somehow. The Rat seems bigger than she did when Dad was here.

Can babies smell fear, like they say dogs can? Still she stares at me with big solemn eyes.

'You needn't look at me like that,' I say. 'I don't want to be stuck here with you either.'

It's a strange, claustrophobic feeling, knowing there's just the two of us in the house. I wonder for a moment if Mum will come and help me out; but the weird thing is I realize I don't want her to. She'd know, if she saw me with The Rat, I know she would. She'd know how I feel about her, however hard I tried to disguise it. I've got enough to worry about without her giving me a hard time too.

I put the radio on, which helps. It makes me less lonely and The Rat seems to like the music. After a while, I realize that perhaps if there are voices talking The Rat will be quite happy to be left in a room on her own. I twiddle the dial and leave her listening to a discussion about sex and relationships after the meno-pause while I go and have a shower.

When I come back downstairs, I check Dad's minute-by-minute schedule, which tells me I need to feed her. I find I can give her a bottle without even getting her out of her chair. I don't even have to look at her while I'm doing it.

The phone rings from the hall. I check the handset and see it's Dad's work number so I answer because I know otherwise he'll probably call the police.or something. Probably the fire brigade and the bomb squad too.

'You've only been gone an hour,' I say. Although to be fair it feels like a very long hour. 'Are you even at the office yet?'

The Rat listens to the radio for quite a long time while I try to pretend she's not there. She gets restless after while, but I turn her chair round so she can see out of the window and put some music on instead and she calms down.

Dad calls again on his mobile after a couple of hours. The Rat is on her play mat now.

'Yes, Dad,' I sigh. 'Everything's fine. Apart from the earthquake. And the herd of stampeding elephants.'

'*What?*'

'I'm kidding. Everything's fine.'

'Pearl, honestly. This is no time for jokes.' He actually sounds relieved, as though he'd genuinely been imagining a herd of elephants stampeding through south London on a Monday morning. 'Have you done her feed?'

'Yep.'

'Has she gone down for her nap yet?'

'Sorry, Dad, you're breaking up,' I lie. 'Better go.'

The Rat is watching me, wide-eyed. She doesn't look like she has any intention of sleeping, but she seems happy enough. Well, not happy exactly. Her face is solemn and watchful, like it always is, as if she's a very old person trapped in the body of a baby. But she's not crying and I want it to stay that way. I'm not going to risk putting her in her cot. Dad's left a whole page on how to get her to go to sleep with the subheadings *Rocking, Music Box, Nightlight* and *Reassuring Hand on Back*. What's the point? So I just leave her where she is.

After a while, she starts to fuss. I can see she's working herself up into a frenzy so I try putting her back in her chair in the sitting room and finding a cartoon channel on the TV. This works brilliantly. The Rat is totally transfixed. I smile, thinking about Dad fussing around with all his advice books and routines and instructions. Why do people make such a big deal about looking after babies? It's easy.

I'm in the kitchen making a coffee when I hear her start to cry. It starts as a snuffle, then a sort of bleat. By the time I get into the sitting room, she's yelling.

At first I think I'll just leave her. She'll probably stop or fall asleep. I go back into the kitchen. But I can still hear her, even when I've put the radio on really loud. I go back into the sitting room. She's bright red and angry now, and her screams go right through my head. What can I do to make her stop? I get another bottle and try to give it to her even though Dad's instructions say she mustn't have it for another couple of hours. She gulps half of it down, but then she won't have any more and, as soon as she stops drinking, she starts screaming again. I start to panic. What if she goes on like this for the rest of the day? I'll go mad.

After ten more minutes, I *am* going mad. It's like torture. I know I ought to pick her up, cuddle her, try to calm her down. I don't even want to touch her, but it's not long before I'm desperate enough to give anything a go. I lift her awkwardly and hold her to my shoulder, trying to remember what Dad does, shushing her, rocking to and fro. But her little body is tense with anger and the crying just gets louder. I wonder suddenly if she knows how I feel about her. Perhaps the feeling's mutual.

That's it. That's why she's doing this. She hates me.

I'm just thinking this when The Rat's sick: all the milk she's just drunk, warm and sour, all down my back and in my hair and dripping down the inside of my top. And she's still screaming. And I know she's doing it just to spite me. I hold her out in front of me, her skinny legs dangling.

'Stop it!' I scream at her. 'Just stop it!'

But even as I'm doing it I think of Mum and what she'd think if she could see me, and I start to cry. I just stand there in the middle of the room, holding The Rat out in front of me, tears and snot running down my face.

I've got to get away from her. If I don't – I don't want to think about what might happen. I just have to get out. I put her down on her play mat, still red and screaming, her sleepsuit wet with sick. And I run out of the room and out of the front door, slamming it hard behind me. And I keep on running: down the garden path, down the road, as far away as I can get. I have to get away.

Just as I'm passing the bus stop, a bus pulls up and opens its doors and without thinking what I'm doing I jump on. I haven't got my purse or my oyster card, but there's some money in my jeans pocket, some loose change and a couple of notes. I pay the driver and sit down at the back as far away from anyone else as I can, partly because my hair and clothes smell of baby sick and partly because I don't want anyone to notice me. If they look at me too closely, they might guess what I've done. The sound of The Rat's screaming is still ringing in my ears and I can't help feeling that if anyone gets too close they might hear it too. I shut my eyes as the bus drives off and I try not to think about anything at all.

When I open my eyes, we've gone further than I thought. We're down by the shops already, a couple of stops away from home. Everything seems far away as though I'm looking at it through the wrong end of a telescope. A girl not that much older than me gets on the bus with a buggy. The baby is crying. I can feel myself tense. As the bus moves off, the girl leans over to pick her baby up and starts to rock him. He's tiny, only a few days old perhaps. The girl's hair is scraped back tight and she has a hard, sharp face, but when she looks at the baby it changes; softens.

Suddenly I can't breathe.

What have I done?

I picture The Rat at home all alone, lying on the floor, her little legs kicking, her cries unheard. I ring the bell and as I push my way clumsily to the front of the bus the memory flashes through my mind of the time I was going to meet Molly and thought I saw Mum through the bus window. I was wrong that time. But what if she's here now? What if I get off the bus and Mum's standing there waiting for me and she knows what I've done?

'Oi, watch it,' says the girl with the baby.

Outside, the air is hot and heavy and full of traffic fumes, but I'm cold with fear.

There's no sign of Mum, but still the panic is almost blinding. I've got to get back.

I run across the road, back up towards the bus stop going the other way. But of course now there's not a bus in sight.

125

'Nice to see the sun at last,' says an old man in a pork-pie hat who's also waiting, leaning on his walking stick. 'I thought that rain wasn't never going to stop. Thought I was going to have to build me an ark.' And he laughs like crazy at his joke.

But all I can think of is The Rat. How long has she been on her own? I check my watch. I don't know when I left, but it must be nearly an hour now. What if Dulcie from next door finds her all alone and calls the police? Would I go to prison? I screw my eyes up, staring down the road into the sun to look for the dot of a bus on the horizon. Nothing. What if Dad decides to come home from work early? I turn and start to run.

After a while, the stitch in my side is so painful I have to slow down and walk. But my mind is racing on ahead of me to what I'll find when I get back. What if The Rat's been sick again and choked? She could have been screaming because she was ill. I think of Dad's warnings about temperatures and how to check for meningitis . . . What if I get back and she's not breathing? Or there's been a fire? What if I get back and she's just not there? Everyone thinks these things can't happen, that they only happen to someone else. But I know better. I force my heavy legs to start running again.

I feel sick with the heat and the smell of the baby puke in my hair and the air so thick with traffic fumes that it feels as though it's sticking to my lungs. But most of all I feel sick at the thought of The Rat, alone. I push myself on along the main road till at last I'm close to our house.

There are no blue flashing lights outside which has to be a good thing. But what will I find when I get inside?

I'm almost crying with fear and exhaustion as I turn in through the gap in the overgrown hedge to our garden. Then I stop dead and the panic rises in my throat.

Someone's there, peering in through the window of the sitting room. And even though I can only see his back I recognize him straight away. It's Finn, Dulcie's grandson. Christ. He already thinks I'm mad. What am I going to do?

He's banging on the front door. I dodge back behind the hedge so he won't see me and watch him through the leaves. He stands there for a few seconds then rings the doorbell several times. He's obviously been trying for a while. He looks around then walks over to the window to look in. He'll see The Rat. I know he will. My mind whirls, trying to think what to do. But I don't have time because now he turns round, his face concerned, and starts walking back up the path. Once he turns out of our garden, he'll see me standing on the pavement. There's nowhere to hide; I'll just have to bluff my way out of it. What would Mum do?

I stroll through the gate, almost bumping into Finn, who stares at me, shocked.

'What are you doing here?' he says.

'I live here,' I say. 'Obviously. What are *you* doing here?'

'But the baby,' he says. 'She's in there.'

'Is she OK?' The words are out before I can stop them.

'She's just lying there asleep,' he says, frowning. I'm so relieved I could almost hug him. 'I could see her through the window.'

'Do you often go round spying through people's windows?'

'My nan sent me round. Dulcie next door. I'm staying with her. My name's Finn.' He hesitates. 'We met before.'

I stare at the pavement. 'I know who you are,' I mutter.

'Nan said you'd definitely be in, looking after the baby.'

'I had to pop out,' I say.

'When you didn't answer the door, I thought something must have happened to you.'

'Like what? I'd been abducted by aliens?'

'I don't know. You could have had an accident or something.'

'Well, you can stop worrying. Look.' I hold my arms out wide. 'I'm fine. No little green men. No severed arteries. Everything's just fine.'

Finn's watching me closely. 'But you left her on her own.'

'Oh,' I say breezily. 'Just for a couple of minutes. I had to run down to the corner shop to get some nappies. We'd run out and she was fast asleep. I didn't want to disturb her so I just let her sleep. After all,' – I take a deep breath, hoping he won't notice I'm shaking – 'what could possibly happen to her?'

But the frown deepens. I know he thinks I'm lying and he's trying to work out why.

'Anyway,' I say, 'what *are* you doing here?'

But he's not listening. 'Where are they?' he asks.

'Where are what?'

'The nappies?'

'What nappies?' As I say it, I realize what I've done.

'The ones you went to buy.' He looks me in the eye. It's a challenge.

'They didn't have the right ones,' I say. I even manage a smile. Maybe I did inherit some of Mum's talent for deception after all.

'Right.'

'Anyway, I can't stand out here chatting,' I say, marching past him up to the front door, reaching into my pocket, my fingers folding gratefully round my keys. 'She could wake up any minute. You can tell your nan I'm fine, thanks very much.'

He looks at me. 'Are you?'

'Course I am,' I snap.

'Nan said you could come round with the baby if you want,' he says. 'If it's getting a bit much.'

'Well, it's not.'

'She said it would really cheer her up seeing the baby.' He blushes as he says it and can't look me in the eye, and I realize he's making it up; he's just trying to find a way of inviting me round there. But why? Because he thinks I'm mad and might be a danger to The Rat? Because he doesn't want Dulcie to be disappointed? Or because *he* wants me to go?

'OK,' I say, desperate to get rid of him and check on The Rat. 'Tell her maybe I'll bring her over.'

He starts to walk down the path. Then he hesitates and turns back.

'Look,' he says, 'whenever I speak to you I feel like I'm saying the wrong thing. I'm sorry. Honestly, I'm only trying to help. Not that I'm saying you need help or anything,' he adds hastily.

His eyes meet mine through his dark curly hair, and I can't help noticing how very blue they are. I'm aware suddenly of how he must see me: sweaty and flushed from running, in old jeans and a top that are far too big for me, reeking of sour milk.

'I'd better go and check on her,' I say, turning away.

Then I think of something. 'You won't say anything to your nan, will you?' I call after him. She'd be bound to tell Dad if she knew I'd left The Rat on her own.

Finn looks back at me and gives a small shrug. 'About what?'

Then he disappears round the corner.

The Rat is fast asleep on her play mat, just as Finn said. I tiptoe up to her and kneel down and rest my hand gently on her chest, just to make sure she's breathing. I leave it there for a moment, feeling the warm rise and fall under my hand. Now she's asleep she looks so small, so vulnerable, just lying there in the middle of the floor.

'I'm back,' I whisper. But she doesn't stir. It makes no difference to her whether I'm there or not.

Once the panic leaves me I'm exhausted. I lie down on the floor next to her and close my eyes and I think that I've never felt so alone. I only told Finn that I'd go round to see Dulcie to get rid of him. But lying here, I know I can't bear it. I can't be on my own in the house with her again. So I lift her into the Moses basket, carefully so as not to wake her, and carry her next door, making sure I don't slam the door, hoping the fresh air and traffic noise won't disturb her.

'Hello,' I say, trying to sound calm and confident as Dulcie opens the door. I'm still in a bit of a state and I'm hoping she won't notice. As I walked over, I told myself anything would be better than staying at home with The Rat screaming at me again. But now I'm here I just feel embarrassed, and terrified she'll suss out how useless I am at looking after babies. 'Finn said I should come round? But I can go if it's not . . .'

But my voice disappears mid-sentence and I find I'm crying. I turn away, horrified, and put my hands over my face and let my hair fall forward so she won't see me, but it smells of sick which just makes everything worse, and my silent sobs keep coming. I've completely messed everything up. Now Dulcie will know that I can't look after The Rat and probably tell Dad I'm having a nervous breakdown or something and that'll be that. He'll hate me and he won't trust me to look after her again and he'll have to quit his job and we'll be homeless and it'll all be my fault and then Mum will never forgive me either . . .

I feel Dulcie's hand on my shoulder. 'Shhhh,' she says as if I'm the baby. The Rat is lying completely silent in her Moses basket. Of course. 'Shhhh. It's all right.'

'It's not,' I try to say. It's really not. But her hand feels calming and gentle and her voice is soothing.

'Sometimes you just need to cry,' she says gently. 'Even at my age. But one thing I have learned over my many years of experience is that doorsteps aren't the best place to do it. Why don't you come in and cry in my kitchen instead? I have tissues and tea. I find they usually help. Possibly some cake too if Finn hasn't eaten it all.'

Gratefully, I turn and follow her inside, hoisting up The Rat as I go.

In the kitchen she makes me tea, moving slowly. I can see it's painful for her.

'Do you want me to do it?' I ask.

'No,' she says. 'You just sit there.'

I look down at The Rat fast asleep in her Moses basket. A brass band could start up right next to her now and she wouldn't notice.

'She wouldn't stop crying,' I say to Dulcie.

'Oh,' she says. 'I've had babies of my own. You don't have to tell me. It's enough to drive you mad. It drove me to tears on many occasions.'

'Really?' I say.

'Oh yes,' she says. 'Of course. And they were *my* babies, who I loved more than anything. In your situation . . .' She looks down at the sleeping Rat. 'Well, it must be very hard for you.'

I watch her for a moment and she looks at me with those fiercely blue eyes and I know that she understands that I *don't* love The Rat more than anything. And it's like a weight shifts from my chest.

'You mustn't worry,' she says. 'It's not your fault.'

I want to say thank you, to tell her how grateful I am, but I can't speak so I just nod.

She makes her way over slowly and gives me the tea and a large slice of cake which I nibble, wondering where Finn is. Perhaps he's gone out. I can't work out whether I hope he has or not.

As I drink, I feel calmer and I look around. Dulcie's house isn't like I thought it would be. It's a mirror image of our house, everything reversed on the other side of the wall. And where our house feels so empty, the walls still without pictures, the mantelpieces bare, Dulcie's house feels as though it's bursting at the seams. There are photos of far-flung places, Manhattan and the Taj Mahal, jungles and deserts, posters from old films and plays, paintings and wall hangings and books. I'd imagined an old lady's house, full of pot-pourri and ornaments of kittens and shepherdesses, but her home is full of the life she has lived.

On the mantelpiece is an old black-and-white photo of a very beautiful, glamorous woman and a 1950s-film-star-looking man.

'Is that you?' I say, incredulous.

She laughs at my surprise. It's an unexpected laugh, open and mischievous. She seems younger suddenly. 'I wasn't born eighty-seven, you know.'

I stare at the younger her in the picture, the curve of her throat and cheekbones, the lipsticked smile, the wide clear eyes fixed on the man next to her. 'You were beautiful,' I say.

'Well,' she says, 'not really. But he thought so.'

'Your husband?'

134

'Yes.' She smiles, but her eyes look far away. She unfolds herself slowly out of her chair and walks over to the mantelpiece. She picks up the photo and brings it over to me.

'He was quite a looker,' I say, smiling at her.

'I always think Finn's just like him,' she says, amused, and I wish for the billionth time in my life that I didn't blush so easily.

I hand it back to her quickly and she sits there, gazing at it for a moment or two, half smiling, and I wonder if she even remembers I'm there.

'It wasn't so very long after that picture was taken that he died,' she says. 'A year. Maybe two.'

'Oh,' I say, shocked. He looks so alive in the picture. 'I'm sorry.'

'Cancer. He smoked like a chimney of course. We all did back then; didn't know it was bad for you.'

I wonder suddenly if that's what she cries about.

'Does it get easier?' The words are out before I've even really thought them.

She looks at me; thinks about it.

'When someone you love first dies, they're all you can see, aren't they? All you can hear? Blotting everything else out.'

I nod, hardly breathing.

'That changes,' she says. 'They get quieter over the years. They still whisper to you sometimes, but the

135

world gets louder. You can see it and hear it again. There's a gap in it, where they used to be. But you get used to the gap; so used to it that you hardly see it.' She takes my hand in her fragile, old one. 'And then some days, out of nowhere, you're making the tea or hanging out the washing or sitting on the bus and it's there again: that aching, empty space that will never be filled.'

There are tears in her eyes. 'I'm sorry,' she says. 'I don't suppose that's what you wanted to hear.'

I look at her and very gently I squeeze her cold, thin hand. 'I'm sorry too.'

She smiles at me, sad.

From upstairs there's the sound of a musical instrument being played, a cello I think.

'Finn,' she says. 'He's good, isn't he?'

We listen for a while. It's so sad and beautiful I can't believe it's Finn who's playing. I don't want it to stop.

'He's got a place at one of the best music colleges in the country,' she says proudly. 'Up in Manchester.'

She looks tired.

'I'd better go,' I say, though I find I'm just the tiniest bit disappointed that Finn didn't make an appearance.

'I wish you could come round again tomorrow, but it's one of my hospital days,' she says as I heave the Moses basket to the front door.

'You won't say anything to Dad about how upset I was, will you? It was silly really and he'd only worry.'

'He's got nothing to worry about,' she calls after me as she closes the door.

When the door slams behind Dad the next morning, I know one thing: I've got to get out of the house. But this time The Rat's coming too.

I collect together all the things on Dad's *Going Outside* list. It takes forever. You'd think we were going on a month-long expedition. By the time I've got it all together, the nappies, wipes, bottle, milk, spare sleep-suit, sun hat, changing mat, muslin squares, The Rat is already almost hoarse with crying. I plonk her down into the pram as quickly as I can and with some difficulty manoeuvre the pram out of the front door.

The funny thing is that as soon as we're outside everything feels different. The Rat seems to shrink. In the house she seems so big and knowing. Out here she just looks like a tiny baby. I feel a bit self-conscious about the huge shiny pram at first. It's so noticeable and steering is trickier than it looks. But once I get going it's easy and after a while I realize that people look at it rather than at me. In fact, it turns out that when you're pushing a pram you might as well not exist. People who do notice are only interested in the baby. I walk right past Jodie and Kev who used to live next door to us in Irwin Street, Phoebe Monks from school and they just don't see me at all. I feel invisible. It's a good feeling. All this time I've been looking for a hiding place, where everyone would leave me alone. And now, with the exception of a few old ladies who want to cluck over The Rat, I've found one.

She goes to sleep almost as soon as we're moving. I find that, if I stand at exactly the right distance, the angle of the pram cover means I can't even see The Rat; her strange, pointy little face is out of view. I pretend the pram is empty as I push it along, letting the breeze push my hair back from my face and neck. Even with all the traffic of the main road it smells faintly of summer. As long as I keep walking, I know she'll sleep. And the sun is warm on my skin and just being out of the house, just walking feels good. I feel alive. I'd forgotten what it was like. So I keep on going, all the way down to the Heath, then take the corner entrance into the park and head for the flower garden. It's in full bloom, the air heavy with the scent of flowers.

I sit down on the grass and park the pram, worrying that The Rat will wake up once we stop. But she doesn't stir. There are a few other people around, a group with toddlers and babies on picnic blankets, but no one's interested in me. I can just sit here in peace. I close my eyes.

'Pearl!' I start, opening my eyes to see a man waving at me. As I squint to get him into focus, I realize it's Mr

138

S, my old science teacher from school. He retired a couple of years ago, but he looks exactly the same as he comes striding over: far too tall, his hair a bit long and untidy.

'Well, fancy meeting you here,' he says. He peeks in at The Rat. 'And just look at this one, eh? She's a little belter, isn't she?'

'She's not mine,' I say hastily.

'No,' he says. 'No, Sheila told me about your mum.' Mrs S is my English teacher. 'I was so sorry to hear about it, Pearl, I really was. She was a lovely woman, your mum.'

Mum loved Mr S. She always used to flirt with him at parents' evening. It was excruciatingly embarrassing.

'So you're looking after the nipper, are you?'

'Just for a week or two.'

'Good for you. Hard work, isn't it?' he grins. 'I look after my little grandson one day a week now. It takes me the rest of the week to recover.'

'Yesterday was a nightmare,' I say in a rush. 'She started crying and I didn't know how to make her stop.'

I'm not sure why I'm telling him. It's just a relief to share the horror of it.

'Occupational hazard,' he says. 'Still, you're obviously doing a good job. Look at her now, happy as you like and fast asleep. You should give me a few tips.'

I smile at him gratefully. 'It's better now we're out of the house.'

'Tell you what, do you want to come and have a cup of tea with me?'

I know he's just saying it because he feels sorry for me, but for some reason I don't mind. I always liked Mr S and I know he won't try to make me talk about how I'm feeling or ask me difficult questions. He'll be too busy telling terrible jokes.

'Go on then,' I say.

He pushes the pram as we walk down to the tea pavilion. 'How did your exams go?'

'I don't know.' And I don't care, I want to add.

'You'll be fine,' he says. 'You're not as green as you're cabbage-looking, you.'

I laugh. 'Is that supposed to be a compliment?'

'And I sincerely hope you're planning to carry on with English next year,' he says. 'Or I'll have Sheila bending my ear about it.'

'I haven't really thought about it.' I haven't even decided whether I'll go back and do A levels. The idea of going back to school doesn't exactly fill me with joy. On the other hand, it's better than being stuck at home with The Rat. And I know everyone will give me a hard time if I don't, including Mum.

We sit at one of the picnic tables outside to drink our tea. Mr S makes me laugh, telling me silly stories about the good old days when his pupils used to blow things up and set fire to their hair in science lessons.

When The Rat wakes up, he volunteers to give her a bottle of milk and he chats away to her while he does it, explaining the names of the different field placings in cricket. Short square leg. Silly mid-off. 'I hope you're listening, young lady,' he says. 'This is an important part of your education.' She stares, intrigued. 'Periodic table next time.'

'Good to see you, Pearl,' he says when it's time to go. 'You're doing a grand job. Good luck with your results.'

It's late by the time I get home and Dad's already there. As I open the front door, he's on the phone.

'I've got to go,' he says quickly as soon as he sees me. 'I'll speak to you about it at the weekend.'

He puts the phone down and comes to help me get the pram through the front door.

'How are my girls?' he says.

'Who were you talking to?'

'Oh,' he says, looking shifty. 'Just something to do with Rose.'

'What about her?'

'Childcare. Sort of. I'll tell you about it later. Anyway, where have you been? I brought some work home so that I could see you both and then you weren't here. I was starting to get worried.'

He lifts The Rat out of the pram and smiles at her.

'We're fine,' I say. 'You don't have to check up on me, you know.'

'So it's going OK?' Dad says. 'You're sure you can cope for the rest of the week?'

'Course,' I say.

When I go up to my room, Mum's sitting on the bed, waiting for me.

'You scared the life out of me,' I say.

'How's Rose?' she says excitedly. 'She's home now, right? I just wanted to check how it's all going.'

She fixes me with her most piercing stare. I know I'm going to have to make this good. I can't let her have any suspicion about what's really been going on. If she knew what a mess I was making of everything, how I'd abandoned The Rat, I'd never see Mum again. I've got to convince her, and I never could lie to her without her seeing through me. *You can't kid a kidder, Pearl,* she used to say, eyebrow raised.

But maybe I can. Suddenly I know how to do it. I won't tell Mum about The Rat. I'll tell her how it would have been if things had gone right; if we'd brought home the baby I'd imagined when Mum was pregnant, the nappy-advert one with the dimples and blonde hair.

'It's great,' I say, picturing in my head how it should have been. 'She's so good. She hardly ever wakes up in the night.'

'Really?' Mum looks surprised. 'You woke up every hour on the hour for the first two years from what I remember.' She'd made a big point of telling Dad about this when she was pregnant with The Rat. Since he'd missed out on the night feeds and nappy changing with me, she'd been determined he'd be making up for it this time round. 'She sounds angelic.'

'Oh, she is,' I gush. 'She's adorable. Everyone says so. Really smiley. I've been looking after her this week while Dad's been at work and she just loves being with me. Dad always says her face lights up when I come into the room.' I remember The Rat screaming at me as I held her out in front of me, her little body rigid with rage. Was it rage? Or was it something else? I push the thought away and focus again on the imaginary baby. 'She loves it when I feed her,' I add for good measure. 'And when I sing to her.'

Hmm. Perhaps that was overdoing it. Mum looks sceptical.

'Have you had her hearing checked?'

'You're not funny.'

'Well,' Mum says, 'she sounds positively perfect. Almost too good to be true. I take it she does produce the occasional smelly nappy? Or does what comes out of her rear end have a faint aroma of meadow flowers?'

I realize I have been overdoing it slightly.

'Oh,' I say. 'Smelly nappies. Yes, of course. Yuck.'

'Well, I'm delighted it's all going so swimmingly,' says Mum and there's a faint edge to her voice. Does she know I'm lying?

'Are you ever here without me knowing?' I ask suddenly.

'What?'

'It's just sometimes I get the feeling you're watching me. Like the other day I was talking to Dad in the sitting room about . . . something. And I thought maybe you could hear.'

'What? You think I'm spying on you?'

'Not exactly . . .'

'Shuffling along, hiding behind a rubber plant? Sitting in cafes, reading newspapers with holes in? Wearing those glasses with the fake nose attached?' She laughs so hard she starts to cough and has to take a swig of my glass of water. After a while, she tries to control herself. 'I always rather fancied myself as a gumshoe actually. Private investigator. Lady detective. I'd be great at it. I have all the necessary attributes. Discreet. Inconspicuous. Very good at blending in, chameleon-like. Don't you think?'

'That's not what I meant,' I snap.

'So what are you so worried I'll find out anyway? Are you keeping secrets?'

For some reason I think of the hidden photo in my bedside table of Mum with James.

'No. Course not.'

144

I'd been thinking perhaps I could ask her some questions about him, but somehow now doesn't seem quite the right time. She'll only bite my head off, take it all the wrong way.

She raises an eyebrow. 'Then why do I get the feeling there are things you're not telling me?'

'Because you have a suspicious mind,' I offer.

She sighs. 'Can't you be honest with me, Pearl? I'm your mum.'

'I *am* being honest.'

She sighs and fishes a packet of cigarettes out of her pocket. 'OK, if you say so.'

'I do.'

'Well I never,' she says as she opens the window. 'Come and look at this.'

'What?'

'There's a rather glorious boy digging up next-door's garden. Come and see.'

I walk over to the window and catch a glimpse of Finn disappearing into Dulcie's house.

'Oh, you've missed him now,' Mum says. 'He's gone indoors. Shame. He was ever so good-looking.'

'No he isn't,' I say, trying hard not to think about how blue his eyes are, and the way his hair falls down over them.

'And how would you know?' She turns to me, interested.

145

'I've met him already.'

Mum's face lights up. 'Oh, *have* you indeed? When?'

'A couple of times.'

'And?'

'And what?'

'Did you speak to him?'

I feel myself blush as I remember the utter horror of the first time I met him, and then the second time when he realized I'd left The Rat on her own. What must he think of me?

'Yes.'

Mum notices the blush, I know she does, and misinterprets it.

'*And?*' she says, grinning.

'And what?'

She sighs. 'You are hard work sometimes, Pearl.'

I shrug. 'And nothing.'

'But what's he like?'

'He's just – I don't know. He was just in the garden. We didn't say much.'

She tuts impatiently. 'Oh, Pearl. Honestly.'

'Well, what do you want me to do?' I say. 'Make stuff up? Fine. His deep-set dark eyes met mine across a herbaceous border. He took me in his strong, muscular arms and I looked up at his chiselled, masculine jawline and—'

'Have you been reading Mills and Boon novels?'

'Molly's gran in Ireland reads them. Molly used to sneak them back in her suitcase.'

Mum smiles. 'Darling Molly. How is she?'

'Fine. Still on holiday. With Ravi.'

'Ah.'

She goes quiet for a while.

'Are you lonely?' she says at last.

I smile. 'No!' I laugh. 'Course not.'

It turns out lying isn't so hard after all.

An asteroid is going to hit the earth. It's all here in the paper Dad left lying on the kitchen table before he took The Rat off to the park. *NASA scientists identify asteroid threat . . . Armageddon . . . Could hit Earth in 2040.* I can see it in my head, this huge, lethal, unstoppable lump of rock with our name on it, hurtling silently through space towards us.

I stare at the piece of burnt toast on my plate and decide I'm definitely not hungry after all. I go upstairs to get dressed; but then I decide that maybe, as it's Saturday and I don't have to look after The Rat, I'll go back to bed. It's not like I've got anything else to do. Molly's still on holiday and no one else bothers trying to get hold of me any more.

I stop for a second, remembering how we all used to hang out together on Saturdays, Molly and me and the others. It seems so long ago, unreal almost, as though it didn't really happen to me at all. I've got used to being on my own, and it turns out it's really easy to avoid people without a phone. And I haven't opened my laptop in months.

I'm just climbing back into bed when I hear some kind of small commotion going on in the street. I peer out of the window to see what's happening. A black taxi has stopped a couple of doors down from us and there's an argument going on between a woman I can't see, because a tree is in the way, and the taxi driver. There's also a yapping dog somewhere. Its bark bounces off the walls.

I head back to my bed and close my eyes. But a few moments later there's a very long ring on the doorbell. I think about ignoring it, but almost immediately there are another two impatient rings. I pull on an old jumper of Mum's over my pyjamas, go downstairs and open the door.

On the doorstep is a small glamorous woman, old but not *really* old: about sixty I'd guess, though she's wearing a lot of make-up and I'm rubbish at ages. She has cropped blonde hair with designer sunglasses perched on top and she's wearing an expensive-looking cream jacket. Behind is the taxi driver I saw from the window, laden down with matching violet-coloured leather luggage.

148

'This "gentleman" is trying to make me pay extra!' she says in a posh Scottish voice, jerking a manicured thumb at the taxi driver. 'For *Hector*.' She looks at me outraged, evidently expecting a response. I stare back at her, bewildered. She's clearly mad. I look to the taxi driver for some kind of explanation, but he's red and sweating both from carrying the cases and from being very angry.

'NO dogs in my taxi. Except for guide dogs obviously,' he adds apologetically to me, as if to prove he's not a monster.

'Well then, you should have said something when we got in,' says the woman, sounding like the Queen.

'Um,' I start to say, not quite knowing where to start. Who is she? Why is she here? Why are they both talking as if I know what's going on? I'm also a bit confused by the fact that she seems to own an invisible dog.

'How was I supposed to know you had a bleedin' dog? You smuggled him on in that!' He points accusingly at the large bag tucked under the madwoman's arm and, as I look at it, I realize there are two large black eyes gleaming out of it suspiciously, which at least answers one question.

'Smuggled him on indeed.' She glares at him. 'I've never heard such nonsense.'

'Excuse me,' I begin again, 'I think you've made a mistake—'

'It's not hygienic I'm afraid, love,' the driver explains to me. 'And I'm allergic.' As if to prove the point, he sneezes loudly, sending the bags and cases tumbling to the ground.

'No, I mean—'

'*Not hygienic?*' For a moment I think the madwoman is actually going to hit him. She covers the gap in the bag where Hector (presumably) is peering out, as if to protect him from the distress of hearing the slur. The bag begins to emit a low grumpy bark, which gets louder as the madwoman gets angrier. 'How dare you? You are a silly, ignorant little man—'

'Now wait a minute.' The taxi driver pulls out a handkerchief and blows his nose loudly, then glares at the woman. 'I'm not putting up with that, not even from an old lady.'

She turns a similar colour to her luggage and draws herself up as tall as she can, which is about chest height to the taxi driver.

'Just who exactly are you calling an *old* lady?'

'*EXCUSE ME! WHAT ARE YOU DOING HERE?*' I shout. They both turn their full attention to me for the first time and I remember I'm still in pyjama bottoms and one of Mum's old jumpers. The woman looks me up and down and clicks her tongue.

'Dear, dear,' she says. 'There's no need to shout, Pearl.'

I stare at her. She knows my name.

'Who are you?' I say it slowly because, as I'm speaking, I realize there *is* something familiar about her, something I know, but can't quite remember . . .

The taxi driver looks from her to me, bemused. 'I thought you said your granddaughter lived here?' He looks at me and taps the side of his head. 'Sorry, love, I think she's got a screw loose.'

'*Granny?*' I stare at her in disbelief. But yes, I know it's her now, even though I haven't seen her since I was four.

She looks at me as if I'm the one who's behaving oddly.

'Of course. Who else would I be? Now enough of this nonsense. Shall we go in?'

'No,' I say. She looks at me.

'Pardon?'

'You can't. It's Mum's house. She wouldn't want you here. You're not welcome.'

She smiles at me as if I'm still the four-year-old I was last time she saw me. 'Don't be silly, Pearl.'

'I mean it,' I say. 'Dad's not going to be too happy if he comes back and finds you've just turned up out of the blue.'

She looks at me, her plucked and pencilled eyebrows arched with surprise. 'Pearl, dear,' she says. 'Who do you think asked me to come? Did he not tell you?'

He wouldn't have gone behind my back. Surely. But of course. The conversation we never got round to having. The phone call I interrupted. That's why he was being so shifty. I shake my head slowly.

'I wasn't supposed to be arriving till next weekend,' she says, 'but I managed to change my plans at the last minute and I thought I'd surprise you both.'

'Looks like you've done that all right,' says the taxi driver.

'You needn't look like that, my girl,' Granny says as if the taxi driver no longer exists. 'I've come to help. To sort you all out.'

She empties Hector, who turns out to be a pug, from her bag. He sniffs at a dandelion growing from the cracks in the garden path with his black, snub nose. Then he cocks his leg against the porch wall and trots into the hall, his little claws tip-tapping on the tiles. Soot, who had been sitting on the bottom stair, licking a paw, puffs her tail up like one of those old-fashioned dusters on a stick and scoots towards the back door.

'I'm not *your girl*,' I say to her. 'And I don't need sorting out.'

She smiles as if I'm a small child who's said something very funny without realizing.

'You really are so like your mother, God rest her soul. Poor dear Stella.' She stops for a moment, puts her hand on my shoulder and looks genuinely sad. But it doesn't last long. 'As for *you*,' she says, turning to the taxi driver, 'you can help me in with these bags if you please.'

'I don't think so, love.' The taxi driver sneezes again.

'You will if you want paying,' she says and grumbling he collects up the bags again and heaves them into the hall.

'London,' she says scathingly as she sweeps past me into the house, leaving a trail of relentlessly floral perfume in her wake. 'There's obscene graffiti on your front wall you know. And it's not even spelt correctly.' I wonder vaguely what she expects me to do about it. Remove it? Or go out with a spray can and correct it?

Within ten minutes it's like Granny's been here forever. She's bustling about the kitchen, making tea, feeding Hector dog biscuits produced from one of her many cases, wondering aloud when Dad and The Rat will be back, complaining about the state of the house. Damp in the hallway. Woodworm in the floorboards. Kitchen hasn't been renovated since the dawn of time. Garden like the jungles of Borneo. I look out through the patio windows. It's wilder than ever out there. *Mature*, the estate agent had said. *A challenge for the keen gardener*.

He'd looked at Dad hopefully and Dad had said, *We'd better hope the baby has green fingers then, hadn't we?*

'Well, we like it,' I lie.

153

'The whole place is a bomb site, Pearl. What on earth possessed them to move into this place with a baby due any minute?'

'Actually, the baby wasn't due for months.' So if you want to blame anyone blame her, I don't add.

'Still.' Granny inspects the range, which is now covered in a thick layer of dust. 'Gracious. My grandmother had one of these.'

'We were supposed to move in months ago. Things kept going wrong. Down the chain. I don't know . . . Mortgages. Surveys. Some boring thing or other. Anyway, Mum said all it needed was a lick of paint and elbow grease.' As it happens, when Mum said this, I told her she was probably clinically insane and should seek medical attention, but I have to defend her against Granny since she's not here to do it for herself.

'Yes, well, she always did have a good imagination,' Granny says disapprovingly. Then she sighs. 'I really am sorry about it, Pearl. About your mum.'

'No you're not,' I say. 'I know how things were with you and her. You hated her. So you needn't pretend to be upset.'

She shakes her head. 'That's not true, dear. Really it isn't. We had our differences, but I didn't hate your mother.'

'You never even wanted her and Dad to get married. You thought she was a horrible single mother.'

Granny puts two cups of tea on the table. 'I worried, like all mothers do,' she says, giving the chair next to me a thorough clean with The Rat's wet wipes which Dad's left lying on the side. 'I just wanted Alex to be happy. And maybe at first I did have reservations. But I could see that he was happy, with Stella. And with you. Happier than I'd ever seen him.' She sits down at last and clicks sweetener into her tea. 'He loved her. And he adored you. I've never seen anyone dote on a baby like he doted on you. Whether I liked Stella or she liked me didn't come into it.'

Well, she would say that now, wouldn't she? I don't speak. Just stare at my tea. Hector comes sniffing round my feet. He seems very at home already. I wonder if we'll ever see Soot again. If I could run off into the garden and hide, I'd do it too.

'Anyway,' Granny says briskly, 'now isn't the time to be going into all that. Let me have a good look at you, darling.'

Darling?

'The last time I saw you, you were about so high and a chubby little thing. I used to call you "my precious Pearl". Do you remember?'

My precious Pearl?

'No,' she says, hoisting Hector up on to her lap, and I realize that she *is* older than she seems, under the make-up. She looks tired. 'I don't suppose you do. Dear me.' She sits there, gazing at me, lost in thought, until I feel so self-conscious I have to get up from the table and pretend I'm searching for something on the other side of the room.

'You do look awfully thin, dear,' she says at last, snapping out of it. 'I'm going to have to feed you up a bit. What shall I cook us for dinner? Shepherd's pie used to be your favourite.'

I'm just turning round to protest when I hear the sound of the key in the front door, followed by the familiar sound of Dad wrestling the stupid pram in. You still have to get it at exactly the right angle or it won't fit, even since Dad moved the chest of drawers in the hallway.

'There they are!' Granny's face lights up. She's so excited she even empties Hector off her knee, and he stands, squat and belligerent, at her feet, looking up at her. Dad comes into the kitchen and Hector starts up his gruff barking again. When Dad sees Granny, he stops, shocked. Then he looks anxiously over at me.

'I thought you weren't coming till next week?' he says to Granny.

'Well, that's a nice welcome,' she says. 'I thought you'd be pleased.'

'I am, Mum, of course I am.' He walks over and gives her a hug, and he looks so relieved and she looks so happy I want to be sick.

'What's she doing here?' I demand, although I know, of course I know. I'm not stupid.

'I wanted to tell you, love, but I never got the chance. Granny's come to look after Rose for a while,' Dad says. 'Just till we can get something else sorted. So you don't have to any more.'

'I was quite capable of looking after her,' I say, though the truth is I'm so relieved that I won't have to look after The Rat any more that part of me is actually quite pleased to see Granny, in spite of everything. Before Dad arrived, I'd been planning a big *If she stays, I go* showdown. But now I think, what's the point? Someone's got to look after The Rat. And it's not going to be me. It's not like I have to have anything to do with Granny. Most of the time I'm in the house I stay in my room anyway, out of the way of Dad and The Rat. I won't even have to talk to Granny if I don't want to.

'But you didn't want to look after her in the first place,' Dad says, bemused. 'And it was always going to be a temporary thing. Anyway, you'll be back at school in a few weeks.'

All this time Granny hasn't taken her eyes off Dad.

'You look older, Alex,' she says. I wonder when she last saw him. I remember he used to go up and see her every now and then for a weekend, but not since I was a kid. Mum would stomp around in a bad mood the whole time he was away. I asked her once why I couldn't

157

go with him and she bit my head off so I never asked again.

'Well, I am older,' he says. 'It's been a while.'

But I know what she means. Dad looks older than he should. Granny's staring at him as if she's trying to get him into focus; trying to see her son in the grey, tired man in front of her.

'Yes,' she says. 'It has.' Hector whines at her feet and she picks him up and strokes him and forces herself to smile. 'Where is she then? My little granddaughter?' Her voice goes all treacly. 'What have you done with the little angel?'

'She's in the pram,' Dad says, smiling. 'Sleeping. Come and have a look.'

She clip-clops off down the hall after him in her heels, and I can hear her cooing. I stand in the doorway of the kitchen and watch them. Granny carefully lifts The Rat out of the pram. The Rat has almost disappeared inside a sleepsuit – her clothes are still far too big for her – and Granny cradles her in the crook of her arm so she can see her sleeping face.

'Hello, Rose,' she whispers.

Dad's watching them, looking happier than I've seen him in a long time. He doesn't care what Mum would think. He doesn't care what I think.

In fact, they've all forgotten I'm even here.

*   *   *

That evening, after Granny's settled The Rat in her cot, Dad hauls all the boxes out of Mum's study and puts up the sofa bed. I watch, furious, as Mum's study becomes Granny's room, filled with the never-ending contents of the violet suitcases.

'Sorry, Mum,' Dad's saying. 'I know it's not exactly luxury accommodation. I was going to have a sort-out before you got here. I don't know where we're going to put it all.'

And suddenly I'm not furious any more.

'Oh,' I say. 'I don't mind having some of the boxes in my room.'

When I'm sure Granny and Dad have gone to bed, I search through the contents of the (PERSONAL) box again, but I can't find anything to do with James.

I try not to feel disappointed, but I do. Then a thought occurs to me. I drag my laptop out from where it's been gathering dust under my bed, plug it in and switch it on. Then I sit in the lamplight staring at the screen. Why do I feel so nervous? I've got nothing to feel guilty about. I just want to find out a bit about my father. Nothing wrong with that. It's not like I'm going to contact him or anything. It's no big deal. I'm just curious. But still, I push one of the removal boxes against the door in case Granny decides to come wandering in. I can already tell she's the sort of person who can sense when something's about to happen that she disapproves of.

159

My other worry is that Mum will decide to appear and stick her nose in.

I type his name – James Sullivan – and, before I can think of reasons not to, I click on the search button. It takes a while to load: the internet connection is always crashing here. Then the screen flashes up. *About 82,700,000 results.*

Oh.

I sit there for a while, staring at the screen, feeling stupid. It's hardly the most unusual name. I should have realized there'd be zillions of them. How was I going to track down the right one? I flick through a few pages. There are doctors and students and solicitors, assorted sportsmen, a lecturer in philosophy, a dog trainer; the pages go on and on. They live all over the world so I add 'UK' to the search, thinking this will narrow it down. It does – to around 21,500,000. And then I realize that, in any case, I have no idea whether he lives in the UK. He might have emigrated. He might not even call himself James. He might be Jamie or Jim or Jimmy, or he might call himself by some stupid nick-name or his middle name. I flick through a few more pages. There are young ones and old ones and dead ones. Mum would have told me if he'd died, wouldn't she? But would she have known? I realize I have no real idea whether they were even still in touch with each other.

I sit and think for a while, trying to remember the conversation we'd had about him all that time ago, vainly struggling to find any forgotten snippet of information that might be useful.

But I realize there's nothing for it. I'm just going to have to ask Mum.

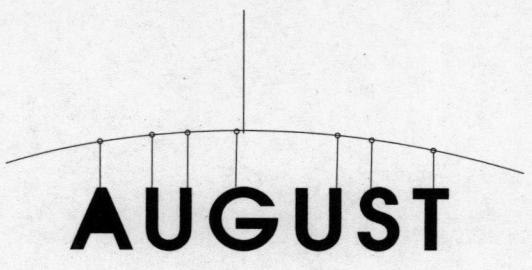

'Don't mind us,' Granny bellows cheerily at me, vacuuming around my feet with The Rat on her hip as I sit on the sofa, pretending to read a book. 'We'll be done in a minute, won't we, Rosie Posie?'

She's only been here three weeks, but it feels like forever, or possibly longer. The house is hardly recognizable. Everything's been scrubbed and bleached and polished to within an inch of its life. You can't put a coffee cup down without her picking it up, tutting loudly and putting a coaster underneath it. The Rat sleeps through the night without a peep. She 'just needed a bit of routine' Granny keeps telling us, sounding very pleased with herself.

'Then perhaps you could help me purée some pears for Rose's lunch,' she says, switching the vacuum cleaner off. 'My little treasure's getting hungry, aren't you?' The Rat smiles and gurgles at her. I seethe silently at her disloyalty.

'Perhaps you could even try your hand at feeding her?' Granny says. She buys mountains of organic fruit and veg which she turns into mush for The Rat, who dribbles it down her chin or splatters it all over the kitchen floor. The whole process is revolting enough to watch, let alone get involved in.

'I can't,' I say quickly, getting up. 'I've got things to do.'

But as I'm heading upstairs the doorbell rings.

'Get that, will you, Pearl?' Granny shouts.

I open the door and standing on the doorstep is Molly, looking tanned and blonder than ever.

'Oh, Pearl!' she says, hugging me. 'How are you? It's been so long, I just had to come round and see you as soon as I got back. I've really missed you.'

'Oh yeah?' I say, sceptical. 'While you were on holiday in your boyfriend's luxury apartment in Spain?'

'It *was* brilliant,' she says, smiling. 'But yes, of course I missed you. I thought about you every day.'

We stand there for a moment.

'Anyway,' she says, 'I can't stay long. I've got to get back to look after the boys. I just wanted to see you and . . .' She pauses. 'I wondered if I might be able to say hello to the baby.'

'Oh right.' So that's why she's here.

I stand in the doorway, trying to think of a reason why she can't come in, but of course Granny appears at that exact moment with Rose in her arms and says,

'You must be Molly. Pearl's told me so much about you.' Which is true, because MI6 and the CIA could learn a lot from Granny's interrogation techniques. She wears you down until you'd tell her anything just to make her go away.

'She's my granny,' I explain in a resigned sort of way. But Molly's not looking at me, or at Granny. She's transfixed by The Rat.

'Rose.' She says it reverently. 'Oh, Pearl. She's *perfect*.'

'Isn't she just?' says Granny, delighted to have found an ally. 'Come in, Molly dear, and have a cup of tea so you can meet her properly. We were just about to give her lunch, weren't we, Pearl?'

I don't say anything, just trail in after them and then sit watching them as they laugh and coo and feed the pear sludge to The Rat.

'Can I hold her?' Molly asks Granny when she's finished.

'Of course,' Granny says, lifting the sticky Rat out of her high chair and placing her gently in Molly's arms.

'Hello, Rose,' Molly says. Her face is lit up with excitement and tenderness, just as I'd known it would be. The Rat gurgles back at her. Molly walks her over to the window and points things out to her in the garden: the birds, leaves on the trees gently moving in the breeze. She looks so natural and happy with The Rat that I can't bear to watch. I pick up Granny's magazine from the table and try to concentrate on *15 Ways With Aubergines* instead.

Eventually, reluctantly, Molly hands The Rat back to Granny.

'I'd better go,' she says. 'Mum's shift starts soon. Shall I come round on Thursday so we can walk in together to get our results?'

I feel a flash of resentment at her, trying to make everything normal, as if we can just pretend it's all fine, just how it used to be.

'I'm not going in to get my results,' I say, flicking through the pages of the magazine.

There's a pause, and I feel Molly and Granny turn to look at me.

'What do you mean?'

I shrug, not looking up. 'I don't care about them. It's a waste of time.'

'Don't be silly, Pearl,' Granny says. 'Of course you're going to get them.'

'I'm not,' I say.

The Rat starts to whine.

'Well, call me if you change your mind, won't you?' Molly says.

'I'm not going to change my mind,' I say, pretending to be riveted by an article on scented candles. 'Didn't you say you were in a hurry?'

*   *   *

168

After she's gone, I head straight up to my room before Granny can start giving me a hard time.

'You know you upset her,' Granny calls after me. 'Such a lovely girl too. You were really quite rude to her, Pearl.'

But I don't care.

I can't forgive Molly for loving The Rat more than I do.

A few days later, The Envelope is sitting on the kitchen table when I come down for breakfast. The Exam Results Envelope. Dad and Granny had been on at me all week since I told them I wasn't going to go in and collect my results. Granny had wheedled and threatened and bribed, but I wasn't having any of it. Now they're both standing, fixed grins on their faces, watching me intently. Even The Rat watches me closely from her high chair, where Granny's propped her up with a cushion.

'Morning,' Granny says brightly. 'Did you sleep well?'

'Would you like a coffee? Or tea?' Dad says before I can answer her.

'Actually, I think I'll give breakfast a miss,' I say. 'I'm not hungry anyway.' I get up and head for the door.

'No!' Granny shrieks. 'You can't!'

'But your results,' says Dad, trying to sound calm. 'Don't you want to open them?'

'No.'

There's a pause.

'Not in front of us perhaps.' Dad smiles at me encouragingly. 'I completely understand. It's a private thing. You take them upstairs with you and you can tell us whenever you're ready.'

'It's not that,' I say. 'I just don't want to know.'

'Look.' Dad comes over and takes hold of my hands. 'You mustn't worry. We all know what a difficult time it was for you, what awful pressure you were under when you sat the exams. No one will be disappointed in you, love. And there's always resits. We'll be proud of you whatever the results are.'

'I'm not worried. I just don't care. What does it matter anyway?'

'What do you mean?' Granny says. 'Of course it matters.'

'Fine,' I snap. 'If it matters so much to you, you open them.'

'We can't do that,' Dad says.

'Oh yes we can,' Granny says, snatching them off the table in case I change my mind.

'You go for it. Knock yourselves out. I'm going to have a shower.'

I stomp upstairs and, as I'm closing the bathroom door, I hear shrieks from downstairs.

'Pearl!' Granny calls up gleefully. 'Pearl? I think you're going to want to see this, dear!'

I close the bathroom door and lock it.

I'm in the middle of shampooing my hair when there's a loud sneeze from the direction of the toilet. I start and turn round, noticing as I do Mum's hazy shape through the blotchy, yellowing shower curtain.

'Can't stop,' she says. 'Just popped by to say well done on the exam results.'

I smile, despite myself. 'I don't even know what they are yet.'

'No, but given the frenzy of delight and excitement that's going on downstairs I'm guessing you didn't fail them all.'

'I suppose.'

'Granny's probably busy thinking of reasons that it's all down to her you're a genius. She won't let tiny details like the fact that she hasn't seen you since you were four and has no genetic input whatsoever get in the way.'

'So you know she's here?' I still can't work out whether Mum knows more than she's letting on about what happens in between her visits. I'd been thinking that I might have to break the bad news about Granny's arrival to her, half dreading her fury, half looking forward to it; it would be good to have an ally against Granny.

171

'Oh yes,' Mum says, sounding very blasé. 'I'd recognize that perfume anywhere. It always did make me—' She breaks off and sneezes again. It's true. Granny's heavy, flowery scent seems to have permeated the whole house. Even in my room I get the occasional whiff of it, probably because she insists on going in there to clean on the rare moments I'm not there. I've been threatening to put a lock on the door. 'And let's be honest you can hardly miss her, can you? I'd forgotten just how loud she is. They can probably still hear her back in Edinburgh, poor things.'

She sounds disappointingly jolly about the whole thing.

'I thought you'd be furious.'

Mum sighs. 'Look, I'm not saying I'm delighted. But with Dad at work and you back at school soon someone has to look after Rose, don't they?'

I know she's right, but I can't help feeling disappointed that she's not more angry with Granny and Dad.

'Easy for you to say,' I grumble. 'You're not the one who has to live with her. She's a nightmare. She's always on at me.' I do my best impression of her drawling, posh Scottish voice. '*You should be out enjoying yourself at your age instead of moping about. You should be eating more. You should have a boyfriend. When I was your age, your Grampy, rest his soul, and I were already courting.* She drives me mad.'

She's also always on at me to do things with Rose. *Ooh, could you just take her a wee minute, Pearl, while I go and spend a penny?* Or *Could you just take over this feed, so I can get on with making our dinner?* Without fail The Rat wails inconsolably when she's thrust into my arms. *Oh, see, she loves her big sister,* Granny always says implausibly. But I don't mention any of this to Mum.

'Oh dear,' Mum laughs. 'Poor you. I do pity you, Pearl, I really do. But Rose has to come first,' she says firmly. 'I know you understand that, darling.'

I'm so shocked that I can't speak, and I'm thankful that the shower curtain means she can't see the expression on my face.

'Anyway, let's not waste time talking about Granny. This is your day. I'm so proud of you. I knew you could do it.'

I don't say anything.

'You could try to be a bit more excited, for heaven's sake.'

'What does it matter?'

Mum's unimpressed face appears round the side of the curtain.

'Oh, don't start all that again, Pearl.'

'Mum!'

'What?'

173

'A bit of privacy wouldn't go amiss'

'Oh really. I've seen it all before.' She looks at me closely. 'Are you OK? Your eyes are all red.'

'I've got shampoo in them,' I lie. She mustn't guess how hurt I am. 'Pass me a towel, will you?'

No towel appears.

'You never go out anywhere any more.'

'Molly's boyfriend's having a party next week.' Molly keeps phoning me about it. She's desperate for me to get to know Ravi. 'I might go to that.'

'Promise me you will.'

'Give me a towel.'

'Promise me or I'm not giving you the towel.'

'OK, I promise.'

She gives me the towel and a peck on the cheek.

'You won't regret it.'

'Fine. Now will you please go away and let me get dressed in peace?'

As I walk up to Ravi's front door, I'm glad I started on the vodka before I got here. I feel nice and warm inside and not at all nervous about the fact that Ravi's house is much posher than I expected, or that I don't know any of his friends, and even if I did I probably wouldn't like them.

I nearly chickened out at the last minute, but, just as I was about to call Molly to say I wasn't going to come after all, Mum stuck her head round my bedroom door and said, 'You needn't think I don't know what you're doing. A promise is a promise, Pearl. Go on, you'll enjoy yourself once you're there.' So I swiped the vodka from the drinks cabinet and after I'd drunk a bit of it I decided maybe the party would be OK after all.

I ring the big brass doorbell and, after a moment, a very beautiful, sparkly woman, who I assume is Ravi's mum, answers the door, which is a surprise. I hadn't realized it was going to be that sort of party. I'm still wearing the clothes I picked up off the bedroom floor this morning with Mum's moth-eaten old cardigan over the top. The woman looks at me as if she's trying to work out whether I've come for the party or I'm going to try and sell her something she doesn't want.

'I'm Molly's friend, Pearl.'

'Oh yes,' she says, flashing white teeth and lipgloss at me. 'Lovely. I'm Sarah, Ravi's mum. Go through, go through. Everyone's in the garden.' She waits to greet more people who have pulled up in a 4 x 4.

Ravi's house has lots of thick cream carpets and shiny floorboards and cut flowers in vases, and the overall effect is very *Hello!* magazine. I imagine a picture of Molly and Ravi, sitting on one of the antique-looking sofas with fixed grins, and maybe a few kids scattered about the place. *Molly and Ravi and the triplets*

175

invite us into their Gracious Home. This thought combined with the vodka makes me giggle and then I hope sparkly, smiley Sarah can't hear, which makes me giggle some more.

The whole back of the house opens on to a veranda overlooking the huge garden where there's a kind of marquee bar area and an industrial-scale barbecue going on. People in uniforms – in *actual uniforms* – are flipping burgers and serving drinks. That's how posh this party is. There's a band playing terrible music at the far end of the garden and fairy lights hanging in the trees and great big candle things stuck in the ground. There are lots and lots of people. Some are obviously Ravi's friends; others look like relatives, aunties and uncles. I don't know any of them, which is good. I take another swig from my bottle then stash it back in my bag.

'Well,' Mum says from behind me. 'This *is* swish.'

'I know,' I say. 'I was expecting cans of beer in the bath and people being sick.'

'Oh well,' she says, 'I wouldn't complain. Just enjoy yourself. Have fun for once. Go easy on the free booze though if you've been on the vodka. You don't want to make a scene at Molly's posh boyfriend's house, do you?'

I head down the veranda steps towards the marquee where the bar is.

Molly comes running over and gives me a hug. 'I'm so glad you're here. I thought you might not come.'

'It's not really what I was expecting.'

'Come on.' She pulls me after her. 'Get a drink and come and dance with me. Ravi's so busy having to talk to all his relatives I've hardly seen him all evening.'

'I'll have a drink, but there's no way I'm dancing.'

'OK,' she says. 'Let's have a chat instead. A proper catch-up.'

We spot some chairs a bit out of the way and sit down.

'Well done on your results,' she says.

'And you.'

'We had such a great time in Spain.' Her face falls a bit. 'Just a shame to come back really.'

'Oh right,' I say. 'Thanks.'

'Oh no!' she says, taking my hand. 'No, I didn't mean that. It's great to see you of course. I really missed *you*. It's just—'

She stops.

'What?'

'It doesn't matter. Come on, just a quick dance?'

But just as she's trying to pull me up Ravi appears.

'Hi, Pearl,' he says and kisses me on both cheeks. Then he stands there, looking awkward and tall. 'Thanks so much for coming. Are you enjoying yourself? Can I get you anything?'

177

'I'm fine thanks,' I mutter to his shoes, which look as though he's probably polished them specially for the occasion.

'Do you mind if I just steal Molly away a minute?' He takes her hand. 'My auntie is dying to meet you.'

'Oh, OK.' Molly looks shy but pleased. 'Back in a minute, Pearl.'

And they disappear into the crowd.

After I've drunk a bit more of the vodka, I find it's quite good fun talking to people who don't know anything about me. One of Ravi's great-aunties in a beautiful purple sari. His godfather. A cousin from Ealing. None of them feel sorry for me. None of them ask me how I'm feeling. I can just tell them anything that pops into my head. *I'm a black belt in karate. I'm at finishing school in Switzerland. I play the ukulele. My dad's a fighter pilot. Oh yes, my mum's an opera singer actually.*

Oh no. No brothers and sisters. No, it's just me.

I nip off to the loo every now and then to drink some more vodka. There are copies of *The Economist* in there which makes me giggle for no good reason. As I stash the vodka bottle back in the bag, I notice that half of it has gone already.

'You're getting through that,' Mum says from somewhere behind me. 'Don't you think that might be enough now? Have a glass or two of water. And I know you don't really do much eating these days, but some food might not be a bad idea.'

'You were the one who told me to enjoy myself,' I say, accidentally squirting expensive hand lotion all over my shoes which sets the giggling off again.

'Just promise me you're not going to make a spectacle of yourself. No vomiting in the water feature or trying to snog an uncle. It can all get very messy very quickly, Pearl. And believe me, I know what I'm talking about here.'

'I'm fine.'

I'm just in the middle of telling someone who works with Ravi's dad that I grew up in the Australian outback when I find the ground seems to be moving about a bit. Maybe Mum was right. I go to the bar and ask for a glass of water. Then I find a table out of the way of everyone where I can just sit on my own for a while and get my head straight.

'Pearl?'

I look round. Oh God. It's Taz. Awful Taz, the 'self-obsessed pillock' who I sort of accidentally used to go out with. What the hell is he doing here? Drinking mainly, by the looks of it. Even I can tell he's had way too much. He comes shambling up to the table, a bit unsteady on his feet, and sits down on the chair next to me.

'Long time no see,' he says, breathing alcohol fumes all over me. 'How are you? You're looking fantastic.'

He leans in close and I remember how much I didn't fancy him even when I was going out with him, which I never was really.

'Taz,' I say with as little enthusiasm as I can manage. 'What are you doing here?'

'I play football with the Ravster.'

Great.

'How are you doing?' he slurs.

'Oh. You know.'

'I heard about your mum.' He tries to look all serious and sympathetic, but his eyes keep sliding down to where my cleavage would be if I still had one. He puts his hand on my hand. It's warm and sweaty, and I carefully remove it with my other hand. 'I'm really sorry,' he slurs. 'Really, really sorry.'

'Right.'

'Really.'

'OK. Got it.'

'If there's anything I can do . . .'

'Taz,' I say, taking my hand away, 'are you trying to be nice about my mum because you think it might get you into my knickers?'

Even in his state he looks a bit taken aback.

'No.' There's a pause and his head sways slightly. 'Not really.'

'That's what I thought,' I say. 'Only a real arsehole would do something like that.'

'Yeah.'

There's another pause and this time he sways so much he almost falls off his chair.

'I think I might go and get a drink,' he says at last.

'Good plan.'

'You want anything?'

'No.'

'OK then. See you later.'

'I doubt it somehow,' I say as he staggers off, almost knocking over one of Ravi's fiercer aunties, who doesn't look best pleased.

The fairy lights are starting to swirl around a bit. I blink to get them to stay still. But everything's just a bit hazy and it turns out I rather like it that way . . .

'You're Molly's friend, aren't you? I'm so sorry, I can't remember your name.'

I look over to see who's talking to me, but it takes me a moment to focus on her. Of course, it's Ravi's mum: sparkly, smiley Sarah.

'Pearl,' I mumble.

'Such a lovely girl, Molly. She and Ravi seem very happy together.'

'Don't they just.'

'It's just a shame she's having such a rotten time at the moment.'

I look up. 'What do you mean?'

'Well, with her parents.'

'What about them?'

'You know. The trial separation.'

I stare at her, thinking maybe she's got muddled. She does look as though she's been on the champagne for a while now: a bit less sparkly, a bit more shiny. But then I think of Molly and how sad she'd seemed earlier, and how she changed the subject instead of telling me what was wrong, and I know Sarah hasn't got the wrong person. Molly just hasn't told me.

'Oh, that,' I say.

She hasn't told me, but she has told Ravi.

'It can be so hard on the children, even when they're your age. Especially when there's so much acrimony. And they're using poor Molly like a pawn in their games. She was in tears the other day just talking about it. I told her she's got nothing to feel guilty about: none of this is her fault. It's selfish, it really is.'

So not only has she told Ravi, but she's told Ravi's bloody mum.

'I think our Spanish break really helped though,' she says. 'A chance to relax and forget about everything. We had such a wonderful time. But I expect she's told you all about it.'

'Oh yes,' I say. 'Of course.'

'I just wonder how things will be when Ravi goes to university.' She sips her champagne thoughtfully. 'Hard to keep a relationship going. But some people do of course. I suppose if it's a strong enough relationship it will last.'

The lights are swirling again. I close my eyes. When I open them again, Ravi's mum has gone. I've no idea how long I've been here, but it's quite cold and I'm definitely feeling quite dizzy now.

There's a slow dance playing and over on the dance floor I can see Molly and Ravi, arms wrapped round each other.

It's definitely time to go.

'I don't think it's a very good idea to be walking home on your own, Pearl,' Mum says, but I don't look at her because I'm having to concentrate quite hard on walking in a straight line. 'Couldn't you and Molly have shared a taxi?'

'Molly's staying over at Ravi's.'

'Oh, I see. Is that a problem?'

'Why would it be a problem?'

'You just sound as though you mind.'

I attempt a disdainful shrug, but I've got hiccups which rather ruins the effect.

'Molly can do whatever the hell she likes. It's no duck off my back.'

Mum sighs. 'Pearl, how much exactly have you had to drink?'

'If she wants to go out with the most boring boy in the entire history of the history of the entire universe, that's up to her.'

'I'm surprised she let you go home in this state.' Mum takes my elbow and steers me out of the way of an oncoming pillar box.

'I didn't say goodbye. She was Otherwise Engaged.' I try to do the air quotes thing with my fingers, but I just end up tipping vodka over my feet. 'She probably hasn't even noticed I've gone.'

'She seems pretty serious about this Ravi. He can't be that bad,' Mum says.

'Well, Molly obviously doesn't think so. She'd much rather spend her time with him than me so that's just fine.'

'Well, you haven't exactly been . . . sociable recently, have you?'

'Oh, so it's my fault, is it?'

'I didn't say that.'

'She even likes his mum better than me. His *mum*.'

'Should you be drinking that, do you think?'

'Yes.'

I've decided I might as well finish the bottle of vodka.

'It's just you're already a bit . . .'

'What?' I try to glare at her, but there seem to be two of her and I can't work out which one to focus on.

'Tipsy?'

184

'I am not.'

'OK. Well then, why do you keep walking into hedges?'

'I don't.'

'Yes you do.'

We walk on for a while and I concentrate very hard on walking in a straight line, but somehow the ground keeps tipping me off towards people's gardens.

'I'm doing it on purpose,' I say.

'Course you are.'

'It's finished now anyway.' I put the bottle down ever so carefully by a lamp post. 'There you go.'

'Why are you talking to a lamp post?'

'I don't know.' I'm laughing uncontrollably.

'Oh, Pearl,' she says. 'Just concentrate on trying to get home, will you? Before you fall asleep or vomit.'

'I feel absolutely fine,' I say. 'Anyway, it's not far.'

My voice sounds loud and annoying so I stop talking. I just keep walking and walking. Walking and walking. It seems so much further than on the way here. It's cold now, and dark, except it's never really dark with the streetlights and car headlights and night buses thundering by. Dark enough though. I want to be home. I want to be in my bed. I'm still hiccuping and it's starting to really get on my nerves. However hard I focus on putting one foot in front of the other, I keep veering off to the side, and concentrating on not falling over is giving me a headache.

'You all right?' asks Mum.

I try to say yes, but it doesn't come out.

'It's really not far now,' she says. 'You can do it.'

My teeth are chattering like mad and my legs have pretty much stopped working. But I'm nearly there. So very nearly . . .

'Just have a little rest,' I mumble.

I lie down on the pavement. It feels rough and cool under my cheek. Everything's whirling like I'm on a fairground ride. But I like the cold stone against my cheek. It stops me feeling like I'm going to be sick. Oh. Yes. I really do feel sick. But if I fall asleep the sick feeling will go . . .

'No, Pearl. Keep going. You're nearly home. You can't sleep here. Think how much more comfortable it will be in your bed.'

'S'nice here.'

I close my eyes and feel everything start to fade away.

'No. It's really not.' Mum's voice is sharp, bringing me back for a moment. 'Think. Lovely soft pillow. Lovely safe house. No Bad People who might take advantage of vodka-filled teenagers. Come on, Pearl. You can do it.'

I try to lift my head, but someone seems to have superglued my face to the pavement.

'It's a bit . . .' I close my eyes. 'Yeah. S'fine. Thanks.'

'No! Keep your eyes open.'

I try to, but it's too much effort. Everything's swimmy and then it fades until there's just dark.

Someone's talking to me, but they're a long way away and I can't hear what they're saying.

Then there's an arm round my middle and it's lifting me up to a standing position.

'No,' I try to say, but it just comes out like a noise.

'You're all right,' says the voice. 'Just lean on me.'

I do and they feel strong.

'Just try to walk a bit. I'll help.'

We stagger along the road a bit and round a corner. I feel shivery.

'No,' I say. 'You're not Mum.' But my mouth won't work properly; it's like trying to talk in a dream. Everything feels wrong.

'I'm going to be sick,' I say.

'OK. Try and lean over the drain.'

I lean forward and retch. There's nothing in my stomach except the alcohol and some apple juice from earlier, but my body keeps convulsing until it's all gone. Hands hold my hair out of my face. Liquid dribbles down my chin. I crouch down on my haunches and the wind cools my cheeks. Everything comes into focus a bit for a moment then fades again.

'Come on.'

The strong arms lift me again.

'It's OK,' says the voice. 'Not far to go.'

Someone is crying. Noisy, horrible, empty crying.

'It's OK, Pearl,' says the voice. 'Don't cry. We're nearly home.'

'You're not Mum,' I try to say.

'Up the steps.'

'I can't.'

'Course you can. I'll help you . . . That's it.'

Then there's a doorway and bright light and Dad's voice says: 'Oh God! Pearl! Christ. Is she OK?'

And then—

Nothing.

I'm in bed. My head is wedged against something hard which turns out to be a washing-up bowl with sick in it. Sunlight's streaming in through the gap in my curtains. I try to sit up, but my head pounds so hard I have to lie down again and pull the duvet up over my head and pretend to be dead.

'You don't need to speak, Pearl. I know exactly how you're feeling.' Mum's voice sounds slightly muffled through the duvet. It also sounds indecently chirpy for someone who's supposed to be concerned for my welfare.

'No,' I croak, pulling the duvet back so I can see her. 'You don't.'

'Oh yes I do. I've had a lot of experience in this area, believe me.' She's sitting on my bed, watching me closely.

'My head—'

'Ah yes. Your head. It feels as though you've woken up mid-lobotomy. Am I right? Agonizing pain?'

She looks at me eagerly, but I can't speak or move my head.

'Or is it more of a thudding? And it feels like someone's pumping up your brain from within and it's about to burst out of your skull?'

I try to nod.

'NO!' she shouts. 'Sorry!' she whispers, grinning as I flinch. 'Don't under any circumstances move your head. The consequences could be catastrophic.'

'I feel . . .'

'As though the room's spinning? Or perhaps rocking? Rising nausea?'

'I didn't. But now . . .'

'It'll pass. Probably. Eating's the best thing. Complex carbohydrates. A fry-up is perfect if you can face it.'

I grab the bowl and retch. When I've finished, I flop back, hot tears running sideways down into my ears.

'Ah yes. The self-loathing. Tempered with a modicum of self-pity. Yes. The perfect hangover storm. I remember it well. The physical and mental misery.'

189

'Can you please—' I stop. The effort of speaking is too much. I close my eyes.

'Yes? Anything. Just say it and I'll do it.'

'*Please*. Stop talking.'

And, to be fair, she does, although she doesn't go away. I can feel that she's still there.

'You seemed upset,' she says tentatively after a while. 'Last night.'

I realize I have absolutely no idea how I got home. The last thing I remember is seeing Molly and Ravi on the dance floor and staggering off into the night. After that, it's a complete blank. Except . . . now I think about it perhaps I *do* remember something. The sound of someone crying . . . And voices. Dad – was it? Granny? *She won't stop. Can you make out what she's saying? I think it's something about Stella. Pearl, it's OK, love, we're here . . .*

'Pearl?' Mum says.

'You're talking,' I say, keeping my eyes closed.

As I lie there, it occurs to me that I'm in my nightie. Did I put it on? Or did Dad or Granny have to do it? I picture the scene. Oh God. I am beyond embarrassed. I am *mortified*.

I roll over on to my side and I must fall asleep because the next thing I know I'm waking up again. I really need the loo, but I can't face trying to get myself vertical again. So I just lie there, wondering if I'll ever feel like a real, living person again, and also trying to piece together the hazy memories I have of last night.

Eventually, I hear the door open.

'Pearl?'

It's Dad.

'Mmm,' I groan from under the duvet.

I hear him come over and put something down on the bedside table.

'There's a pint of water, a vitamin C tablet and some painkillers. How are you feeling?' I can tell from his voice he can't decide whether to be angry or sorry for me.

'Bad.'

He sits down on the bed. 'You're bloody lucky, Pearl. If Finn hadn't found you—'

'*Finn?*'

'He found you lying on the pavement almost unconscious. Don't you remember?'

'No.' But of course. It would be him that found me. I know I should be glad it wasn't a rapist or murderer or something, but why does Finn *always* have to turn up at the worst possible moment? Not that I care what he thinks of me. Obviously. It's just I'd rather not develop a reputation for being a dangerous lunatic.

'You could have got hypothermia. Or worse, someone else could have found you. Someone who didn't have such good intentions. What were you thinking?'

191

I don't say anything.

'I'm worried about you, Pearl. And Granny is too. You're not seeing your friends. You're too thin. You're obviously very unhappy—'

'I'm fine.'

'You were talking last night. About Mum . . .'

'Dad. Don't.'

'I wish you'd talk to me about her when you were sober,' he says. 'You know you can.'

I close my eyes and try to pretend he's not there.

'Or if you can't talk to me . . .' He pauses. 'Perhaps you should talk to someone else. A professional.'

'You want me to see a shrink?' I croak. 'Dad, I got drunk. That's all. Don't worry. The way I feel today it's not going to happen again any time soon.'

'Just think about it, Pearl.' He walks to the door. 'Oh and I went round to thank Finn this morning. Ever such a nice lad. He's going to come round next week to paint the kitchen and do a few odd jobs around the house. You know how Granny's been nagging me about getting the place sorted out a bit.' Oh *brilliant*. 'He seemed very keen when I suggested it. I expect he could do with the money. He's off to music college next month. Very talented apparently. Plays the violin.'

'Cello,' I try to say. But all I can manage is a low moan of despair.

*   *   *

Much later, after another long sleep, I manage to stagger out of bed down to the kitchen. All I want is some more water, but Granny sits me down at the kitchen table and insists on trying to make me eat something, throwing out suggestions – *toad-in-the-hole? macaroni cheese?* – which only make me feel like vomiting all over again. In the end she settles for giving me sugary tea and a short lecture. I'm too weak to argue so I sit there, limp, watching Granny spoon orange gunge of some sort into the mouth of The Rat, who's in her high chair.

It strikes me suddenly how different she's looking, rounder, more contented, as if she's grown into herself somehow. Granny's going on and on, telling me how concerned they are about me, and how Dad's got enough to be worried about without me, and how they want to help, but they can't if I won't help myself, all interspersed with the whole 'Here comes the little aeroplane' bit with The Rat.

But all I can think about is how The Rat is becoming more of a person, more solid and real, and I'm becoming less of one. I think of the ghost girl in the window, my moment of confusion about which of us was real. I feel as though I'm blurring at the edges somehow, the me that I was before leaching away until one day I'll wake up and she'll be gone completely.

I decide I really need to go back upstairs and sleep. It's probably just the hangover making me feel like this.

But, just as I'm trying to find the strength to stand up, the doorbell goes.

'Oh good,' Granny says. 'That'll be Molly.'

'*What?*' She's the last person I want to see.

'Yes, she called earlier, worried about you. I said you'd got home OK, but I told her I knew you'd be pleased to see her.'

She gives me a Look and, before I can argue with her, I hear Dad answer the door and Molly comes through to the kitchen.

'Hi,' she says. 'I was so worried when you disappeared last night. I just came to check you're OK.'

'I'm fine,' I say, feeling about two hundred years old. Molly looks perfect and fresh.

'Good. That's a relief.' She looks over to The Rat.

'Hello, Rose,' she says, smiling, and The Rat waves her spoon at her excitedly.

'Come on,' I say, anxious to get her away from The Rat. 'Let's go upstairs.'

When we get to my room, we just sit there awkwardly in silence.

'Are you sure you're OK?' she says. 'Are you angry with me?'

I look at her. 'Why didn't you tell me? About your parents splitting up?'

'I didn't want to worry you,' she says, forcing a smile. 'I'm sure Mum and Dad will sort themselves out. It's just a temporary thing. Dad just needed a bit of space, that's all. Just needed to get his head straight. You know what it's like in our flat with the boys and the bloody dog; it's enough to drive anyone insane. And Mum's been doing loads of late shifts which hasn't exactly been helping.'

'But you didn't tell me. You told Ravi.'

'You've had enough going on. It didn't feel right to be moaning on about my problems. And . . .' She stops.

'What?'

'It doesn't matter.'

'Yes it does.'

Molly hesitates. 'You haven't wanted to talk to me. Not about your mum or Rose. I thought . . . Well, we've always talked about everything, haven't we?'

I think of all the things we've shared over the years: silly jokes, embarrassing secrets.

She takes a deep breath. 'I just feel like, if I could find the right thing to say or do, or if I could be a better friend, you'd be able to tell me how you're feeling.' The words tumble out of her mouth. 'I've tried to be there for you. I've tried to give you space. I know I always talk too much and sometimes I say the wrong thing without realizing. I want to help. I feel like I've failed you some-how, but I don't know how.'

I look away from her. 'You haven't.'

I can feel her watching me.

'I brought you this.' She hands me a small package wrapped in tissue paper. 'Me and Mum were having a clear-out the other day and I found it. I thought you might like it.'

I unfold the tissue paper. Inside is a faded old photo in a frame of me and Molly when we were only five or six. We're out in the back garden at our old house in our school uniforms, arms round each other, gap-toothed smiles on our faces.

I look up into Molly's concerned face. She looks prettier than ever, older somehow, more grown-up. Hard to believe we were ever the two little girls in the photo. I wish so much that I could explain to her; that I could get everything that's inside me out, to share it, be rid of it. But I can't. I can't even find the words for what's inside me. It's just noise; or maybe it's just silence. Whatever it is, it's not something I can share. I've locked it away out of sight, like you do with things that are very precious or very dangerous. It cannot be allowed out.

I shake my head.

Molly flicks a tear from her eye with the back of her hand as she pushes back her hair, hoping I won't notice. Then she stands up.

'I'd better get going,' she says, her voice catching in her throat.

After she's gone, I look at the picture for a while longer and silent tears trickle down my cheeks. Then I

196

wrap it up back up in the tissue paper and I put it away where I can't see it.

'Pearl,' Granny calls down from upstairs. 'Could you fetch me the wet wipes, please, dear? I think I left them on the side in the kitchen.'

I know exactly what she's doing. Finn's painting in the kitchen and she's trying to engineer situations where we have to talk to each other.

'You get them,' I call back.

'I'm changing Rose's nappy.'

'Can't Dad get them?'

'He's in the garden.'

I sigh. Finn started work yesterday and I've done a brilliant job of avoiding him so far. I know I should thank him for getting me home after the party, but the thought of it is just too humiliating. I haul myself off the sofa and scurry into the kitchen, keeping my head down, hoping he'll be too busy painting to notice me.

'Hello,' he says from the top of a ladder.

'Hi,' I mutter, trying not to think about the fact that last time he saw me properly I was so drunk I couldn't walk. I grab the wipes off the side and head for the door.

At the last minute, I turn back, my conscience getting the better of me.

'Thanks for getting me home safe. Before, I mean.' I feel myself blush.

197

'That's OK,' he says. He puts the roller down in the paint tray and grins. 'How was your head the next day?'

I half smile back. 'Not great.'

He climbs down the ladder. 'You were . . . upset,' he says tentatively. 'Really upset. Do you remember?'

I shake my head.

'I guess you're off to music college soon?' I say, changing the subject. 'I heard you playing round at Dulcie's. It was beautiful.'

'Thanks,' he says, looking embarrassed. 'Yeah, I'm off next week.'

'Aren't students supposed to spend their summers backpacking round India or something? How come you ended up here?'

'I haven't got the money to go backpacking round India,' he says. 'Nan hasn't been well and she needed stuff doing to the house and garden. She asked if I wanted to come and stay, and said she'd pay me for the work. It's better than being at home anyway.'

'Why's that?'

'My parents run a B. & B. in the middle of nowhere. If I was at home, I'd have spent the summer cleaning toilets and making beds. I thought it would be more exciting to be in London.'

'And has it been?'

'Well, I don't know anyone and I can't afford to go anywhere,' he says, smiling. 'But it's still better than cleaning toilets at home.' He pauses. 'It's a shame we didn't get to know each other.'

I smile.

'Well, you know me now. Sort of.'

'I suppose I do,' he says. 'Sort of.'

'You've got paint in your hair by the way,' I say with a smile as I walk out of the door. Then I take the wipes up to Granny.

'And what are you looking so pleased about?' she says.

'I'm not.'

'Kitchen looking good, is it?' She gives me a knowing smile.

'Didn't notice,' I say.

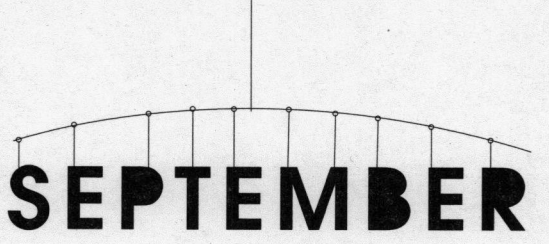

SEPTEMBER

'Of course it would be the longest, hottest summer in living memory the year I'm too dead to get a tan.'

In the heat of the sun my limbs feel heavy. I can't be bothered to sit up so I just turn my head and squint over to where Mum's sitting in the shade of a nearby tree.

'Oh please,' I say. 'That is just so . . . *British*.'

'What do you mean?'

'Moaning about the weather. Even from beyond the grave.'

She gives me a look that I assume is meant to be withering, but since she's wearing sunglasses all I can see is myself reflected back and the glare of the sun.

'I'm not moaning. I'm just making an observation. Rather a poignant one actually.'

'No you're not. You're moaning. About the weather. Next it'll be how the buses are always late. And how nobody queues properly in . . . heaven. Or . . . wherever.' I roll over to look at her properly, propping myself up on my elbow. 'Wherever it is you go.'

She looks at me over her sunglasses.

'And what exactly is it you think people would be queuing for in heaven, Pearl, just out of interest?'

'Ah! So heaven does exist,' I say triumphantly.

'I didn't say that.'

'So it doesn't exist?'

'I didn't say that either. Anyway, shouldn't you be at school?'

'No,' I say. As it happens, I'm missing an appointment with the school counsellor. I nearly did go, just to get Dad and Granny and school off my back. But then, as I was walking down the corridor, it suddenly didn't seem such a good idea. It was such a lovely day and I sort of had this feeling that if I went to the park and just lay back in the sunshine that Mum would turn up. 'It's all different now we're in the sixth form,' I tell her. 'Lots of free periods and stuff.'

'I see.'

I can't resist the urge to lie back in the sun. The grass is cool and tickly under my neck. I close my eyes and feel the warmth on my eyelids and cheekbones. I roll on to my side and prop myself up on my elbow to look at Mum.

'So about heaven,' I begin.

Mum tuts. 'Pearl. I've told you. I'm not going to talk about this.'

'I'm not asking what it's like. I'm just asking does it exist?'

'Well, that's fine, but don't ask me. Ask Father O'What's-his-name who did my funeral. Ask Stephen Hawking. And then make your own mind up.'

'I mean, I know it can't be angels and harps and fluffy clouds and all that . . .'

'La-la-la-la.' She puts her fingers in her ears. 'I can't hear you.'

'But if it's not like that,' I persevere, 'then what could it be like?'

I try to sound casual, as if I'm just musing to myself, but I watch her closely to see if her reaction gives anything away. She swats irritably at a fly that's buzzing round her nose.

'And *where* is it?' I muse. 'I mean, it can't be up there, in the sky. Obviously. Or can it?'

But she doesn't reply.

'Is it there?'

'Yes.'

'Yes, what?'

'Yes. You're exactly right. There's a big magic garden in the sky with angels and rainbows and frolicking bloody unicorns. We all skip around, hand in hand, singing all day long. Happy now?'

'Well, there's no need to be like that.'

'Yes there is actually,' she says sharply. 'You shouldn't be wasting your time worrying about what's going to happen after you die. It's pointless. Think about what's happening now. In your life. That's what's important. So change the subject, will you?'

'OK,' I say, annoyed. 'I've got an interesting subject we can talk about.'

'Go on,' she says. 'I'm all ears.'

'James,' I say. 'Tell me about him.'

She sits up sharply and pushes her sunglasses back on her head. 'What?'

'James. Sullivan. My father.'

She stares at me. 'Yes, Pearl. I'm well aware of who he is.'

'Well, go on then,' I say, meeting her gaze. 'Tell me about him.'

She shakes her head, confused. 'What's brought this on?'

'Nothing. I'm just interested. I've got every right to be. He is my father after all. You always said if I wanted to know about him I could ask you. So now I am.'

'But why now? It's the worst possible time you could be bringing all this up.'

'Why?'

'Well, have you thought about how Dad will feel for a start? He's got enough on his plate without you

206

stirring things up, causing complications. He'll be hurt, Pearl. He needs you at the moment. He's already lost me. He'll think he's losing you too.'

'Well,' I say, 'that's his problem.'

'What did you say?'

She looks so furious I backtrack a bit. 'I just mean I don't think it's such a big deal. And Dad's got the baby now, hasn't he? So he probably won't be that bothered.'

She stares at me as if she can't believe what I'm saying. 'That's ridiculous, Pearl, and you know it. You're being childish and selfish.' She pulls her sunglasses back down over her eyes and lies back. 'I'm not going to discuss this with you.'

'So that's it, is it?'

'Yep.'

'Fine,' I say. 'I'll find out for myself. I don't need your help.'

And I scramble to my feet and walk off, leaving her lying there on the grass.

I walk straight home, working out excuses for Granny as I go about why I'm home so early. But when I get there she's taken The Rat out somewhere. The house is empty. I go up to my room and open the drawer of my bedside table. In it are the passport pictures of Mum and James. Who is he now? Where does he live?

Did Mum even know? Perhaps they'd lost contact completely. But they can't have done. Mum had said if I ever wanted to get in touch with him we'd talk about it. She must have kept his address somewhere. But there was nothing in the box. And then I have an idea. Her computer is still on the desk in Granny's room.

I creep in there, listening out for the sound of the front door, telling myself I'm not doing anything wrong. I switch the computer on and find her contacts. *Yes!* There he is. James Sullivan. He lives in Hastings – isn't that by the sea? – assuming this is still his address. I scribble it down and close the computer.

I was right. I don't need Mum's help. I can find him all by myself if I want to.

'Stop gawping at the boy and go and take him this cup of tea,' Granny says.

I'm standing at the kitchen sink, washing dishes, and, however hard I try, I keep finding that my eyes are drawn to Finn. He's working in the garden, his dark hair sticking out from under a battered trilby. His T-shirt clings to his back and as he digs I can see the muscles of his shoulders move under it. I look down quickly to the plate I'm washing up, rinse the foam from it, stack it carefully in the drainer. But my eyes drift back to the garden. To him. To the curls of hair that cling to his neck and the slow rhythm of his movement as he turns over the soil with his spade.

He's finished painting the kitchen now. It's not dark and shadowy any more; it's light and airy and he's cut back all the wisteria that was hanging down over the patio doors and window so the sunshine floods in. Dad persuaded him to sort out the garden too before he leaves. Dulcie's given us a load of seeds and bulbs and cuttings from her garden, and Finn's going to plant some before he leaves tomorrow.

As I watch, Finn turns to the house, as if he can feel my eyes on him. He doesn't wave, just gives a half-nod and then carries on with what he's doing. I grab another plate quickly and sink it into the bubbles, feeling as I always do that he's caught me out.

'I'm not gawping,' I say to Granny. 'I'm standing in front of a window that he happens to be on the other side of. I can hardly avoid seeing him. Unless you want me to do the washing-up blindfold.'

'Talk about protesting too much,' Granny smirks. 'Just take him the tea, will you?'

Finn's totally absorbed in what he's doing, paying no attention to me.

'I brought you some tea,' I say, blushing.

'Oh,' he says, taking it from me. 'Thanks.'

I wait for him to say something more, but he doesn't, just takes a sip of tea, then puts it down and carries on, picking up a rake that's leaning against the wall and making a line in the soil with it.

'What are you doing?' I ask.

'This is a drill,' he explains, as if to a small child, pointing to the dip he's made in the soil. 'It's where I'm going to plant these seeds. I used to do this with Nan when I was a kid.' He picks up a packet of seeds and opens it. Then he shakes some seeds into his palm, picks them out a pinch at a time with his other hand and sprinkles them into the soil.

'It always seemed like magic when I was a kid,' he says. 'We'd bury these tiny seeds in the soil. And then next school holidays I'd come back and . . .' He holds out a packet with a mass of red and orange flowers pictured on the front.

I look at the dry, greyish seeds again, and the black earth, and then back at the fluorescent flowers in the picture.

'It still seems like magic to me.' I smile at him. 'You're a magician.'

As I'm walking back to the house, he calls after me.

'You don't—' He stops.

'What?' I ask, turning back towards him.

He doesn't look me in the eye. 'You don't want to go out later, do you? As it's my last night here?'

'Oh,' I say. 'No. I can't. Sorry.' The words are out before I can stop them.

He looks confused and a bit embarrassed. 'Oh right. Fair enough. Just thought I'd ask.'

'Sorry,' I say again, and I turn back to the house and rush inside, my cheeks burning.

In the kitchen Granny's looking pleased. I know she's been watching me.

'What?' I say at last, not really concentrating on her. I'm still thinking about Finn.

'Oh, nothing,' she says, meaning the opposite. She smiles at me as if we're sharing a secret. 'Lovely boy, isn't he?'

'If you say so.' I pour myself a glass of water.

'And going to one of the top music colleges in the country too, so your dad was saying,' she calls back to me as she goes to take the rubbish out. 'Plays the cello.'

'Oh *well*,' I say, pulling a face at The Rat who's in her little chair, gnawing on a fist. 'He *must* be nice then.'

The Rat gurgles.

And then she smiles at me.

She smiles. At me. Her whole face changes. She looks like a person. She's happy.

Happy to see me.

I stand, staring at her. It's as though something's pressing on my chest. I can't breathe.

'Stop it.'

I want to shout at her, but it comes out as a whisper. 'Stop it.'

And the glass I've forgotten I'm holding slips from my hand on to the stone floor and shatters. The crack of it startles her and she starts to cry. I watch the smile disappear, her little face redden and crease. I kneel down to pick up the pieces of glass. My hands are shaking.

I drop the shards of glass on to a newspaper on the table and a trickle of blood drips down. As it does, I realize how much my hand hurts. When I open it up, it's full of blood.

Dad comes up to see me when he gets in from work. It's late and I'm already in bed. 'Granny said you cut your hand badly,' he says, looking anxious. 'She said you should have gone to the hospital to get it stitched.'

'It's fine,' I say, waving my bandaged hand at him. 'She was just fussing as usual.'

He sits down on the bed and looks at me.

'What?'

He pauses uncomfortably. 'It was an accident, wasn't it?'

I remember how, when Granny bathed my cut in a bowl of boiled water, the blood had blossomed from my hand like an exotic flower.

'What do you mean?' I say. 'You think I did it on purpose?'

'Did you?'

'No. Of course not. It was an accident.'

He watches me closely, the lamplight picking out shadows under his eyes, making him look tired. 'OK.' He kisses the top of my head.

When he's gone, I find myself thinking about how upset I was that time when I was a kid and Dad shouted at me after I ran into the road. I didn't know whether my tears were because I was scared of the car, or of Dad shouting, or because I knew I'd upset him. He hugged me so tight it hurt, but I didn't care. I felt safe. *Promise me you'll never, ever do that again*, he said. *What would I do without my Pearl?*

Next door The Rat starts to cry. I hear Dad go in the room to comfort her. It all goes quiet, then after a while I hear him singing softly to her to get her back to sleep.

Why did he have to ruin it all? Why did he have to want a baby? He had me. Why wasn't that enough?

I switch the lamp off and lie back in the dark. I just want to sleep, but I find I'm thinking of Finn. Why did I say no? He'll be gone tomorrow and I'll probably never see him again.

Not that it matters. Not that any of it really matters.

I press gently on the blank white of the bandage and the pain makes my ears ring.

213

OCTOBER

'Pearl, could I just have a quick word with you before you go?'

Mrs S smiles at me as Molly and the others file out of the classroom and I try to smile back. I have a feeling I know why she wants to speak to me.

'I'm really glad you've chosen to carry on with English,' she says. 'How are you finding it so far?'

'Fine,' I say.

'And how's everything at home now? Is your little sister doing well?'

'Yes.'

'And you? How are you doing, Pearl?'

'Fine,' I say.

'You're sure about that?'

'Course.'

'It's just you've missed a couple of classes already. And we've only been back a few weeks. I wondered if there was a problem?'

217

'No,' I say, thinking fast. 'Sorry. It's just I've had to help out with the baby.'

'But your dad told the school that your grandmother was caring for her now?'

'She is,' I say. 'But she's quite old. It's a bit much for her.'

I try not to smile, imagining Granny's face if she could hear me saying this.

'I see,' Mrs S says. 'All the same, it's important that you don't miss classes, Pearl. You can't afford to get behind.'

'I know,' I say.

'And in yourself, you feel that you're coping?'

'Yes.'

She looks at me with gimlet eyes. Mr S always used to say, *You have to get up pretty bloody early to fool my wife. Believe me, I know.*

'Well,' she says, 'you know where to find me if you ever want to talk about anything.'

'I'd better be getting to my next class.'

Molly's waiting for me outside in the corridor, looking pale. She's been moping around like mad since Ravi left for university a couple of weeks ago.

'What did she want?' she says as we walk downstairs.

'Oh, you know. Just asking why I've missed classes.'

'What did you say?'

'I told her I'd been looking after the baby.'

'You haven't though, have you?'

I look at her, surprised. That's the excuse I've been giving Molly. I had no idea she'd seen through me. I wonder how long she's known I've been lying. Since the beginning of term? Since Mum died?

'Course I have. Why would I lie?' I say.

She looks at me. 'I don't know. How would I? You never talk to me.' Her voice wobbles a bit. Then she walks off and leaves me standing on my own.

It's half-term and Granny's got me looking after The Rat for the morning while she goes to the dentist.

'If you're just going to lurk around the house doing nothing, you might as well make yourself useful,' she'd said briskly. 'I've had this rotten toothache for weeks. It'll only be for an hour or so.'

I grumble about it, but it's not so bad. The Rat doesn't cry like she used to. She can't crawl yet so I just sit her on her play mat propped up by a cushion, surrounded by the gazillions of toys that Granny has bought for her, and she keeps herself occupied while I try to read a magazine. But I keep getting distracted by what she's doing: chatting away to herself, making excited little noises and chuckles as she reaches out for toys, chews them, bashes them together. She's changed so much.

219

I turn away from her and walk over to the big bay window. The clouds are low in the sky and the wind blows leaves from the trees and rattles the windowpane. I shiver. And then I notice it: a FOR SALE sign outside Dulcie's house. I stare at it, thinking about how kind she was to me in the summer. I've hardly seen her since then. Dad says she hasn't been well. I won't see Finn again if she moves. I push the thought away. What does it matter?

I think of him digging in our garden, about the seeds, the bright flowers on the packet. The colours seem impossible on a raw grey day like today. I wonder what he's doing now?

Perhaps I'll go round and see Dulcie. I'll take The Rat; she'll like that. I scoop her up and squeeze her into her little coat.

When Dulcie opens the door, I'm shocked by how thin and exhausted she looks, her skin almost translucent. But she smiles when she sees me and her eyes are as bright and blue as ever.

'Pearl!' she says. 'And little Rose too. What a lovely surprise.'

She takes us inside and I make the tea while she sits down and plays with The Rat on her lap.

'You're moving,' I say.

'Yes,' she says. 'It had to happen eventually I'm afraid. I'm not well and the house is too much for me to cope with. I'm moving into a home after Christmas.'

'I'm sorry,' I say.

She smiles sadly. 'So am I.'

'How's Finn getting on?' I ask, trying to sound casual.

'Oh, he's fine,' she says. 'Having a great time.'

I try to smile. 'Great.' I wait, hoping she'll say that he's coming down to visit her soon, or that he's asked after me, but she doesn't.

We don't stay long; I can see Dulcie is exhausted.

'She's really growing up,' she says as she hands The Rat back to me at the door. 'She looks just like you, you know.'

'Like me?'

'Yes,' she smiles. 'Can't you see it?'

'No,' I say.

'It's Molly on the phone,' Dad calls from downstairs.

I'm surprised. I thought she'd be off visiting Ravi over half-term. I also thought she'd given up phoning me.

'She sounds a bit upset,' Dad whispers as he hands the phone over.

'Can you meet me at the park later?' she says.

'Oh,' I say, trying to think of an excuse. 'I'm not sure.'

'Please, Pearl. I need to talk to you.'

My heart sinks. But she sounds desperate and anyway Granny keeps hassling me about spending so much time in my room on my own. *It's not right, a girl your age. You should be out with your friends, having fun. You can't just droop around all day doing nothing.* At least this will get her off my back.

Molly's waiting for me by the gate. Her eyes are red and her face is blotchy and she doesn't smile when she sees me.

'Shall we go and get a drink?' I say.

She shakes her head. 'I'd rather walk.'

It's getting cold, the sun already dropping low in the sky, but we stick our hands in our pockets and walk off along a tree-lined path. The trees stand in pools of leaves, red and orange, lit like fire by the light of the setting sun. Our shadows stretch long and thin in front of us.

I wait for Molly to say something, but she doesn't. It must be Ravi. He must have broken up with her. I know I shouldn't, but I can't help feeling pleased. He was never right for her. We walk on, right down the hill and past the swings, our breath puffing out in white clouds.

'Do you remember we used to come here when we were little kids?' Molly says, pausing as we reach the boating lake. 'Mum and Dad would bring us down here on Sunday afternoons in the summer. Or take us up to the bandstand and we'd have a picnic.'

'Yeah, I remember. In the winter we'd fly kites on the Heath and then go to the tea pavilion for hot chocolate. Seems so long ago, doesn't it?'

Molly doesn't reply; when I look at her, there are tears in her eyes.

'What is it, Molls?' I say, trying not to sound impatient. 'Please don't tell me it's Ravi. If he's gone off with someone else then there really is no justice in the world.'

'No!' She looks shocked. 'Of course not. He'd never do that.'

And yet the tears still come.

'Oh my God,' I say. 'You're not pregnant, are you?'

'No. It's nothing like that.'

'What then?'

'It's Mum and Dad.' It all comes out in a rush. 'Dad's left. For good. He's not coming back. They're getting a divorce.'

'Oh.' I can't really say I'm surprised.

'Turns out Dad's been having an affair with some woman in the Swindon office. Can you believe it?'

I can, as it happens. I've never liked Molly's dad much. All mouth and trousers, Mum used to say. And her mum's so nice and always looking so tired and stressed. But I try to look sympathetic. Molly thinks the sun shines out of his backside. And at least she's telling me this time, not Ravi.

'I'm sorry,' I say.

We walk on in silence.

'I just can't believe it. I can't believe he'd do it. First of all it was like I was in shock. Now I just can't stop crying.'

I look at her, irritated. I know she's upset, but it's hardly the end of the world. 'Maybe it's for the best,' I say.

Molly stops and looks at me, her eyes wide and uncomprehending.

'What?'

'Maybe it'll turn out to be for the best.'

I've never seen Molly look so angry. In fact, I've never seen her look angry at all. But she certainly is now.

'How can you say that?' she shouts, and a couple of pram-pushing mums in front of us turn round disapprovingly. 'My mum's in pieces. The boys can't sleep at night. I'm trying to hold everything together.'

'I just meant—'

'I should have known you'd be like this.'

'Like what?'

She thinks about it, searching for the right word. 'Cold. I don't know why I'm even surprised. It's what you're like now. It's as if you're a different person from the Pearl I knew.' She shakes her head. 'You're so

224

distant. Nothing gets through to you, does it? It's like you just don't care about anyone. I thought after everything you've been through you might be sympathetic. I thought you'd understand how I feel—'

And now it's my turn to lose it.

'Are you seriously comparing your dad running off with some slapper from Swindon to my mum dying?'

'No.'

'Good. Because you'll never understand how I feel.'

'No, I don't suppose I will. Because it doesn't matter how many times I've asked you, or tried to help, you just shut me out. I feel like I don't even know you.'

'I'll never see my mum again. So don't expect me to be all heartbroken just because your dad can't keep it in his trousers.'

The pram-pushers tut and shake their heads.

Molly puts her face up close to mine. She's shaking. For a second I think she's going to slap me. 'At least your mum didn't choose to leave you,' she whispers, tears sliding down her cheeks.

Then she turns away from me and walks off into the dusk.

'Ravi was right about you,' she shouts over her shoulder.

'Why? What did he say?' I call.

But she doesn't answer.

*   *   *

225

I'm so angry I just walk, rerunning the argument over and over in my head. How dare she? How *dare* she? I'm shaking with anger and with cold too. The sky darkens as the sun drops below the houses on the far side of the park. Everyone else has left, but I just keep walking, along the paths and avenues, not caring where I'm going.

Eventually, I find I'm back at the kids' playground. It's deserted now. The light is dim and shadowy, and the wind is bitter. I don't care. I sit on a swing and push with my feet, trying to let the motion soothe me. The metal chains are freezing under my fingers. The cold ache is satisfying.

I tip my head back as I swing, back and forth, back and forth, until I'm dizzy. The sky is already flecked with dim stars.

'Well, this is nice.'

I start at the sound of her voice. It's Mum, sitting on the swing furthest away from me.

'Oh. Hello.'

'Everything OK?'

I remember the look on Molly's face just before she walked away from me.

'Course,' I say. 'Why shouldn't it be?'

I look over to see if she's buying it, but in the falling dark I can't really make out her face.

'Oh, I don't know, Pearl. You're hanging out on your own in a kids' playground in the middle of the night . . .'

226

I can feel her staring at me, waiting for an explanation, but I just carry on swinging.

'With no coat . . .'

'It's not the middle of the night.'

'Even though it's minus thirty—'

'Why do you *always* have to exaggerate?' I snap. 'I
know you think it's funny. But it's not. It's just
annoying.'

'Oh.'

'And childish.'

Mum lights a cigarette. She doesn't say anything for
a moment and I wonder if I've gone too far. 'Well, that's
me told,' she says at last, her face still masked in shadow.

'Sorry,' I say. 'But you're always going on at me.'

'Am I not allowed to worry about you?'

'You're always nagging. Always asking me
questions.'

'I know you're not telling me what's really going on.'
She says it carefully, the precision and weight of her
words concealing the emotion beneath them, whatever
it is. 'You won't ever tell me the truth.'

I watch the amber tip of her cigarette glow bright as
she takes a drag.

I take a deep breath. 'I told you. There's nothing
wrong.'

We sit on our swings in silence, not looking at each
other.

'I know you told me,' she says eventually. 'And I know you're lying.'

'How do you know?'

'I'm your mum, Pearl.'

I think about it. It's so tempting just to tell her. About Molly. About everything. Dad and school and The Rat. What a mess everything is. How lonely and small and grey my life has become without her.

'Well, you're wrong,' I say. 'I'm fine.'

I shut my eyes and feel the cold against my eyelids as I swing. Mum doesn't say anything.

I lean back again. The stars blur and I feel hot tears brimming in my eyes.

I sit up suddenly and stop the swing with my foot.

'Mum?'

But I know before I look that her swing is empty, still swaying a little in the cold night.

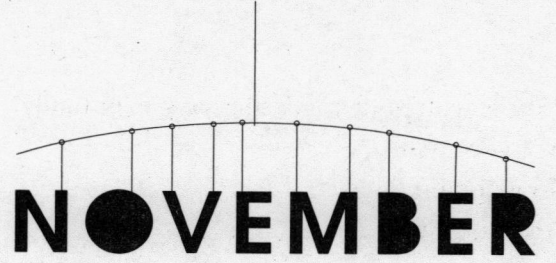

I stare at the piece of paper with James's phone number on it, feeling sick. I've waited until a Saturday morning when Dad and Granny have gone out and taken The Rat with them. They're off to meet a cousin of Dad's who's in London for the day so they'll be gone for ages. No doubt there'll be lots of cooing over The Rat.

I go downstairs and get the phone. Then I sit on my bed and start dialling. My finger is poised over the last number when I stop. What will I say if he answers? I try to imagine it. *Hello, is that James? It's Pearl here* . . . Or should I say *your daughter Pearl*, just to be clear? It's unlikely he knows anyone else called Pearl, but it might be best, just to make sure there are no embarrassing misunderstandings. What then? Maybe once I hear his voice I'll know what to say. Or maybe he'll be so pleased to hear from me he'll just start talking. Perhaps he's been waiting for me to call all this time and he's got years and years of things to tell me. Or there might just be one of those awkward pauses where no one knows what to say and the longer it goes on the worse it gets . . .

I throw the phone down on the bed. I know I'm not going to be able to do it. I could write to him instead. That way I could get everything straight in my head and write it all down properly and make myself sound clever.

I walk over to the window and look outside. It's a bleak day, the wind whipping the bare branches of the trees, squeezing in through the gaps around the window-pane. They'll be freezing up on the South Bank. I imagine Granny tutting as her perfectly coiffed hairdo is dismantled by the gales and smile.

As I watch, I hear Dulcie's front door slam and Finn walks down the path. I run downstairs.

'Hector,' I call. 'Walkies.' He comes trotting out of the kitchen and I grab him, attach the lead to his collar, pull my coat on and run out of the front door. Hector trots along beside me, surprised and delighted by this unexpected turn of events. As we get to the gate, I slow down and try to look surprised as we turn on to the pavement and almost run into Finn.

'Oh,' I say. 'Hello.'

He looks up and as he sees me there's a flicker – isn't there? – of a smile.

'Hi,' he says. 'How are you?'

'Good,' I say. Then I look down and see he's carry-ing a bunch of flowers and my heart thuds. Flowers.

He's going to see a girl. He's taking her flowers.

Well, so what if he is? It's nothing to do with me. It's a free country. Why should I care? Hector's pulling at the lead and whining, desperate to get going on his unexpected walk.

'Shut *up*, Hector,' I snap, still looking at the flowers in Finn's hand, deep red roses, the colour so vibrant it seems to imprint itself on my eyes so I can see them even when I blink.

'They're for my nan,' he says quickly, noticing my stare. 'She's had to go into hospital again. I've just cut them from her garden. I thought it would cheer her up.'

'Oh no,' I say, trying not to look relieved. 'Poor Dulcie, is she OK?'

'No, not really. She's been ill for a while now and . . .' He looks away. 'Well, she's not going to get any better.'

'I'm sorry,' I say uselessly.

He nods. 'I'd better get going,' he says. 'I'm staying at the house tonight so don't worry if you see the lights on. Mum's coming down later too, as soon as she can get away from work. We're staying for a few days while we sort things out.'

'OK,' I say. 'Give Dulcie my love, won't you?'

'I will.'

'Oh!' I say. 'I just remembered. You can't take flowers to the hospital.'

'What?'

'They won't let you. It's some health and safety thing.' Granny had sent a massive bouquet for The Rat when she was first in hospital and Dad had to bring it home. It had sat in its cellophane and tissue paper on the side in the hall until it went dry and brown and he had to throw it away.

'Oh right.' He looks so disappointed I think for an instant he's going to cry. 'You have them,' he says suddenly and thrusts them at me.

I can feel myself blushing. 'Are you sure?'

'Take them,' he says. So I do. 'See you then.'

'See you.'

I let Hector pull me away, his nose to the ground, on the trail of something or other. I'll probably never see Finn again. *What does it matter?* I tell myself. *What does any of it matter?*

But even as I'm thinking it I'm turning back, pulling an unwilling Hector after me. Finn's just crossing the road.

'It's the fireworks down on the Heath tonight.' I can feel myself going as red as the roses as the words tumble out of my mouth. 'I don't suppose you want to go?'

He looks surprised and for a moment I'm worried he'll say no. Then he smiles. 'Sure,' he calls back.

I turn away and smile. Hector is watching me eagerly. 'Come on then,' I say. 'We might as well go for a walk now we're here.'

The wind is stinging as we walk down the road, but I don't care.

Granny soon gets over her sulk about me refusing to go with them to be frozen to death by the Thames when she finds out I'm going out with Finn. She's been moaning all week about the fireworks, due to the unfortunate effect they have on Hector. But now suddenly they're not so bad after all.

'But you can't possibly go looking like that,' she says when I come down in jeans and my parka.

'We're going to the fireworks,' I say. 'What do you want me to wear? Stilettos and a little black dress?'

She shakes her head in despair. 'Let me do your make-up at least.'

'It's not a date,' I say.

'Course it's not.'

She looks so smug I wear Dad's West Ham bobble hat just to annoy her. I take it off once I'm out of the front door.

It's bitterly cold on the Heath, crowded with people wrapped in scarves and hats waving glow sticks and sparklers. I was nervous about seeing Finn and at first

235

it's a bit awkward, but after a few minutes it's fine. We *ooh* and *aah* at the fireworks: fiery flowers blooming in the clear night sky. It's like magic. I feel like a kid again, swept up in the moment.

'You look happy,' Finn says at last. 'I've never really seen you look happy.' And I realize he's been watching me, not the fireworks.

'I am happy,' I say. And when he takes my hand I don't let go.

We don't say much as we walk back. As the crowds thin out, Finn seems lost in thought and we walk along in silence, but it doesn't feel awkward now. It feels right. I find I'm still smiling. But, when I look at Finn, he's not.

'Are you thinking about Dulcie?'

'Yes,' he says, surprised. 'How did you know?'

'You looked sad.'

'Sorry.'

'Don't be.'

He pushes the hair back out of his eyes. 'It's hard, watching someone you love grow old.'

'It's hard not having the chance to see them grow old.'

'I know,' he says, squeezing my hand.

As we walk past the chippy, the smell of chips and vinegar wafts out into the cold night.

'Shall we get some?' Finn says. 'I'm starving.'

And, to my surprise, so am I. We share a bag as we walk.

When we get to the house, we stop under the lamp post, bathed in golden light, the dark all around us.

'Thanks,' I say. 'I'd forgotten about feeling happy.'

He carefully pushes the hair back from my face so he can see me properly.

'That first time I met you,' he says, 'when you yelled at me over the garden wall?'

'Yes?' I still blush thinking about it.

'It was your mum you were shouting at, wasn't it?'

I hesitate. 'Yes.'

He looks me right in the eyes and for a second it's as if he's looking inside my head, right inside to where no one else sees, and I can't breathe.

And then he kisses me.

And the world swoops off into the distance and there's nothing, nothing except him and me, his lips on mine, his hand on my neck, the warmth of him against me, and I kiss him back—

'No!' I pull away.

'What's wrong?'

'I've got to go,' I say. 'I've got to go.'

And I run up the path towards the house.

'Pearl!' he calls after me. But I don't look back.

I pull the keys out of my pocket as I go and slam the door behind me.

Then I lean against it, breathing hard in the darkness, and I realize I'm crying.

There's a noise upstairs and the landing light comes on.

'Pearl? Is that you?'

Granny appears at the top of the stairs. She's in her 1920s-film-star-style Chinese embroidered silk dressing gown and has cold cream smeared on her face and neck.

'I was just off to bed when I heard the door go.' As she comes closer, she realizes I'm crying. 'Whatever's the matter, dear? What happened? Did you argue? Did Finn . . .'

She leaves what he might have done to my imagination.

'No. Nothing like that.' I try to wipe the tears away with my sleeve.

'Then what happened? He obviously upset you in some way.'

'No,' I say.

'So what went wrong?'

'Nothing,' I say. 'Nothing at all.'

She looks at me and her brow creases and she takes my hand.

'Oh, Pearl,' she says. 'You're allowed to be happy. It's OK.'

'No,' I shake my head. 'No it's not.'

And I push her hand away and run upstairs.

I go into the bathroom and splash cold water on my face. Then I look at myself in the mirror. I look tired; bruised under the eyes, pale, thin. But still the same person I was before Mum died. It doesn't seem right. I should look different; changed completely. I push my hair back, just as Finn had. What did he see when he looked at me? Did he see someone beautiful?

Mum's face appears in the mirror behind me. 'But you *are* beautiful,' she says. 'Please, Pearl. Granny's right. I do want you to be happy.'

'It's not up to you,' I whisper.

There's a pair of nail scissors lying on the side and, without thinking about what I'm doing, I pick them up and start to cut my hair off. My hair is long and thick and it takes a long time. When it's done, I look at myself and the person I see looks more like how I feel on the inside.

'There,' I say, turning to Mum. 'Not so beautiful now.'

But she's not there.

'Pearl. Come in, come in.'

Miss Lomax flashes me a self-assured smile as she ushers me into her office.

'Sit down. Would you like a coffee? I'm just having one myself.'

'No.'

'Biscuits? We've got some left over from a very boring meeting I've just been in.'

I shake my head. Presumably, this whole routine is supposed to put me at ease. She's pretending we're going to have a Cosy Chat.

I perch on the edge of my chair.

'So, Pearl.' She takes another sip of coffee and smiles sympathetically. 'How are you doing?'

I shrug.

'Really,' she says, pushing her hair back. She's wearing too much hairspray and it all moves in one solid chunk. 'Tell me. I'm not just asking to be polite. I really want to know.'

I look at my hands. They look bony and the nails are bluish.

She sighs. 'Pearl. I know how tough it must be.'

One of my nails has a jaggedy split in it, low down. I fiddle with it, bending it to and fro, pulling at it. It hurts like hell.

'Really I do.'

Course you do. But . . .

'But the thing is, Pearl, there are some things we just can't turn a blind eye to.'

She waits for me to say something. I don't.

'We all understood that in the first few weeks it was hard for you to focus. Of course it was. And you did

240

very well to get through your exams with the results that you did.'

There's an ugly red smear of lipstick on the rim of her coffee cup. When Molly was in her hardcore vegan phase, she told me lipstick is made from pig fat and ground-up beetles. At the time I didn't believe her, but maybe it was true after all.

'The thing is, Pearl, this can't go on indefinitely. We've shown you understanding and patience for several months. But there comes a point where this sort of behaviour becomes simply unacceptable. You can't keep skipping lessons and expect to get away with it.'

I pull the broken bit of nail so hard it tears right off. The skin underneath it is raw and red and agonizing.

'I don't expect anything,' I say.

'Look. You're a clever girl, Pearl. But if you don't get your act together soon,' – she pauses for dramatic effect and gives me a look to emphasize how serious she is – 'you could find yourself seriously behind. You could even risk failing your A levels.'

I burst out laughing. I can't help it. A levels! The causes of the Second World War and *Pride and Prejudice*. She actually expects me to care about it all.

She bristles. She doesn't like being laughed at so I try to stop.

'It's no laughing matter, Pearl. University. Your career. It could all depend on this. Your whole future.'

241

'It doesn't matter.'

'What doesn't matter?'

I almost feel sorry for her. She really doesn't know. Where do I begin? How can I tell her that all of it – not just A levels and university, but all of it: watching TV and plucking your eyebrows and friendship and ambitions and *love* – it's all just stuff we surround ourselves with to distract ourselves from the fact that anything could happen at any time. Swine flu. Nuclear war. Being struck by lightning. Asteroids hitting the earth and wiping us all out like the dinosaurs.

None of it matters.

'No, forget it,' I say. I feel old.

She purses her lips till they're just a thin scarlet line. I wonder what the name of her lipstick is. *Passione*. Something pretentious and sexy, that's what she'd go for. I reckon she thinks she's pretty hot, Miss Lomax, with her high heels and her blouse you can see her bra through.

'Look, Pearl. I think we've been more than understanding, but I'm beginning to feel that you're abusing that understanding. There comes a point where it stops being about bereavement and starts being about behaviour. If your attitude doesn't change, Pearl, I'm going to have no option but to call your father in. And we may have to take more serious action.'

242

Now we're getting to it. So much for the Cosy Chat. Suddenly I don't feel sorry for her any more.

'Do you really think I care?' I say. 'Do you really think anything you do actually matters?'

She doesn't like that. She's used to getting her own way.

'Don't be childish, Pearl,' she snaps. 'This immature, attention-seeking behaviour is exactly what I'm talking about. I'm sure this isn't what your mother would want.'

My breath catches in my throat. 'You don't know my mother,' I blurt, then blush stupidly. 'Didn't.'

'No. But I *know* this isn't what she would want. She wouldn't want you to wallow in self-pity. She'd want you to get on with your life.'

I look at her face closely as she's talking, hardly hearing the words. Her stupid, smug mouth daubed in pig fat and beetles.

'Well, Pearl, is there anything you'd like to say?'

'Yes,' I say. 'You've got lipstick on your teeth. And everyone knows you're shagging Mr Jackson.'

She stares at me, her face turning red.

'Right. I've had enough of this,' she says. 'Get out of my office.'

'With pleasure,' I say. I grab my bag and head for the door.

My heart's pumping; it's a good feeling.

243

'I will be arranging a meeting with your father as soon as possible.'

I decide against slamming the door. I leave it wide open instead.

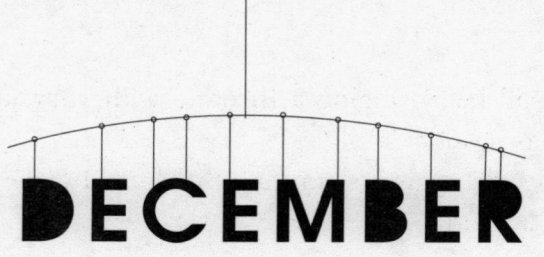

There's a knock on my bedroom door.

'Can I come in?' Dad's trying to make peace. 'I've brought you a cup of tea.'

We had a massive row last week about school. Miss Lomax called us both in to talk about my 'behaviour'. Dad went. I didn't.

When he got back, he'd sighed and said, 'Well, I've done my best, Pearl. I told Miss Lomax you were a good girl really and you'd been through a lot. I said that when you'd had time to think I was sure you'd come to your senses and apologize.'

'I'm not apologizing,' I told him. 'And I'm not going back. I'll get a job.'

'I don't know why I bother,' he said.

And I said, 'I don't know either.' And we haven't spoken to each other since.

Now he sits down beside me on the bed. 'You can't

247

just hide away up here. I don't want us to fight,' he sighs. 'Forget about school and all that. We can talk about it later, when we've had time to think and calm down a bit.'

'I have had time to think,' I say. 'I am calm.' Through the window the sky is heavy and tinged yellow. They say it's going to snow.

'Please, Pearl. It's only a couple of weeks till Christmas. Let's just try to enjoy it, shall we? Together. As a family.'

But how can we?

'We're going to decorate the tree in a minute. Will you come and help us?'

That was always Mum's job. She only ever let me help under sufferance. She loved Christmas, all of it, the carols and presents and wrapping. We always had to have an advent calendar. She was like a big kid.

Dad waits for me to answer. Eventually, he says, 'We can't go on like this, Pearl.' He's not angry; it's just a statement of fact.

'No.' For once we agree.

I hear the door close behind him.

The garden is winter bare now. Just a few months ago it was like a jungle. Finn transformed it, cutting back, weeding, mowing, planting. But now the trees are stark and leafless, the earth dark. I think of the seeds he planted, shoots growing under the surface. It's hard to believe they're still there. Even if they are, he won't be here to see them. There's a big SALE AGREED sign in Dulcie's front garden. The house has been empty since she went into hospital. It'll be someone else's soon. I look at the roses Finn gave me, dried out now, but still vivid red on my desk. He's back at college. I'll never see him again, I suppose. Probably just as well. He must hate me.

I think about calling for Mum, but what's the point? She won't come. She only turns up when she feels like it.

I realize with a shock that I don't want to see her. I'm tired of lying, pretending things are OK with Dad and The Rat. I'm tired of her nagging me about school and Molly. I'm sick of her avoiding my questions about James.

I remember the Christmas card I was going to send him, with the letter inside. It's too late now. Tomorrow is Christmas Eve; it'll never get there in time even if I send it today. I go and pick it up, looking at his name written in my best, most ornate handwriting, whispering it under my breath, even now trying to conjure him up from the sound of it. And, as I look at the envelope, suddenly a terrifying, wonderful idea slips into my head: I don't have to spend Christmas here. There is somewhere else I can go. I read his address. Hastings isn't that far. I looked it up. It's just down on the south coast, through Kent down into Sussex. I could be there in a few hours. My heart beats fast. Could I do it? Am I brave enough just to turn up on his doorstep?

Yes. I'm his daughter. He couldn't turn away his own daughter at Christmas. It's a time for family. He'll be pleased, I know he will. More than pleased. He'll say, 'I've imagined this moment for so long . . .'

Or maybe he won't. But, whatever, it's better than sitting around here.

I know that if I think about it for too long I might lose my nerve. So I don't. I check the train times on my phone. I haul the trolley case that Mum got me last year for the school ski trip from under my bed and I throw in as many clothes as I can fit. Who knows how long I'll stay? Maybe forever. I think about bringing the card and letter to give to him. But what's the point? I can say it all myself.

I pause in the hall. Dad and Granny are laughing and chatting in the sitting room, carols playing on the radio. I think about just leaving, sneaking out without telling them. But I want to see the look on their faces when I say I'm going.

I push the door open and step far enough into the room so that they'll see the rucksack on my back and the trolley case. But no one looks up. Dad's fiddling with the Christmas lights, twisting the bulbs and muttering. Granny's pulling tangles of tinsel out of the decorations box, covered in festive paper, that we've had as long as I can remember. The Rat is watching from her chair, her wide eyes following the sparkly decorations. And it hits me that they don't need me at all. I'm always lurking unnoticed in the doorway, on the fringes of whatever they're doing. Well, good. It proves I'm right to go.

'Right,' I say breezily. 'I'm going. Bye.'

'Oh,' Dad says, looking up, pushing his reading glasses back on to his head. 'I hadn't realized you were going out.'

Granny tuts. 'But you were going to help me ice the Christmas cake.'

'No I wasn't.'

'Where is it you're going?' Dad says, his eyes pausing uncertainly on my suitcase. 'Staying round at Molly's?'

'Hardly.'

He pauses. 'Where then?'

'What do you care?'

He puts down the string of lights. 'What?'

I smile brightly. 'You've made it clear you don't want me here. You said it yourself. We can't go on like this. So I'm going somewhere I'll be a bit more welcome.'

Dad stares at me. 'Is this a joke?'

251

'Nope.'

'I don't understand,' he says.

'You'll be happier without me. Just the three of you.'

Granny snorts loudly from behind the Christmas tree where she's hanging baubles. 'I never heard such self-pitying claptrap, Pearl, really.'

But Dad's just staring at me. 'Where could you possibly be more welcome than your own home?'

I pause for a heartbeat. 'This isn't my home,' I say. 'Not any more.'

Dad rubs his eyes. 'So where are you going?'

'She's not going anywhere,' says Granny. 'She's just being silly.'

I watch his face as I say it. 'To my dad's.'

'What?' He genuinely doesn't know what I mean. But Granny does; her lips tighten into a pale thin line.

'James,' I say. 'My dad.'

He's silent for a moment as he takes in what I'm saying.

'Are you just saying this to hurt me?' he says at last. 'Because if you are I've got to tell you're doing a bloody good job, Pearl.' He shakes his head, as if he's trying to shake my words out, to unhear them.

'Well,' Granny says, not quite under her breath, 'we all know who she learned that from.'

'Mum, *please*,' Dad snaps.

I turn on her. 'What exactly do you mean by that?'

'She didn't mean anything,' Dad says wearily.

'I mean,' Granny says, 'that your mother had a knack for cruelty too, when she felt like it. Oh, she could turn on the charm all right. But she could turn it off again pretty damn quick if she wasn't getting her own way.'

'Mum! For God's sake, shut up!' For a second we both just stare at him in surprise. 'Pearl,' he says. 'Listen to me. You can't go.'

'Yes I can.'

The Rat starts to grizzle.

'Have you spoken to him? James?'

'That's none of your business,' I snap.

'Please, Pearl,' Dad says. 'Don't do this. This is your home. I'm your dad.'

'Look, you don't have to put on an act,' I say. 'We all know you don't want me here now you've got Rose, so let's stop pretending.'

Granny slams down the box of little wooden angels she's holding and they spill all over the floor with a clatter. The Rat's crying gets louder.

'I know things have been difficult for you, Pearl, and I'm sorry about that. But I am not going to stand here and listen to this.' Granny's voice shakes with the force of what she's saying. 'I know that before all this you were the centre of the universe in this family. But things have changed. Not just for you. For everyone. We're all just doing our best to get through it. And you—' She jabs a finger at me. 'You are behaving like a selfish little girl and it's time you grew up!'

'Selfish? I'm not the one who's selfish. *He's* the one who's selfish. If he hadn't forced Mum to have a baby, she'd still be alive.'

Granny stares at me. 'Forced her to have a baby? What on earth are you talking about?'

'He wanted her to have a baby, so that he'd have a daughter of his own.'

'No!' Dad says. 'You've got this all wrong, Pearl. I love Rose, of course I do. But it was Mum who wanted another baby.'

I stare at him. 'No it wasn't.'

'Honestly. I was happy with how things were. You must know that.'

'You're a liar.'

Granny turns on me. 'Don't you call him a liar. Your father didn't want another baby. And I'll tell you why as well. He was trying to protect your mother. He didn't want her ending up in the state she was after she had you—'

'Mum!' Dad interrupts, but Granny's standing right in front of me, cheeks flushed, tense with fury, and she doesn't hear him.

'So depressed she couldn't even look after you properly.'

'Mum, that's *enough*!'

It takes a second for her words to sink in.

'Don't you lie . . .' I try to carry on, but my voice gets choked up and stuck in my throat.

'Oh, I'm not the liar, Pearl. I don't suppose your mother ever mentioned that I looked after you for months when you were a baby, did she?'

I look to Dad, hoping he'll contradict her, but he's silent, his face etched with sadness.

'No? I thought not. She was too busy telling you what an interfering old bitch I was I expect.' She watches my expression and smiles grimly. 'Well, I did look after you because *she* was in such a state for a while she couldn't even get out of bed in the morning. Your dad was working all hours. So I moved down here, left my little job and my house and my friends, and I took care of you. I'm not complaining. I didn't mind doing it. In fact, I loved it. I loved you. I really did. As much as if you were my own baby . . .'

She looks at me, remembering, and her face softens. I know she's not lying.

'We persuaded her to get help. And then, as soon as she was better, that was it. She didn't want me around. She couldn't pack me back off to Scotland quick enough. And she kept me so distant after that. She'd always make excuses why I couldn't come and visit or you couldn't come and see me. I got on with things, picked

up my old life eventually. But I missed you so much.'
Hector whines plaintively at her feet as she wipes her
eyes. 'My precious Pearl . . .'

The Rat is screaming. Dad bends down to pick her
up.

I turn awkwardly with the rucksack on my back, and
I walk down the hall.

'Pearl!' Dad calls after me. 'Wait! You can't just go.'

'Yes I can,' I shout.

'Then I'm coming with you,' Dad says. He looks like
he means it as well, grabbing his coat off the hook.

I stare at him. 'No you're not. It's all arranged. James
wants me to go. I don't want you there, ruining everything. It's none of your business.'

'Just let her go,' Granny shouts from the sitting room.
'She'll be back before tea.'

I slam the door behind me and walk out into the cold,
pale light of the afternoon.

'Pearl? What's going on?'

It's Mum, behind me.

'Wait.'

I walk faster, my trolley case clattering along the
pavement.

'Pearl! Where are you going?' She's panting, trying
to keep up with me.

'What do you care?'

'Of course I care.' She tries to grab my arm, but I shake her off. 'Pearl, *please*. Stop. Tell me what's happened.'

'You lied to me,' I say. 'That's what happened.'

'Me?' she says, mock-innocent. 'Nah, not me, guv, you must have the wrong person. I'm honest as the day is long, me.'

I ignore her.

I cut through the park to get to the station. It's quiet; everyone's off Christmas shopping or staying in the warm. The grass is stiff with frost.

'Oh wait. This isn't about that time when I missed your dance show and I told you it was because the cat collapsed and I saved her life by giving her emergency CPR?'

I still don't say anything, just keep on walking.

'Because if it is I'm afraid you've got me bang to rights. I admit it: I forgot. There, I said it. Can you find it in your heart to forgive me?'

'Why do you do this?'

'Do what?'

'Whenever things get serious. You always have to try and turn everything into a joke.'

'I don't know. Defence mechanism? Low self-esteem? Probably all due to something in my childhood. I suppose it's a bit late to consider psychoanalysis now.'

She smiles hopefully.

257

'You lied about everything.'

'What do you mean?'

I look at her and I realize there's so much I don't know about her, that maybe I never will know about her. I think about everything I've found out. But only one thing really seems to matter.

'You told me it was Dad who wanted the baby. You told me you did it for him. But it was you. You wanted her.'

'Yes,' she says. 'Well, maybe I did. But that's not such a big deal, is it?'

I look away. 'All this time I've been blaming him for making you have the baby.'

There's no pretence now. No jokes from Mum.

'I thought if it wasn't for them, him and the baby, you'd still be here. But it wasn't him. It was you.'

'Pearl, listen to me.' She grasps my shoulders hard. Her voice is shaking. 'No one is to blame. Not Dad. Not me.' She looks me in the eye. 'And not my poor baby girl, who's going to grow up without ever knowing her mother.'

I look back at her and at last I understand. I understand just how much she loves The Rat.

I turn and walk away from her into the stinging wind.

'Pearl? Where are you going?' The wind whips her voice away from me.

I don't look round.

*   *   *

258

It's cold on the train and I wriggle down into my seat with my headphones on in case anyone tries to speak to me. I'm shaking, I don't know whether from cold or anger. My head is full of Mum and Dad and Granny and The Rat, and my thoughts are so loud and angry I almost think people will hear them.

But the world racing past outside the window is soothing: first the backs of houses and gardens, little squares of people's lives, then fields and trees and a man walking his dogs, there and then gone, there and then gone, all under a big white sky.

As we plunge into a tunnel, my reflection comes suddenly into focus, pale against the black. My hair has grown a bit, but it still looks mad. What will James think when he sees me? I begin to wish I'd let Granny persuade me to go to the hairdresser's to sort out the hacked remains I'd left. The window is double-glazed so there are two overlapping reflections looking back at me, one clear and solid, one fainter, transparent, blurry around the edges, and for a second I think that I feel more like that one, that it is the real me and the other one is the one I left behind that day outside the cinema when I listened to Dad's message and the world stood still.

The road gets steeper the further along it I go, and in the falling light it's getting harder to read the house numbers. I know I'm getting close though: 49, 51. My heart's thumping. Number 57.

This is it.

I stop for a moment at the gate. It's exactly the same as all the other houses in the road: a normal-looking semi, with cream-painted pebbledash and an ugly glass porch stuck on the front. It's got those plasticky windows with the diamond patterns that are meant to look all olde worlde.

I'll be honest: it's not exactly the home you'd dream your long-lost father would live in. On the long train journey here I'd imagined a rambling Gothic mansion perched on a clifftop. But, on the plus side, it's not a crack den. And, looking back over the brow of the hill I've just climbed, I can at least see the sea, stretching away to a blurry grey horizon.

The garden looks like someone takes good care of it. Him? I wonder. Or has he got a wife?

There's a battered black estate car in the drive, with one of those *Little Princess On Board* signs on the back windscreen. I stop dead.

A daughter.

He's got another daughter.

Why hadn't it occurred to me that he might have kids?

I realize suddenly how little I've thought this whole thing through. I can't go in. What am I doing here?

But then I think of Dad and Granny and The Rat, all cosy and happy together, and I know I don't have a choice because I can't go back.

I clench my teeth and, before I can think of a reason not to, I stride up the crazy-paved drive. The lights in the front room are on and I want to peek in. I don't though, in case what I see makes me change my mind. I keep my eyes fixed on the Neighbourhood Watch sticker on the porch door as I march up to it and push the bell hard.

There's squealing from the front room and a dog starts yapping somewhere at the back of the house. Footsteps. I feel light-headed for a moment, imagining James's face, what his reaction will be when he sees me. Will he look like me? Will he know who I am or will I have to tell him?

Then I see a small nose press against the opaque glass of the front door at about waist height and a mouth squished beneath it. The mouth works its way across the glass, leaving a slimy trail like a pink-and-white snail.

'Verity!'

A dark shape looms behind the child, but it's not him. It's a woman's voice.

'Go and put some clothes on, Verity, for heaven's sake,' it says.

This is a mistake, I know it now. But it's too late. The door's opening.

Behind it there's a pretty, harassed-looking woman, about Mum's age I'd say. She's got a snotty toddler on her hip and behind her, disappearing up the stairs, is a child – Verity, I assume – naked except for a pair of socks.

'Yes?' the woman says, obviously wishing I'd go away.

I take a breath as if I'm about to speak, but I can't think what to say. So I just stand there, mouth hanging gormlessly, not making the sophisticated first impression I might have hoped for. The toddler starts to screech.

'Look,' she says, putting the child down so that he can make his wobbly escape back down the hallway. 'I don't want to be rude or anything, but it's the kids' teatime. I'd love to give to charity and all that, but—'

'Oh no,' I say, laughing manically. Nerves I suppose. 'No, I'm not a charity.'

'Who are you then?'

'I'm . . .' I stop, taking in the wedding ring on her finger. 'I'm looking for James.'

'James?' She looks at me properly now, taking in my suitcase and rucksack. 'You mean Jim. What do you want with him?'

'I'm his . . .' I can't say it. 'He's my . . .' No, that's worse. 'I'm Pearl.'

Her expression changes. It closes up. I know she knows who I am. At least he must have mentioned me, acknowledged my existence.

'No one calls him James,' she says, folding her arms.

We stand staring at each other, her inside, filling the doorway, me out in the cold. I search desperately through my head for things that might be appropriate to say to the hostile wife of the father you've never met and draw a blank. So instead, I just stand and shiver because I was in such a rush to leave that I didn't even think about putting on a proper coat. I'm wearing Mum's old leather jacket, the one she wore in the garden when she first told me about The Rat. I'm so angry with her now that if it wasn't for the sub-zero temperatures I'd have left it on the train. As it is, I try to pull the sleeves down over my numb fingers. My teeth are chattering.

'You'd better come in,' she says flatly, though her face is saying something else.

I step over wellies and trainers into the hall, hoisting my stupid case after me, knowing how presumptuous it must look.

The house smells unfamiliar. Not horrible, just like someone else's house.

'He'll be back any minute.' She takes me to the toy-strewn sitting room. 'You can wait in here. I've got to go and get on with the dinner.'

She stops at the door. I know she wants to ask me what the hell I think I'm doing here. Verity reappears in a sparkly leotard.

'Come on, Verity,' the woman says eventually. 'Come and help Mummy.'

There's a crash and a loud wailing from the kitchen.

'Christ, Alfie,' she says and disappears.

Verity doesn't follow her. She stands in front of me, watching closely. I sit uncomfortably on the sofa, crossing and then uncrossing my legs. My fingers and toes are burning with the shock of being out of the cold. There's a Christmas tree in the corner with flashing lights that are making my head ache; *Teletubbies* is blasting out from the TV at about a billion decibels.

'Do you like our Christmas tree?' she asks proudly. All the decorations are at exactly Verity height, leaving the upper half completely bare except for an angel balanced precariously on top.

'It's lovely,' I say. 'Did you decorate it yourself?'

She nods. 'Yep.'

'Very . . . Christmassy.'

She stares at me some more. 'Who are you?'

I'm stuck for a moment. Obviously, I can't tell her.

'I'm Pearl,' I say.

'I'm Verity,' she says and holds her hand out for me to shake. 'Pleased to meet you. I'm a famous gymnast. Can you do gymnastics?'

264

'No,' I say.

'Oh.' She looks disappointed. I can't think of anything to say so I just stare at the TV.

'Do you like *Teletubbies*?' she asks.

I shrug. 'Sure,' I say. 'Laa-Laa. Po. What's not to like?'

She gives me a rather scathing look. 'I'm far too grown-up for them,' she explains. 'They're for babies. Like Alfie.'

Which makes me feel pretty stupid.

She carries on staring. You know how some kids can stare in a way that makes you feel they're boring into your brain? Like they can hear what you're thinking? I shift in my seat and try not to think about what a cow her mum's being, not even introducing herself or asking me if I'd like a cup of tea.

'Would you like a cup of tea?' Verity says.

I start. 'Oh. Yes.'

The kid's starting to freak me out.

'Yes *please*,' she says sternly.

She disappears under a coffee table and comes out again with a plastic teapot which she hands to me.

'The whole pot? Just for me?'

'Yep. Alfie hides the cups. Sugar?'

'No thanks.'

'Milk?'

'Just a splash.'

I pretend to swig imaginary tea from the pot. What am I doing here? I wonder if I should just make a run for it. But where would I go? Verity looks at me expectantly.

'Is it delicious?'

'Mmmm, delicious,' I say.

There's a smell of burning fish fingers wafting through from the kitchen now, and what with being so hungry and tired and nervous, and the *Teletubbies* music jangling through my brain, it's making me queasy. This isn't what I expected. I think for a moment I might cry.

'Verity!' The woman yells from the kitchen over the wailing which hasn't let up. 'I want you in here *now*.'

She ignores her mum, just carries on with the staring.

'You don't look very well,' she says to me. 'Do you smoke?'

'No.'

'Smoking makes you ill.'

'Yes. But I don't. I'm just tired.'

'My daddy smokes.'

I look at her. 'Does he?'

'Except after Christmas. He gives up after Christmas.'

So many things this little kid must know about my father that I don't.

The nausea rises again. Will he be angry that I've come? Will he shout and push me out of the door?

That's what *she*'d like him to do, the fish-finger burner, whatever her name is. I know she would.

'*Verity!*' She sounds angry now. I guess she doesn't want her in here with me. 'Come here *right now*. Tea's ready.'

I grimace at her, like a co-conspirator. 'S'pose you'd better go. Smells good,' I lie. Once she's gone, I'm going to do it. I'm going to sneak out of the front door and run. I don't know where I'll go. But I've got to get out of here.

She pulls a face. 'You can have mine if you like.'

'You're all right, thanks.'

She's about to say something else when the yappy dog starts up again, getting louder and louder, as it runs into the hall. Suddenly I realize why.

'Daddy's home!' Verity squeals and runs off.

The front door slams and I hear her jumping up and squeaking at him, and him laughing and groaning, trying to talk to her, but it's muffled because she's climbing on him and kissing him. And I sit, bum rooted to the sofa, wishing I could just disappear or time travel or *something*, because I know, I *know* I've made a terrible mistake.

I know I shouldn't be here.

I peer round the door, hoping to see him before he sees me, but he looks up at that exact moment and he slowly puts Verity down and straightens up to look at me properly, and I have to come out from behind the door.

'Hello,' he says, puzzled. He's tall and thin, greying hair in a ponytail, thinning at the front so it looks like his hair has slipped backwards off his head. I feel my face drop as I take him in; he is not any of the James's I imagined. He's not even James. He's Jim.

'Hello.' It sounds like an apology. 'I'm Pearl.'

'Pearl?' he says. He stands there, staring at me with an expression on his face like he's in a cartoon and has just been hit over the head with a frying pan. 'Pearl. Of course you are. I'm Jim.' There's an awkward silence while he presumably tries to work out what the hell I'm doing there. 'You look just like your mum,' he says at last.

'No I don't,' I say quickly, because I'm so angry with her I don't want to, and anyway it's rubbish. I look nothing like her.

'Yes you do,' he says. 'Your expression. Around the eyes.'

I'm aware suddenly of the Fish-finger Burner's looming presence in the kitchen doorway, holding Alfie tightly in front of her like a shield, and emitting vibes of doom into the hallway, though I can't work out whether they're directed at me or him or both of us.

'Hello, love,' he says and goes over and gives her a kiss on the cheek, but she hoists the sleepy Alfie up so he gets the kiss instead, and gives James – Jim – a look that screams Don't You Hello Love Me. She has to clamp her lips shut to stop it actually escaping. But I know she doesn't want to shout at him because I'm there watching.

'So . . .' Jim says nervously, and I can see in his eyes that he's mentally spooling back the afternoon, wondering how long I've been there and how things are panning out between everyone, and probably working out that we haven't been sitting around exchanging stories over home-made lemonade and cake. 'You two have met.'

'Yes,' I say.

'And, er . . .' I can see that what he really wants to say is *What the hell are you doing here?* but he can't think of a polite way to do it.

'Pearl's come to stay,' sings Verity loudly and does a little dance. 'Pearl's come to stay, hurray hurray hurray!' The dog, who turns out to be large and very hairy, joins in with the singing and dancing. I wish again for any kind of natural disaster that might cause the ground to open and swallow us all.

'Is it time for your bath yet, Verity?' Jim says.

The Fish-finger Burner turns to him. 'Can I have a word?' she says icily. '*In private.*'

'It's OK,' I say. 'You needn't bother. I'm just going.'

'Going?' Verity bellows. 'But you can't. You only just arrived.'

'Sorry,' I say. 'I only popped in to say hello. I was just . . . in the area.'

James looks at me, half surprised, half relieved. 'You were just passing?'

'Yes,' I say, looking away.

'How did you know the address?'

'I found it on Mum's computer.'

'Why didn't you call to let me know?'

'I don't know.'

I look at my feet and feel him watching me, trying to work out what's really going on. What if he gets angry? I can feel the panic rising again. I just have to get out of here.

'Didn't your mum and dad mind you coming?'

I don't answer.

'They do know you're here, don't they?'

'Dad does. Mum's . . . well, she died.'

Verity hugs my legs. 'Is that why you're sad?' she says.

'What?' James says. 'Stella's dead? When?'

'Last February.'

'I'm so sorry,' he says. 'How?'

'She had a baby. She got ill suddenly.'

270

'I'm so sorry,' he says again.

'I'd really better be going. It was lovely to meet you,' I say to Verity, pointedly ignoring the glowering Fish-finger Burner.

'Tell you what,' Jim says, 'why don't we go for a walk?'

'Can I come, can I come?' says Verity, bouncing from foot to foot.

'No, sweetheart, just me and Pearl.'

'But you can't' says the FB. 'We've got all the Christmas presents to wrap.'

He takes hold of her hand. 'We won't be long, I promise. Come on, Bel.' He gives her a look I can't read. 'Imagine if it was Verity.'

'Imagine if what was me?' she squeaks and slides down the banister, landing in a heap at the bottom. I help her up. 'Thanks,' she says. 'I'm getting really good at that, aren't I?'

'OK,' the FB says and maybe she's not a total cow because I think there's a tiny hint of a smile as he kisses her on the cheek again. 'See you in a while.'

We walk along in silence. What must he be thinking? What had *I* been thinking? That he'd be waiting for me, arms outstretched? That he'd have a bed made up for me in the spare room, just in case I should turn up one day? I shrink down inside my coat with embarrassment.

271

'Don't mind if I smoke, do you?' he says at last.

'No.'

'I'm giving up soon.'

'I know. Verity told me.'

He laughs. 'She's always giving me grief about it.'

'I was the same with Mum. Not that she ever listened to me. She only gave up when she was pregnant.'

'I'm so sorry about your mum,' he says.

I don't say anything. It's freezing and the ground is slippy with frost.

'Here, hold on to my arm,' he says. 'It's like an ice rink.'

'No, I'm OK.'

I look at him sideways and catch a little smile at the corner of his mouth.

'What?' I say.

'I was right,' he says. 'You are like your mum.'

Down on the seafront the wind is sharp as a blade. Jim ushers me into a cafe. Inside, it's warm and busy, festooned with shiny Christmas decorations. We order and sit down at a table with a faded red gingham cloth.

'So what's really going on?' he says at last.

'What do you mean?'

'You weren't really passing through, were you?'

I think about lying, but it seems such an effort, I just haven't got the energy.

'So,' he says gently. 'What's happened to make you pack your bags and turn up on my doorstep after sixteen years?'

Everything I think of saying to explain why I'm there sounds stupid and childish.

'Does your dad really know you're here? If he doesn't, you've got to let him know, Pearl. He'll be worried sick.'

'I told him I was coming here.'

'And what did he say?'

I fiddle with a serviette on the table. 'I didn't give him much of a chance to say anything.'

'You had a row?'

I nod.

'A big one?'

'You could say so.'

'What about?'

I feel so stupid. 'Everything.'

The waitress puts a bowl of chips down on the table, with a hot chocolate for me and a bottle of beer for Jim.

'Yeah, well. It can be like that. I remember me and my old man almost coming to blows when I was your age.'

'Me and Dad always got on all right. Before.'

Jim nods. 'I can't imagine what you must both have been through the last few months. It's bound to put you both under pressure.'

He pushes the bowl of chips over to me and I'm so hungry and they smell so good I can't resist taking a few. I start to feel a little bit warmer.

As I sip my hot chocolate, I look at Jim out of the corner of my eye, trying to see the kid in the passport photo.

'How come things didn't work out with you and Mum?'

'We were only seeing each other for a little while,' he says. 'We got on all right, but we realized pretty quick that we didn't have much in common. She was at art college, I was doing my plumbing apprenticeship, we had totally different friends. Didn't even like the same music.' He takes a swig of beer. 'So we called it a day. We didn't even split up as such because we were never really going out with each other as such. I didn't phone her and she didn't phone me. Then, a couple of months later, she rang me up out of the blue saying she was expecting you. It was a bit of a shock, I can tell you.'

I imagine for the first time what it must have felt like for Mum, only a couple of years older than I am now, finding out she was pregnant.

'Was she happy about it?'

Jim looks uncomfortable. 'It was a shock. I told her I'd stand by her whatever she decided to do. But she knew her own mind, your mum. Said she was going to do it by herself. About a year later, she sent me a photo of you. She told me she'd met your dad and they were getting married.'

'Did you keep in touch?'

'Not really.'

'But Mum had your address?'

'We agreed that if you ever wanted to know more about me when you were older you could get in touch.'

'But you never wanted to get in touch? You didn't want to see me?' I try not to feel hurt. I know it's silly; after all, I never wanted to see him either.

'I did, as it happens. I suppose eventually I grew up a bit. I started to feel bad, that I'd let you down somehow. So I got in touch with your mum and said maybe we could meet up or something. Or maybe I could send you birthday cards or Christmas presents, that kind of thing. But Stella said no. She said it would be confusing for you. You already had a dad you loved. She said you knew he wasn't your birth dad, but that didn't matter. You knew my name and that was it. She said maybe when you were a bit older we could talk about it again. I didn't want to cause any trouble or upset you. I suppose I just wanted you to know I wasn't a complete loser who'd abandoned his kid. But then I met Bel and everything changed. She already had Verity; she was just coming up for two then.' His face lights up when he mentions them. 'Look here, I've got a picture of Verity on our wedding day.'

He opens his wallet and shows me a picture of a smaller chubbier Verity in a bridesmaid's dress, tiara askew, face covered in chocolate.

'She seems like a great kid,' I say.

'Bel says I'm a sentimental old fool,' he says, 'but when I look at her it's like I know why I was born. I know what the point of my life is. Sounds daft, I know.'

'No,' I say. 'It doesn't sound daft.'

'And the thing is, I realized that was how your dad must feel about you. And I thought how I'd feel if Verity's birth father got in touch with her and wanted to see her — not that he's likely to; he's a total bloody waste of space.'

He stops and takes another drink of his beer.

'And the point is I knew I couldn't do that to your dad. I knew it'd break his heart. He'd brought you up from a baby; he'd looked after you, hadn't he? Worried about you when you were ill, and picked you up when you fell over, and made you feel safe when you'd had a nightmare or were scared about the monsters under the bed. Am I right?'

I can't speak.

'I had no right to call myself your dad.'

He looks at me. 'Oh no, I've made you cry. Please don't. I'm sorry.' He rummages around in his pocket and passes me a handkerchief. 'It's clean,' he says.

I blow my nose.

'I didn't mean to upset you,' he says. 'That's the last thing I wanted to do.'

'It's not your fault,' I say.

'It is,' he says. 'Raking over the past. And look at you, you're exhausted. Let's get you back to the house. We'll phone your dad and if he's OK with it you can stay the night at ours and we'll see about getting you home tomorrow.'

I think about Dad and his face when I said I was coming here, and I can't stop the silent slide of tears down my cheeks.

'Everything'll look better after a good night's sleep,' Jim says. 'I promise.'

'I can't come back with you. What will Bel say? Something tells me she won't be too keen on me staying.'

He smiles. 'She'll be all right once I've explained.'

We step out into the cold.

'Do you mind if I just have a few minutes by myself?' I say. 'I just need to walk. Clear my head a bit. I'll find my way back to the house.'

'What now? In the dark? I'm not sure it's a good idea. You don't know where you're going.'

'I won't be long.'

He doesn't look convinced. I lean over and give him a very quick peck on the cheek.

'I'll see you back at the house.'

And I walk away before he can speak, his hand raised to his cheek in surprise.

I walk down to the main road that runs along the front. It's dark, but the amusement arcades are all lit up and there are Christmas lights on the lamp posts. There's snow in the air, just a few flakes, glowing as they float through the light, and then disappearing into the dark. The fairground and the crazy golf are deserted, the boating lake frozen round the edges.

Further along I see some stone steps leading to the seashore. I make my way down on to the stony beach, the large pebbles crunching as I step on to them. The wind is fierce. I lean into it, walking down towards the wild sea, the noise deafening. I stand, the wind tearing at my hair, watching the foaming waves crash against the shore.

My head's spinning with tiredness and hunger and with everything Jim's just told me. I can't keep the thoughts straight in my head. I think about Mum, and what it must have felt like to be young and scared and pregnant. I think about Jim and how his face lit up when he was with Verity, when he even talked about her. And, most of all, I think about Dad. I think about how much he loved Mum. I think about how he looked after me when I was a little baby who wasn't his. *I've never seen anyone dote on a baby like he doted on you.* That's what Granny said.

The sea is big and dark and cold. I am so small and so tired. I just want to lie down. If I lie down, the sea will just come and take me. It will carry me away and drag me under.

I think about the car and the football and how Dad saved me. *What would I do without my Pearl?*

I'm not going to lie down.

I sit on the bed in the little lamp-lit spare room back at Jim's house, hugging my knees to myself, but I can't stop shivering.

There's a small desk in the corner and a pinboard behind it with photos on, of Verity and Alfie and the Fish-finger Burner and Jim all doing happy family things: holidays, birthdays, trips to the park.

When I was a little kid, I sometimes used to play a game where I'd pretend that my bed was a raft floating alone in the middle of the ocean, waiting for someone to rescue me.

But there's no one to come and rescue me now.

When I wake up, the room is filled with a strange brightness. Verity's shouting downstairs.

'It's snowing! It's really, really snowing!'

I go to the window and pull the curtains back. Everything is dusted with snow and it's still falling. For a moment all I can feel is childish excitement.

But how am I going to get home? Will the trains be running?

I feel more alone than ever.

There's a knock on the door and Verity comes in, carrying a cup of tea. Most of the tea is in the saucer, but I thank her anyway.

'Mum says come and have some breakfast,' she says.

'No, I don't think so,' I say. 'I've got to go.'

'Mum said you'd say that,' she says. 'So she said I have to use my persuasive charms because you need to eat.'

'Go on then,' I say.

'PLEASE PLEASE PLEASE PLEASE PLEEEEEEEASE—'

'OK,' I say. 'OK, I'm coming.' And she leads me downstairs, gripping my hand tightly in hers.

'How old are you?' Verity asks as we sit at the kitchen table.

'Sixteen,' I say.

'That's old,' she says. 'Have you got a job?'

'No.'

'Have you got a boyfriend?'

'No.'

'Why not? You're quite pretty really.'

Great.

'Thanks.'

She looks me up and down thoughtfully.

280

'A bit thin though.'

God, she's worse than Granny.

'Are you anorexic?'

'Verity!' The FB – Bel – gives me an embarrassed look as she spoons food into Alfie's mouth.

'No,' I say.

I pick up a piece of toast to prove the point, but it's dry and cold and I put it back down again.

'Bulimic?'

'Verity, that's *enough.*'

'You know a lot for someone who's seven,' I say accusingly.

'I like reading.' She carries on assessing me as she crunches on her toast. 'So why haven't you got a boyfriend?'

I try not to think about Finn and take a swig of coffee which burns my mouth.

'It's not compulsory.'

'Have you got a girlfriend instead?'

'No.'

'It's OK if you have.'

'I know. But I haven't.'

'But—'

'Have *you* got a boyfriend?' There's only so much interrogation by a seven-year-old you can take over breakfast.

She looks at me like I'm mad.

'Me? Why would I want a boyfriend?'

'Exactly,' I say.

She watches me for a moment. Then she smiles.

'Want to come and build a snowman with me?'

I shake my head. 'I can't. I have to go home.'

I go back up to my room to get my bags. The snow is still falling, slow and steady, and I go to the window to look at it.

And then, as I watch, out of it, slowly through the falling flakes, a red car appears.

I watch it pull up and see Dad and Finn get out. And then I run downstairs and out of the front door without my coat or even my boots. And when Dad sees me his face looks like Jim's did when he saw Verity last night and I want to explain everything to him: everything that I've done wrong, and everything that he's done wrong, and how angry and lonely and scared I've been and how I want things to be different, but I don't know how to change them. But when I get to him I'm crying too much to speak and he hugs me so tight that I couldn't speak anyway.

But it doesn't matter, because I realize he already knows.

'Yes,' Dad's saying. 'Thank goodness for Finn here. My car wouldn't start with the cold and he and his family are down staying with our neighbour, Dulcie, who's just out of hospital. He saw me trying to start the car and offered to drive me. Very good of him.'

We're all squashed into Jim and Bel's tiny kitchen, drinking tea, and I'd be lying if I said there wasn't a certain amount of awkwardness. Dad and Jim have shaken hands and done a manly sort of 'Thanks' and 'No problem' and now they're talking about roads and gritters ('It's fine once you're on the A21'); Finn is drinking tea and being interrogated by Verity ('But why the cello? It's just a big violin'); Bel is trying to unpack the groceries that have just been delivered, battling to fit a turkey that's almost as big as Alfie into the fridge; and Alfie is eating old breakfast cereal off the floor, assisted by the dog, who I now know is called Dottie ('Because she is,' Verity had told me proudly). I just watch them all. And I find I'm smiling.

'You said you didn't have a boyfriend,' Verity says accusingly as we leave.

'I don't,' I say.

'I may be seven, but I'm not stupid,' she says.

Dad phones Granny on his mobile as we walk down to the car. I can hear her exclaiming even from several metres away. Dad can hardly get a word in.

'There's no need to cry, Mum,' he says at last. 'She's fine. You'll see her yourself soon enough. We're just setting off now.'

While no one's looking I take Finn's hand.

'I'm glad you came,' I say.

He looks at me, surprised. Then he smiles. 'Me too.'

Before I get in the car, I look out over the snowy rooftops and the cliffs, everything white now, everything new. The world is transformed.

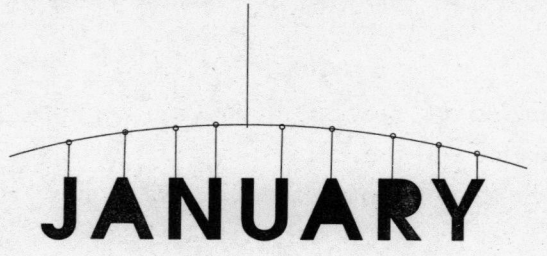

Granny takes me to an unbelievably posh hairdresser's in Chelsea. She won't take no for an answer.

'Your dad's looking after Rose for the day. It's all booked,' she says. 'We can't cancel now.' When she tells me how much it costs, I nearly choke on my cornflakes.

They bring me a cappuccino and a little biscuit and I have a hand massage and manicure. I have to admit it's quite nice.

Afterwards, we go for lunch at an equally posh restaurant, despite the fact that I've told Granny a hundred times I'm not hungry. Granny orders us both a glass of wine and the waiter doesn't dare to contradict her. She tells me embarrassing things that Dad did when he was young that make me laugh, and about his dad, my grandad, who died before I was born. She tells me about her lovely flat in Edinburgh and how I must go and visit her there when she goes back.

'Go back?' I say. 'But what will we do?'

She laughs. 'You'll be fine. Now the insurance is sorted out Rose can have a proper nanny or go to nursery. I'll miss you all, but I have got a life of my own you know. I haven't been to a Pilates class for months. And Hector misses his little friends, I know he does.'

'Oh.'

Halfway through her second glass of wine, Granny stops and looks serious.

'I said some unfair things about your mum, Pearl.'

'I've talked about this with Dad,' I say. 'It's OK.'

'It's not OK,' she says. 'I do understand why she didn't want me around when you were a baby. Once she was over the postnatal depression I mean. I know I can be a bit opinionated. Perhaps I did give her the impression that I didn't think she was good enough for Alex. But, more important than that, she wanted you to herself. She felt so guilty about the time she'd missed out on. And all that time you'd been with me. I'd been like a mother to you for those months. It was hard for her. I can see that now. Perhaps I should have been a bit more understanding.'

I think about it and smile. I catch sight of myself in the mirror on the far wall. My face is a bit flushed from the wine and I can't deny that my hair looks a lot better.

'Shall we order pudding?' I say. 'I'm hungrier than I thought.'

That afternoon I go and get a new mobile phone. The first person I text is Molly. *Can I come and see you? Pearl xxx*

I don't get a reply, but I go anyway. I'm so nervous as I walk along the slushy pavements to Molly's that I almost bottle out. What would I do if I was in her shoes? I picture her shouting, slamming the door in my face. I wouldn't blame her.

I take the stairs up to her flat, all four flights of them, rehearsing what I'm going to say as I go. It starts with 'I'm really sorry . . .' But then I can't decide what order to put it all in. There's just so much to apologize for; so much to explain.

I knock on the door and then wait, trying to catch my breath, running through it again in my head. *I'm really sorry* . . . There's the sound of pounding feet from inside and the door opens to reveal one of the twins dressed as Darth Vader.

'Hi, Jake,' I say. 'Or Callum. Is Molly in?'

The small Darth Vader just breathes at me loudly through his mask. It's kind of unnerving. Then he raises his red lightsaber slowly and growls, 'Now *I* am the master,' before running off into the flat, cloak billowing, yelling, '*Molleeeeee!* It's Pearl. I thought you said you hated her?'

289

There's another wait. Liam's music is pounding out from inside the flat. My heart's still thumping, from nerves now rather than the climb up the stairs. Where should I start? . . . *about your dad*? *About Ravi*? Or maybe just *I've been a bitch* to encapsulate everything?

But in the end, when she comes to the door, it all goes out of my head.

'I lied,' I say, before she can say anything.

'What?' Molly stares at me, unimpressed, arms folded.

'When I told you about the day Mum died. Do you remember? That time at *Angelo's*.' The unexpected words keep coming. I don't know where from. 'I said I got to the hospital in time to say goodbye. I said she hugged me and told me she loved me?'

'Yes?'

I shut my eyes.

And in my head I'm running. I'm running down green hospital corridors, lungs burning, panic pounding in my chest, and I can't go on, I can't keep running. But Dad's voicemail message keeps playing and replaying in my head and I do. I keep on running. And now I'm there and Dad's walking towards me with a look on his face, carved into his face, that makes my stomach lurch.

What's going on? I say. *I want to see Mum.*

Let's sit down.

He tries to take my hand, but I shake him off.

No! I'm shouting. *Just take me to see Mum.*

And he just stands there, helpless.

I can't, Pearl. Tears spill down his cheeks.

For a split second I don't understand. And then I'm dizzy suddenly, as though I'm looking over the edge of a cliff.

Why not? I start to say. But my voice falters.

Because I know why not. I know what he's going to say.

No, I whisper.

And inside my head I'm yelling *SHE CAN'T BE. SHE CAN'T BE. DON'T SAY IT*—

But he says it anyway.

I open my eyes. I'm standing outside Molly's flat again. Her face is wet with tears. Mine is too.

'You didn't say goodbye?' she asks.

'No.'

And now I never will.

We walk across the Heath, arm in arm. The melting snow is grey-brown and slippery

'Why didn't you tell me before?' Molly says. 'About your mum?'

'I couldn't.'

'So why are you telling me now?'

'Because I can.'

She smiles. 'Good.'

'Yeah.'

'Oh my God,' Molly says. 'Look! Isn't that . . .'

I look to where she's pointing and see Mr S who's jogging slowly across the Heath, wearing a highly improbable tracksuit and sports cap. On his feet are dazzling white trainers. We wave and he makes his way over to us, breathing hard.

'Hello,' I say, smiling. 'You look unusual.'

'Never mind all that,' he says. 'I've a bone to pick with you. My wife's been in a rotten mood all Christmas because one of her star pupils says she isn't going back after the holidays.' He gives me a hard look. 'And who do you think is suffering as a result? Muggins here, that's who.'

I look at my feet. 'Sorry,' I say. 'And say sorry to Mrs S too. But I'm not going back.'

He stands and stares at me, hands on hips, shaking his head.

'Even if I wanted to, I bet the Lomax wouldn't let me,' I say. 'She never liked me.'

'Course she will,' he says. 'All that woman cares about is results and she knows you'll get good ones. Anyway, can't stop. You see if you can talk some sense into the girl, Molly.'

And he jogs off. 'Happy New Year to you both,' he calls back. 'Maybe see you at the park with the littlun sometime, Pearl.'

292

'Are you really not coming back to school?' Molly looks horrified.

'I don't know.'

'Oh, please do,' she says. 'Pearl, you've got to.'

'It's too late,' I say.

'Mr S is right. She's bound to let you back. If you're prepared to grovel.'

'I'm not very good at grovelling.'

'No,' Molly laughs. 'You're really not.'

There are people flying kites, some kids and their dads, and we stop to watch, turning our eyes to the sky.

'I'm sorry about everything,' I say.

Molly squeezes my arm. 'I know.'

The clouds are thin above us, silvery with the light of the sun that hides behind them. The laughter and shouts of the children are carried to us on the wind.

'How're things with your dad?'

She grimaces. 'They're getting divorced.'

'Sorry,' I say.

'It's OK,' she says. 'I mean, it's not. But things have been so bad between them for so long. At least they're not rowing any more. Come on,' she says. 'Let's go and get a coffee.'

'Is Ravi back from uni?' I say as we walk.

'Yes,' she says, smiling. 'For four whole weeks.'

'What was it he said about me?' I ask. 'You know, that day in the park. You said, "Ravi was right about you." What did he say?'

'It doesn't matter,' she says.

'Whatever it was I won't be angry,' I say. 'I know.'

'He said maybe sometimes, when people lose someone they love, it's like they die too. It's like perhaps that's the only way they can stay close to the person who's gone. They stop living.'

I stare at her. 'That was what he said?'

'Yep.'

'Ravi?'

'Uh-huh.'

I shake my head. 'I thought he'd said I was a miserable, sarcastic bitch from hell and you should stay away from me.'

'Oh yeah. He said that too.'

'Did he?'

She laughs. 'No, course not.'

'Do you want to come out for my birthday next week?' I say as we walk. 'You and Ravi, I mean?'

Molly kisses me on the cheek. 'We'd love to.'

The next day a postcard from Verity arrives. It says:

Dear Purl, it was grate to meet you but
can you stay longa next tyme? And Fin
   Luv Verity xoxoxoxoxo

I'm so pleased I stick it up on the fridge. I find a notelet among the things in Mum's study. I write:

294

Dear Verity,
It was great to meet you too. I'll be back soon and maybe one day you'll come and see me here?
Love from Pearl xxx

Dulcie is moving into the home today. I've told her I'll go and visit. I watch the removal men carrying all her things out: paintings, furniture, photos. A whole life fitted into the back of a van. Most of it's going up to Finn's parents' B. & B. She can't take much to the home.

Finn comes round to say goodbye.

And this time when he kisses me I don't pull away.

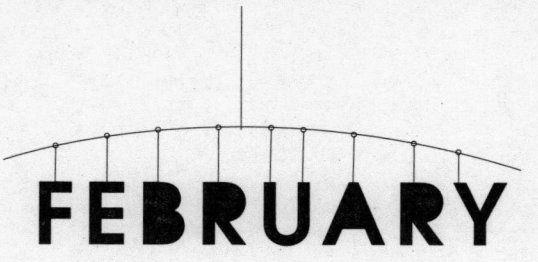

I know she's here before I've even opened my eyes. She's sitting on my bed; I can feel the warmth of her against my arm. I just lie like that for a while, eyes closed, knowing she's next to me.

When I open my eyes, I'm already smiling. She's leaning over me, her face pale in the dawn light. She's been watching me sleep.

'I thought you'd gone,' I say sleepily, full of wonder and relief. She came back, today: on this day when I needed so badly to see her. 'And it was my fault. I was so angry . . .'

'Shhh.' Mum brushes a strand of hair back from my face. 'Come and see this. The sun's rising.'

She takes me by the hand and leads me over to the window, and when I'm standing next to her she pulls back the net curtain. Above us the sky is purple, lightening to blue even as I look at it. But behind the bare black branches of the trees at the end of the garden it's alight: rose and gold and scarlet above the black horizon of trees and rooftops sloping down the hill to the where the Thames flows, cold and out of sight. Vapour trails of aeroplanes glow apricot in the early sunlight, the ghosts of night-time journeys across the sky.

I push the window open and we lean out and breathe in the cold, fresh morning.

'It's beautiful,' I say.

She smiles. I see the little crinkles it makes around her eyes. I see the scatter of freckles across her nose. I see her clearly.

'Yes,' she says and despite the smile her voice catches. In the early morning light her hair looks like fire. She closes her eyes and turns her face into the pale orange glow, which is growing stronger all the time. It picks out the faint lines on her face, exaggerates them. For a second I can imagine what she would have looked like if she'd grown old.

'You look beautiful too,' I say.

She opens one eye and raises an eyebrow.

'You haven't been drinking again, have you, Pearl?'

'No.'

'Not dabbling in hallucinogenic drugs?'

'No.'

She laughs. 'The last time you told me I was beautiful you were four years old. And even then it was only

300

because you'd done my make-up for me. Do you remember? Smeary lipstick all over the place.'

I smile. And once I've started I can't stop. I stand there in the sunlight, leaning against the window sill and grinning like a loon.

'I've been dreading today,' I say.

I know I have been, my heart skittering every time I thought about it; but that fear feels far away now, as though it belonged to someone else.

'I know,' Mum says and she turns her head away for a moment, looks out of the window again.

'Let's go outside,' she says suddenly.

And I smile some more because it's exactly what I want to do.

I unlock the patio doors and put on Mum's coat, which still hangs on the peg it's always been on, over my nightie. Then I slide my bare feet into a pair of wellies and we step out into the garden. The grass is stiff with frost. It sparkles in the dawn light.

'Aren't you cold?' Mum says.

I shake my head, though I ought to be.

'Come on.' I take her hand and we walk over the crunchy grass down to the bench at the end of the garden and sit down, the gnarled, knotted branches of the trees bare above our heads.

For a long time we sit in silence. The world is perfectly

still. It's as if there's only us in it. I can't remember feeling so happy, so peaceful, so at one with everything around me.

But when I look at Mum I see her cheeks are wet with tears.

'What is it?' I say, taking her hand again.

'I'm so sorry, Pearl,' she says at last, and I can feel it, the sorrow that's inside her. It's like a wound.

'What for?' I say. 'What are you sorry for?'

She shakes her head, unable to speak, and I hug her for a while, feeling her ribs shudder as she sobs silently.

'For all of it,' she says, her voice cracking. 'For every single tear you've shed because of me.'

She looks up at me, her eyes red-rimmed.

'I'm sorry too,' I say. 'I was angry with you. I shouldn't have been.'

'I wasn't honest with you,' she said. 'About James. About me. I'm sorry. I never wanted to hurt you.'

'Why didn't you tell me? About how things were after I was born? How hard it was?'

'I wanted to make things how they should have been. I should have been so happy when you were born. But it was exhausting and I was scared and I struggled.' She takes my hand. 'I thought I could make things how I wanted them to be. I wanted to make the world perfect for you. I felt so guilty.'

'That's what Granny said.'

'Well, she's not wrong about everything.' Mum sighs.

302

'She's interfering and bossy and an appalling snob, but – well. She loves you.'

'I've been so angry. With everyone. But most of all—' I take a deep breath. I can hear my heartbeat. But I have to tell her. 'With the baby.'

'I know.'

I look at her. And I realize she does know. All the things I've tried to hide. Dad. The Rat. The lies I've told. She knows all of it.

'How do you know?' I think of all the things I've thought and said and my eyes fill with tears.

'Because I know *you*.'

'I'm sorry.'

She takes my hand. 'I know,' she says. 'I'm sorry too.'

A blackbird is singing in the tall trees behind us. I sit, head leaning on Mum's shoulder, listening. It's so sad and perfect I think maybe it's coming from inside me. And in this moment I understand something; something she can't tell me.

'You wouldn't change it, would you?' I say. 'Even if you could? If the alternative was not having had her at all. You'd choose this.'

As I say it, I realize I've known it all along.

She nods, tears spilling from her eyes. 'I'm sorry. Can you forgive me?'

I shut my eyes. The blackbird sings.

I'm so tired. Tired of being angry. Tired of being sad. I lean further into Mum and she puts her arm round me and we sit like that until I'm so sleepy I can't keep the thoughts straight in my head. I open my eyes and try to look at Mum, but my eyelids droop. I feel myself falling and sleep rising up to catch me.

'Come on.' Mum's voice seems far away. I'm half aware of her arm round my shoulders. I let her guide me back into the house.

The bed is soft around me. I'm almost asleep.

But I know she's still there. I can feel the warmth of her pressing against my arm . . .

'Can you forgive *her*?' she says as I slip towards sleep.

'Maybe,' I try to say. 'I think I want to.'

'I didn't need to make the world perfect for you,' she whispers. 'You're strong. Stronger than me. Strong enough to see life as it is. Messy and terrifying and unbearable—' she kisses me on the lips – 'and wonderful.'

Then she says: 'I love you.'

And I feel her get up; the warmth of her is gone. I feel her leave.

'Wait . . .' I try to grab her hand, but I'm too slow and heavy and full of sleep. 'I don't want you to go yet . . .'

When I wake again, the hot yellow sun is streaming in through the window; it's late. Too late.

I sit up, blind with panic.

She's gone. I know it.

She's gone.

She's gone.

She's gone.

I hide my face. I sob and I sob and I don't know how I'm ever going to stop.

I hear Dad's footsteps. And then his arms are round me and they feel strong and safe, just like they have ever since I was a baby.

'She's gone, Dad,' I say at last. 'She's really gone.'

'Yes,' he says.

And he cries too.

I'm wrung out and empty and weak and still I can't stop crying. The tears just keep falling and falling. My cheeks are tight and itchy. My eyes are swollen.

'I don't know what to do,' I say to Dad. 'What are we going to do?'

He doesn't say anything, just holds me.

Then he kisses the top of my head and takes my hand.

'Come on,' he says.

I follow him. 'Look,' he says. We're standing in front of The Rat's cot. She's sleeping, her arms flung out above her head.

It's her birthday.

I hear the sigh of her breath, in and out, between her

305

slightly parted lips, watch her chest rise and fall, rise and fall.

'Rose,' I whisper.

I walk downstairs and out into the garden. The sun is so bright that when I shut my eyes I can still see the shadow patterns of the trees against my lids.

On the other side of the wall I can hear the children who have moved into Dulcie's house playing, jumping on their trampoline and laughing.

Above are the birds and the constant drone of the planes.

Behind me is my home.

In the soil at my feet there are green shoots; pale petals ready to unfurl.

The world may tip at any moment. But for now—

For now the world keeps turning and I keep breathing, in and out, in and out. I breathe in the life that is all around me, in this garden, in this city, in the fields beyond it, in the seas beyond them and the shores on the other side; life that reaches out towards the unreachable, unknowable space that is beyond all of us and the stars that burn there.

The world may tip at any moment.

But for now that doesn't matter.

Acknowledgements

Huge love and thanks to my mum and dad, Helen and Brian Furniss. Without your support – emotional, practical, financial and editorial – I couldn't possibly have written this book. Also to David, for your blind faith that I would write a book worth reading, and for the sacrifices you made so that I could try.

Thank you to Julia Green and Steve Voake for your gentle guidance, and to my fellow students on the Bath Spa MA Writing for Young People: Blondie Camps, Alex Hart, Helen Herdman, Lu Hersey, David Hofmeyr and Sasha Busbridge. You all helped to make this book what it is.

Thank you to Linda Newbery, Malorie Blackman and Melvin Burgess. Your belief in my writing kept me going when I felt like giving up.

Thanks to the team at Simon and Schuster and Riot for your enthusiasm and hard work, especially to Ingrid Selberg, Jane Griffiths, Elisa Offord, Kat McKenna, Laura Hough, Maura Brickell and Preena Gadher.

And finally, thanks to my agent, Catherine Clarke, for always being right about everything.

Turn the page

for extra content
including a bonus
short story by
Clare Furniss,
Reading Group
questions and
much more . . .

In conversation with Clare Furniss

What was the inspiration behind THE YEAR OF THE RAT?

I was pregnant when I started writing the story and already had two children, although my two were still very young, not teenagers like Pearl. I remember people being surprised that I was writing about a woman dying in child-birth at this time, but I think writing is often a way of exploring fears or preoccupations, of externalising them and working them through.

There was also a very specific incident that became the starting point for the book. The previous summer I'd had to go into hospital for an operation. The night before I baked a cake and the thought popped into my head of what would happen to the cake if I died during the opera-tion (I'm a terrible pessimist – I think, like many writers, I find it very easy to imagine terrible things happening!). Would they eat it? Would it get thrown away? This thought obviously lurked in the back of my mind and appeared unexpectedly when I started writing *The Year of The Rat*. This very small detail became a scene that was then a powerful trigger for the rest of the book; it told me so much about the relationship between Pearl and her dad, and gave me a very tangible sense of the huge loss they were both feeling.

There are several very strong female characters in THE YEAR OF THE RAT and in many ways it's their different experiences and outlook on life that define the novel. Did you intentionally set out to write a book with female relationships at its centre?

It wasn't a conscious aim in the sense of having an agenda, but the mother-daughter relationship felt like a very natural subject to write about, as a daughter and a mother myself. The complexities of relationships within families fascinate me and all the women in my family are strong personalities in their different ways!

Dulcie is an important figure too, even though she plays a cameo role in the story. I was close to my own grandmothers growing up and I wanted to explore how we look at old people and the assumptions we make about them. A big part of growing up is the realisation that your parents and grandparents had lives before you were born, that they were young and very different from the version of them that you know, and that you may have more in common than you think. This plays out in the relationship between Pearl and Dulcie.

But it's not just the women who are strong in this story. Alex, Pearl's Dad, is the hero of the book in many ways. He's under pressure and he doesn't deal with everything perfectly. He makes mistakes, but he's Pearl's rock.

Part of the strength of the female characters is the dynamics between them, and especially the different roles of mothers and daughters. Do you think being a mother has changed your outlook on life? Do you relate most to Pearl or Stella?

Being a mother has definitely changed my outlook, and I think this book comes entirely as a result of that. The strength of what you feel for your children is something I couldn't imagine before having them. Suddenly someone other than yourself is the centre of the world, and that's both liberating and terrifying, because there's a loss of control that comes with that and a huge responsibility. Abandoning your child and causing them pain is the worst thing you can imagine doing, and that's part of what I'm exploring in the book too, because that's exactly what Stella does, albeit completely unintentionally.

I think Stella is my alter ego! She walked onto the page and took over her scenes while I took a back seat, letting her get on with it. If I'm honest I think she probably has an exaggerated version of both my best and worst characteristics. But writing her really felt like taking dictation. Sometimes I'd laugh out loud at things she said and my husband would say, 'You do realise you're laughing at your own jokes?', and I'd say, 'It wasn't me making the joke, it was Stella.' Needless to say, he thought I was crazy.

Having said that, I relate to Pearl very strongly too, and of course while I was writing the book I saw things from

Pearl's point of view, since I was writing in the first person. I remember vividly how it felt to be a teenager, so it didn't feel difficult to see the world through her eyes. I didn't have to deal with the things that Pearl does, but I remember clearly the feeling of being lost and a bit out of my depth and determined not to show it. Pearl's hostility and the distance she creates between herself and those around her is a defence mechanism. And although I didn't lose my mother, I did experience the loss of a friend when I was a little older than Pearl. I think the first time someone very close to you dies, particularly if it's unexpected and they are young, you don't just suffer the loss of that individual but it shakes your entire world, your sense of what life is about and what the point of everything is. That was part of what I wanted to explore in the book.

THE YEAR OF THE RAT is about Pearl's journey after her mother's death. Did you do much research into the processes of grief before you started writing?

I did do some reading around the psychology of grief and the five stages of grieving, and this was useful and thought-provoking as background. But at the same time I knew it was important not to get too bogged down in the theory. The truth is that grief isn't a series of boxes to be ticked, it is incredibly personal, and everyone will both experience and express it differently.

In the course of writing the book I read and listened to

first-hand accounts of young people who had suffered the loss of a parent, and again and again what came across incredibly strongly was that each person reacts in a different way. Some people seem OK on the surface and bottle up their emotions. Some are angry. Some people are brought together by grief, others are isolated by their inability to grieve together or by their different ways of dealing with their loss. For some it is a trigger for other serious problems: depression, anorexia, self-harm. I had to allow myself to be led by my character and believe that, if I knew my character well enough, her responses to particular situations would be true and right and believable for her. I had a very clear sense from the start of how grief would freeze her, how all her sorrow and fear and anger would feel so overwhelming that she would keep them locked inside her, and cut her off from the rest of the world.

While I was writing the book I also came across newspaper articles and interviews and features on the sudden loss of a loved one. The thing that came through again and again was how long it took to accept that the person was really dead; that they were gone and wouldn't be coming back. People referred to the fact that the first anniversary of a death was incredibly hard for them and that it was only really at this point that they really accepted the person was gone. This shaped the way I approached the ending of the book. It was important for me that Pearl isn't 'OK' by the end of the book, that she isn't happy and ready to move on. In many ways she is still at the start of the grieving process. She has simply accepted that her mum is gone.

The make-up of Pearl's family is an unconventional one. Was it important to you to reflect the fact that children and teenagers aren't necessarily living in a traditional nuclear family?

Yes. For the book to be believable it was important for the story to reflect the real world, where families come in all shapes and sizes. Also, one of the things that's really important in this story is Pearl's realisation that people and their relationships are more complicated than they might appear, and that life throws unexpected things at you. I wanted to show that this isn't always a bad thing; positive things can come out of the untidiness and unpredictability of life too. Stella wished that Alex, Pearl's stepdad, was her biological father; she wanted to make everything neat and perfect for Pearl. But Alex's love for Pearl is what makes him her 'real' dad; no one could love her more than he does. And in fact Pearl gains something by discovering her biological father and his family and making a connection with them.

How did you become a full-time writer?

I loved creative writing at school but it never occurred to me that I could do it for a living. When my children were very young and I was at home with them I had a really strong desire to write again but I didn't know where to start. I had very little time, and when I did occasionally manage to sit down at my computer I'd sit and stare at the blank screen, filled with horror, wondering what on earth to do next. In the end I plucked up the courage to go on a week-long residential writing course with the Arvon foundation. It was wonderful, and while I was there I forced myself to start writing – in fact I wrote the opening of *The Year of The Rat* while I was there. I got some really encouraging feedback and began to take the idea of writing a bit more seriously. When my children were old enough I applied to do a part-time MA in Writing for Young People at Bath Spa University. I went back to *The Year of The Rat* for my MA manuscript and after an awful lot of hard work, sleepless nights, blood, sweat and many tears, I got it finished and sent it off to Catherine Clarke, who is now my agent. To my surprise and delight she loved it, and within a month I had a book deal.

What books or writers have most inspired you?
There are so many that I hardly know where to start! Every good book I read inspires me to try to write better. In terms of writing this particular book I would say that Meg Rosoff's *How I Live Now* was a big inspiration. It's a book with a teenage protagonist that speaks to readers of any age because it doesn't limit itself. It deals with big issues, it's funny and moving and clever, it has the most wonderful voice and it's beautifully written. I read it before I had any serious thought of becoming a writer and it

genuinely made me think I'd love to give it a go. I also re-read Jane Gardam's *Bilgewater* and *Crusoe's Daughter* for inspiration when I got stuck with the book. Both are books I have loved for many years, and have wonderful quirky teenage protagonists, as does Dodie Smith's *I Capture the Castle*, another old favourite that I went back to for inspiration. While I was writing this book I was also reading Hilary Mantel's *Wolf Hall* and *Bring Up the Bodies*. They are extraordinary books, and reading her makes me want to write every single sentence perfectly. Of course I don't manage it, but she inspires me to keep trying!

What are you working on next?

My next book is a very different story but again focuses on family relationships, love and loss. This one will have a bit more of a mystery to it though, and also has an element of historical drama set in the 1960s alongside a very contemporary storyline, which is something new and exciting for me. It's great to be working on a brand new project and getting to know my characters – there are some very interesting personalities in the mix! Expect fireworks, a few giggles and possibly a tear or two . . .

READING GROUP QUESTIONS

1) Which techniques does Clare Furniss use to establish Mum as a three-dimensional character, even after her death? Does she feel as 'real' as the other (living) characters?

2) *'She's yours and I'm not'* (Pearl to Dad, about The Rat.) Does the fact that Pearl's dad is her step-father, rather than her natural father, change anything about their relationship, and the way in which they cope with Mum's death and the birth of The Rat?

3) What do you think the different relationships in the book tell us about the true definition of family?

4) The author has added many funny touches to this book. What does humour add to a book that focuses on the theme of bereavement?

5) How do our perceptions of The Rat change throughout the book? Do they correspond to Pearl's feelings about her?

6) What do you make of The Rat's nickname? Discuss the effect that a character's name can have on our perception of that character.

THE LAST DAY

A bonus short story by Clare Furniss

When I was asked to write a short story about one of the characters from *The Year of The Rat* I knew straight away that I wanted to write about Dulcie. She was a character I loved writing, and I wanted to know more about her backstory, which I had only had a glimpse of when writing the novel. I wanted to discover more about her teenage years and her love for her husband who died so many years before, but whose memory still made her cry. The fact that she was leaving the home she'd lived in for most of her life would stir up these memories, so it seemed the obvious subject for the short story. It made me think of my own nan when she moved into a home near the end of her life. Like Dulcie she was a strong, intelligent and independent woman who had lived through a lot. Dulcie's story certainly isn't my nan's story, but thinking about her helped me to imagine Dulcie's emotions. One of my preoccupations is how we see and treat older people – it's something I'm exploring further in my next book. We seem to forget that they have ever been young, or felt the things we feel and done the things we do. As we get older, all the people we've ever been are still there inside us, just below the surface, and this was something I wanted to bring out in the story. I hope you enjoy it.

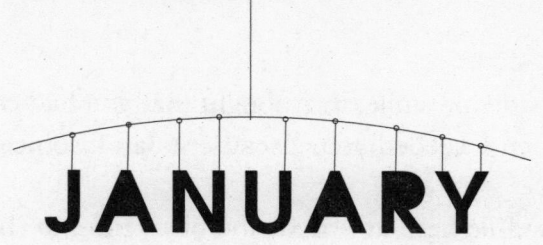

JANUARY

This morning, when I woke – barely morning, the winter sun not yet risen – I caught the scent of your cigarette smoke in the dark, just as I used to. Do you remember, Ted, how you would wake in the night, restless, and light a cigarette and pace about until I'd tell you to come back to bed, or go away and do something useful instead of keeping me awake?

I had been dreaming of you, I think; it was one of those dreams where I woke and was surprised to find myself old. And as I opened my eyes and breathed in that faint trace of smoke, hanging, invisible, in the darkness, I knew you had been there. *Thank you, my love*, I said in my head. Could you hear it? I think perhaps you could. You always could hear what was in my head, somehow; right from that first night we met at the Hammersmith Palais.

It made me smile, the thought that you had come to me when I needed you. Because today I do need you, my love.

Now I lie here in bed, as the black thins to shadowy grey around me, listening to the house. This house that was our home, and then mine and, in a few hours, will be someone else's. In the quiet I can hear it breathe: its night time creakings, the hiss and gurgle of water moving through unseen pipes, the rustling of invisible mice. The nocturnal rhythm of this place is as familiar to me as my own voice, my own heartbeat, I let it soothe me.

This house has kept me company on many sleepless nights. That's one of the things they don't tell you about getting old: the way night time sleep eludes you. Perhaps it's because we sense Death waiting for us in the shadows; best not to let your guard down.

'Don't say that, Gran,' Finn said, the other day when I suggested it, after he'd found me drinking tea in the kitchen at five am. I laughed, but would have given anything for him not to look so pained by the thought of it, of me being gone. I haven't told him yet, what the doctor told me: that there isn't long. I haven't told any of them, I can't bring myself to do it. Not yet. Though his mother guesses, I think. She always did guess things, Caroline, our firstborn child. She senses dangers and secrets, hears the unsaid.

Yes, I have lain here often, listening. But this is the

last time. I will leave here today and I will never come back.

I will leave here today and I will never come back. I say it out loud, to the house, trying to convince myself that it is possible. The house just clanks and hums, impassive. It has seen many occupants come and go.

It seems such a very short time since you and I lay here together, in this same room, our bodies warm and entwined, and were woken by giggles and small slippered feet in the half-light, by small bodies launching themselves upon us. You'd groan and throw them over your shoulders as you went downstairs, threatening imminent dispatch to the nearest dustbin or stewpot. Lizzie would squeal and punch, and Caroline would beg, *Please don't, Daddy, we're very sorry*, never quite certain that she wouldn't end up in tomorrow's casserole.

Sometimes time seems stretched so long and thin it might snap, might cut me quite adrift from all those things that went before. And yet now it concertinas, the past folded up so tight against the present it seems I could reach out and close my hand around it, feel its heat again beneath my fingers, hold it in my arms . . .

Enough, I tell myself, sharply. What is it they say? *Nostalgia ain't what it used to be.* Painfully, I ease my stiffened limbs out of bed and make my way downstairs. I go quietly, not wanting to wake Finn and Caroline. They'll be up soon enough. I want a little time to myself.

But I can't shake you off, it seems, because here again, as I push open the kitchen door, I half expect to find you in there at the kitchen table, bashing away on your old typewriter, a cigarette in your mouth, the girls eating porridge and arguing amiably about the relative merits of dogs and cats, or meccano and dolls. You'll look up and smile, unshaven but dazzling as you always were. 'Morning darling. Now listen, I've had a splendid idea, wait till you hear . . .' It might be anything: a piece you're going to persuade your editor to let you write, perhaps, exposing some corruption or injustice. Or an unseasonal day trip to the seaside. An idea for a film that you'd had in the middle of the night and were going to mention to that chap Walter with the friend in Hollywood. You were going to buy a piano and teach yourself and the girls to play. Or chickens. We should keep chickens! Imagine, fresh eggs for breakfast every morning . . .

How nearby you feel, suddenly, after all these years, you and all your splendid ideas. It's as though I've stumbled back to that blur of time just after you were ill; just after you'd gone. I keep walking into rooms and feeling that you've just been there, keep seeing your shadow out of the corner of my eye.

But the kitchen is empty and dark. Bare now, too, of all but essentials: kettle, mugs, the scant remains of a packet of chocolate digestives, demolished yesterday by the removal men. I make laborious tea, then sit at the table to drink it, exhausted by the exertion. I've made it as you like it – *liked* it – strong, three sugars. It's revoltingly sweet. I take a gulp of water and line up my daily array of pills ready to take.

It's good to have a few moments of peace. Ever since I came back from hospital I've been scrutinised and tended to, organised, hustled and bustled. First there was Christmas, the whole family relieved and surprised I wasn't dead, but trying not to show it. And now – again, to their relief – the move.

After you died, they were always on at me to sell the house . . . *It'll be a new start for you, Mum. You could live by the sea, you always said you wanted to.* Later on it was *Why don't you come and live nearer to us? Somewhere modern, somewhere without drafts and dry rot and rodents. Somewhere with a smaller garden, easier to maintain. A bungalow, perhaps?* They treat me like a child, these children of ours. They don't realise it was only last week I was pinning their nappies and rocking them to sleep. Only yesterday I was bathing their scraped knees and wiping their noses, reading them bedtime stories.

Lizzie arrived last weekend, lipsticked and efficient, armed with colour-coded sticky notes and an ominous number of rubbish bags. She spent days sifting methodically through a lifetime of accumulated nick-nacks, things that might have come in useful one day, forgotten treasures. Practical, unemotional. Box after box taken to the charity shop or the rubbish tip.

'Heavens! Look at this ugly old thing,' she said, holding up some once precious gift or other; the turquoise brooch you gave me for a birthday, I think. 'And look! This frightful old dinner service. Half of it's missing or chipped. Do you suppose the charity shop would even want it?'

It was my mother's, used only for special occasions, gilt-edged, patterned with purple flowers. I remember standing on tiptoes to stare at it on the dresser in the parlour, awed by its beauty.

'Do they not need you at work, darling?' I said eventually. 'You know what a terrible mess they make of everything without you.' I have to confess a sneaking sympathy for our dear girl's colleagues.

'No, no,' she said, brisk. 'Family comes first, Mum.'

'I would understand, you know. You've done more than enough. And Finn and Caroline will be here in a couple of days.'

'I've booked the whole week off,' she insisted, taping yet another box shut. 'And that's that.'

'Do you remember Daddy rigging up that swing for us in the garden, from the apple tree?' she said one afternoon, while taking a break from her ruthless cull of my wardrobe.

I had quite forgotten the swing till she mentioned it. Another one of your splendid ideas, one that actually came to fruition. Such an unlikely thing, you were so hopeless at anything practical as a rule.

'You're right,' I said. 'For your birthday.' I looked up, and saw that there were tears on her cheeks. They never cease to surprise you, your own children.

Lizzie left soon after Caroline and Finn arrived, called away to some emergency or other that required her immediate presence in Copenhagen.

'I was born in this house,' she said as she climbed into her taxi, shaking her head and looking up at the bedroom where the momentous event had taken place.

'I know, my darling,' I said, hugging her. 'I was there.'

And then the removal men came, loud and cheery, whistling and arguing, packing and dismantling.

'You don't have to be here, Mum,' Caroline had said. 'Won't you let Finn take you up to the B&B for a few days? We've no bookings at the moment. You'd be waited on hand and foot.'

'I want to be here,' I told her. 'I don't want to leave until I have to.'

Not long now. Caroline and Finn will be up soon. The sky through the window is pale apricot now, deepening to pink, like the inside of a shell. I have a sudden memory of the beach at Brancaster, of walking into the eye-stinging wind, you and a toddling Caroline ahead of me, collecting shells in a bucket. Lizzie barely even thought of yet. Funny how clear it is, fresh and pristine, every shade vivid, every edge clear and sharp. Yet the present goes in and out of focus, faded, blurred at the edges. I kept those shells for years, in a little glass dish. Whatever happened to them, I wonder.

There are gaps on the kitchen walls, where the pictures used to be: photos, prints, posters for shows we'd seen long ago, those old watercolours my father painted when he retired. Now they are just blank spaces, framed grey, their absence conspicuous. But I can see in those spaces every detail of what was there before.

'You OK, Mum?'

Caroline's voice from the doorway makes me start. I stare at her in wonder. How did our baby girl, our first-born, cherished and fussed over, come to be this woman? This wide-hipped, tired, middle-aged woman? Overnight it seems. Perhaps this is why old people know not to fall asleep at night; to stop the hurtling forward of time while they slumber.

'Mum?'

'Yes,' I say, and I hold my hand out to her, because she is a good girl, she is kind, and anxious. She always did worry. She'd crawl into our bed in the middle of the night and confess her fears: murderers and floods and stray dogs with no one to care for them. She cried about rabbits squashed on the road, and the mousetraps you once set on this very kitchen floor. We came down in the morning to find the traps quite vanished, the mice still happily scuffling in the skirting boards; ancestors, no doubt, of the ones I can hear now. Finn gets that from her: his kindness, his concern.

'Yes, love,' I repeat. 'I'm OK.'

When she turns her back I close my eyes to stop tears from falling.

My skin is tissue-paper thin now, translucent with age. The slightest touch and it bruises, the smallest knock and it bleeds. But today I feel skinless, blood and bone and soul exposed. There is nothing to protect me from the world and everything in it, seen and unseen, real and imagined, it is all part of me and I am part of it and it is hard to bear.

It's almost time to go. The removal men left hours ago, Caroline has taken the hire van with my last few possessions in it to Haven Lodge.

Finn has stayed with me. He is to drive me north. But he's hesitating, and I realise why.

'Go and see her,' I say. 'Go and see Pearl.'

I don't add: Life is short. It's too short to be scared. It's too short to worry about making a fool of yourself, not to show your feelings. You'd have told him, if you were here. You were always so spontaneous. It drove me mad at times, of course, back then. But I admire it more as time passes. It's a rare thing, to be so open, so unafraid.

But it seems he doesn't need us to tell him, because he says, 'OK, I'll be back in a minute.' He's gone for almost an hour.

I think about Pearl while he is gone, about her unhappiness, and the unlikely bond that has formed between us, and most of all about what the future might hold for her. This is the thing about dying; I am not afraid of it, but I do so want to know what will happen next.

I remember the day they moved in next door, Pearl's mother at the centre of everything, her pregnancy evident, barking orders, making rather bawdy jokes. Melodramatic, capricious, rather mesmerising. How would it be to live with such a person? And then to live without them? I know something of that particular agony. Seeing Pearl last summer, when she turned up, tearful, on my doorstep with the baby, brought back the rawness of it, the anger, the emptiness.

The world gets louder, I told her. And it's true. And yet now it seems to be receding again, moving further away as you, my love, come closer.

Pearl came to see me again, last week, before Finn and Caroline arrived. She looked less strained, I thought, seemed, less withdrawn. But still thin, her cheekbones sharp, her dark hair cropped short. I'm not surprised

Finn is drawn to her, with his inherited love of vulnerable things. But looks can deceive. She's tougher than she looks.

'I wish you didn't have to go,' she said.

'So do I.' I didn't mean to say it. I didn't mean to think it. I have told myself leaving is the right thing, the natural way of things, that I am lucky to have stayed here this long, to have lived the life I have lived. I have told myself these things and they are true. But there it is. I wish I didn't have to go.

'Are you scared?' she said.

'Yes,' I told her. 'A little.' Which was half true.

She nodded.

'It's hard, letting go,' I said. 'But you already know that, don't you?'

The baby watched us, serious, self-possessed. There's something sturdy about her, somehow, purposeful. You get to know babies when you've been around a few of them. You begin to sense what sort of person is budding within them. She'll be all right, that one. She won't be easily deflected from whatever path she chooses.

Pearl scooped her up. She's able to look at the baby now, I noticed. She couldn't bring herself to do it before.

'I'll come and visit you,' she said when she left.

'Good,' I said. She's not the sort to say things she doesn't mean. 'And Finn? Will you visit him?'

She looked away and shrugged.

'He might not want to see me,' she said. But was that – could it possibly have been? – the hint of a smile?

And then I think about Finn, our grandson, and what an unexpected gift he has been. Caroline and Stuart had wished for a child for so long, they'd given up all hope of ever having one. The doctors had told them it wasn't going to happen. And then – miraculously – Finn, a tiny scrap wrapped in blankets, being carried down our garden path. He towers above me now. It still takes me by surprise. How odd that we should continually be taken aback by the passing of time, by the fact that babies grow up. 'Haven't you grown?' we say accusingly, as if it's the last thing we expected.

You'd be so proud of him, Ted. All your love of music – the way you'd drag me off to dubious clubs in Soho and to the Proms at the Albert Hall, the fruitless music lessons for the girls, (remember those tortured hours listening to Caroline labouring at that terribly out of tune piano, Lizzie scraping away at the violin?) – it has found its way, gloriously, to Finn. He got that gift from you. And from me? Well, I like to think he gets his determination from me. Though you, my love, might have called it stubbornness . . .

Of course we can take no real credit, much as I would like to. Finn is his own person and will live his own life. How I wish I could be there to see it. I must console myself that he will remember me, and that eventually he will do so happily.

'That was a long minute,' I say when Finn returns, shaking me from my thoughts of the past and the future.

'Sorry,' he says, his face flushed.

I smile and say, 'no you're not.'

He smiles too. So like you, my love, our grandson when he smiles.

He helps me into my coat. 'Thank you, Ted,' I say.

'Finn, Gran,' he says. 'I'm Finn.'

He holds my arm as we walk down the path, slippery with frost still where the ground is shadowed by the hedge, and helps me into the car. It's a slow, undignified manoeuvre these days. I don't mind much usually, the unhelpfulness of my body amuses as much as frustrates me. But today I am impatient with it.

I remember the feeling of slipping elegantly into your first car – an Austin wasn't it? how impressed I was by that car! – knees together in a pencil skirt.

The first time you came to call for me in that car the whole street was peering out of their windows to see. I knew they were watching, as I walked out of the front door and got in, you holding the door for me, tipping your trilby jokily as I passed you. I remember it so precisely, the feeling of walking in high heels, confident and neat-ankled, hips swaying slightly as my shoes clip-clopped.

'A "*journalist*".' Mother had told Mrs Mason next door, as if it was a euphemism for some especially heinous form of criminal activity. Mrs Mason had looked at me severely, a hand on one hip, a snivelling grandchild on the other. 'No good will come of it,' she admonished.

'You be careful,' Mother called after me as we drove off. 'And *you*, look after my daughter, or you'll have me to answer to.'

I can remember the sensation of having long hair, swept back by the wind as we drove in that car, along the Embankment, or over to Richmond, or around the Kent countryside. I can feel it, the excitement, the free-dom, the *joy*.

It was only a couple of months later I walked down the steps of Woolwich Town Hall, arm in arm with you, a small posy of violets in my hand, a wedding ring on my finger. Your mother stood behind us with a face that suggested she'd been sucking lemons, mine looking as though she'd like nothing more than to clout you about the head with her heaviest frying pan. My father checking his watch, anxious to get to the pub. I can see all this in the black and white photo that will come with me to Haven Lodge. At the time I noticed nothing but you. Our wedding, another one of your splendid ideas; the best one of all.

*　　*　　*

Finn does up the seat belt for me, it's too much for my useless fingers in this cold. I feel stubborn suddenly, like a child. It's not fair. I won't go. Self-pity wells up inside me until I fear tears once more. I squash it down. I can't let Finn see.

'OK, Gran?' Finn says. 'You all set?'

'All set,' I say, and I even manage a smile. I turn myself, painfully, as he starts the engine, to watch my home slip out of view through the back window. There. It is gone now.

I turn myself back and look at the grey road ahead.

'Could we take a little detour?'

He looks at me. 'Course,' he says. 'Where do you want to go?'

We drive along the bottom of Blackheath, the last remains of the snow almost gone now, and in through the gates of the park. I can see it, for a moment, as I did when I was a little girl, the heath stretching for miles it seemed, the trees towering above me. I remember how it felt to do a cartwheel on the grass in the sunshine, to run and spin, to roll down the hill and land breathless and laughing, covered in grass at the bottom. It astounds me, briefly, that I can no longer do these things, that I never shall again. Finn parks as close to the Observatory as he can and then we get out and walk, past the Wolfe statue, until we are overlooking the hill and park and the river and the city are spread out before us. Then I stand and look at my city, where I have lived all my life. During the war the park was turned into allotments, down there below us, where the children are playing. There were guns in the flower garden, to shoot down German planes. Behind us, on the heath I remember Nissen huts. They kept German prisoners there, they said, though I never saw one. It seems impossible to believe it all now. It was another world we lived in, you and I.

The sky is bright and cloudless. I look beyond the green slope of the park, beyond the river below us. We walked here when the Isle of Dogs and the docks were just ruins across the Thames, after the war. Skyscrapers have grown there now, made of metal and glass and sunlight.

'Beautiful, isn't it?' Finn says.

I nod. 'I'll never see it again.'

He doesn't contradict me. He takes my hand and warms it in his. Eventually we turn back to the car. There is no putting it off now. I am leaving and I am never coming back.

Once we're past the heath I close my eyes, exhausted. I feel sleep coming to ambush me. And as it does, I think – I'm certain – I feel your hand on my shoulder.

'Thank you, Ted,' I say. 'For coming with me.'

'Finn, Gran. I'm Finn.'

I smile as sleep takes me. I dream again of being young.

CLARE FURNISS'S TOP
LIFE-AFIRMING READS

So what exactly is a 'life-affirming' read? For me, the very act of reading is life affirming. It's all about making connections with the world and the people in it, seeing through the eyes of another person. You might love them, you might hate them; even better you might do both. What matters is you care about them enough to keep turning the pages. Reading a story and thinking: 'Wow, I thought I was the only person who felt like that', or alternatively, 'Wow, I'd never thought of it like that before', is what makes a book special for me, whether I'm reading fantasy, fiction, non-fiction or poetry. A book that makes you laugh and feel good about the world can be life-affirming, but so can a book that makes you angry or that brings you to tears – what could be more life affirming than empathy? In fact a thread that runs through many of the books I've chosen (and, I hope, in the book I've written) is that they show the flaws and imperfections and in some cases the horror of what being alive means and they still some-how manage to show that life is beautiful, life is funny, life is worth fighting for, life is unimaginably precious, life must be lived.

The Secret Garden by Frances Hodgson Burnett

I loved this book as a child and it wasn't until I re-read it recently that I realised it had influenced *The Year of The Rat*. Sour-faced orphan Mary Lennox discovers the secret garden which was once cherished by her aunt, who died in childbirth. With nature-loving Dickon and her unloved cousin Colin she brings the garden back to life, and as it begins to blossom, so do Mary and Colin. 'Being alive is the Magic,' cries Colin as the story reaches its denouement – it really doesn't get much more life-affirming than that.

I Capture the Castle by Dodie Smith

From the moment I read its famous opening line – 'I write this sitting in the kitchen sink' – I was captivated by this book. We see the world instantly through the eyes of bookish, clever, self-deprecating Cassandra Mortmain and we love her and the world of impoverished eccentric English gentility she lives in. Not only that, we love every character in the book, despite the fact that every character in the book is flawed. No, we love them because they are flawed, which for me is the essence of a life affirming book – the embracing of imperfections. It's also hilarious and touching and romantic. It's impossible to read this book without feeling that being alive is a wonderful thing.

A Room of One's Own by Virginia Woolf

'There is no gate, no lock, no bolt that you can set upon the freedom of my mind', Virginia Woolf wrote in her essay on women and fiction in 1928. I first read this book as a teenager and it felt life-changing. I was a girl who loved writing, and this made me feel that I could – and should – take this seriously. It made me feel that I was a part of something bigger, something exciting and daring, that creativity and unconventionality were to be celebrated. It is passionate and bold and I still find it utterly inspiring.

Skellig by David Almond

An astonishingly beautiful book about Michael, who finds the mysterious Skellig in the garage of his new house, an ancient man with wings on his back and a love of Chinese takeaways. As Michael's family struggles with the fact that his prematurely born baby sister may die, Michael's relationship with Skellig and with Mina, the precocious girl next door, develops. This book is about love and family and friendship, magic and dreams and things we don't understand that are at the edges of everyday life. 'Sometimes we think we should be able to know everything. But we can't. We have to allow ourselves to see what there is to see, and we have to imagine.'

Staying Alive edited by Neil Astley

I often turn to poetry when I'm in need of a quick fix of life-affirmation. This wonderful poetry anthology encapsulates all the joy and pain of every stage of life: not only the more usual stuff of poetry (love, death, war) but also home, family, pets, travel, growing up and much more besides. Even if you don't think you're a 'poetry person', you'll find a poem in here that speaks to you.

The Red Tree by Shaun Tan

I only recently discovered this beautiful picture book which explores the unhappy, scary, lonely place the world can sometimes feel. We don't often give children the chance to explore darker emotions, trying to make the world jolly and perfect and cuddly for them, but this book acknowledges the fear and sadness and isolation we all feel and shows that hope is always there, even if we can't always see it. Definitely a picture book that isn't just for little ones.

To Kill a Mockingbird by Harper Lee

The story of Scout and Jem, set in the American Deep South of the 1950s, whose lawyer father Atticus defends a black man accused of rape, incurring the wrath of the townsfolk. It is about prejudice of many kinds, about standing up for what you know is right, and about seeing things from another person's point of view. Most of all it's about courage. 'I wanted you to see what real courage is, instead of getting the idea that courage is a man with a gun in his hand,' Atticus says to his children. 'It's when you know you're licked before you begin, but you begin anyway and see it through no matter what.' We all need an Atticus in our lives.

How I Live Now by Meg Rosoff

It's the voice of spiky, vulnerable, funny Daisy that makes this book so instantly appealing and memorable but there's much more to it than that. It's an adventure set against the background of an imagined war in the near future, which disrupts the idyllic, adult-free life that New Yorker Daisy has found with her English cousins. Rosoff uncompromisingly shows the devastating and brutal effects of war. But at its heart it's a love story, the story of Daisy and Edmund, how their love sustains them. It's full of energy and humour and life and emotion, and for me personally it was reading this book that made me want to go off and write a book of my own.

A Monster Calls by Patrick Ness

To be honest I could have chosen any of Patrick Ness's books. He's so honest about his characters' failings or weaknesses or mistakes, and so compassionate towards them – as the Monster says in this book, most people aren't good guys or bad guys, but somewhere in between. This one stands out for me though. Based on an idea by another great author Siobhan Dowd, who sadly wasn't able to write it before she died, it tells the story of Conor, whose mum is terminally ill. It is about letting go, allowing yourself to accept feelings you think you shouldn't have, and most of all it's about love.

The Complete Works of Shakespeare

Yes, OK, I know this is a bit of a cheat, but I couldn't leave him out. I fell in love with Shakespeare as a teenager, thanks to an English teacher who helped me see past the language to the truth and humour and drama of his plays. They have everything: teenagers falling in love and rebelling against their parents, power-hungry politicians, dysfunctional families, racism, murder, suicide, fathers and daughters, mothers and sons, sibling rivalry, people falling in and out of love with the wrong people, and some brilliant (very rude) jokes. All of life is there to loved, laughed at, wept over and marvelled at.

Clare Furniss grew up in London, and moved to Birmingham in her teens. After brief stints as a waitress, a shop assistant and working at the Shakespeare Centre Library in Stratford-upon-Avon, she studied at Cambridge and Aberdeen. Clare went on to work in media relations for the homelessness charity Shelter and spent several years as a press officer for the then Mayor of London, Ken Livingstone. She now lives in Bath and has completed an MA in writing at Bath Spa University.